EVIDENCE
OF LOVE

EVIDENCE
OF LOVE

Melissa McConnell

A Harvest Original • *Harcourt, Inc.*

ORLANDO   AUSTIN   NEW YORK   SAN DIEGO   TORONTO   LONDON

www.HarcourtBooks.com

Library of Congress Cataloging-in-Publication Data
McConnell, Melissa.
Evidence of love/Melissa McConnell.—1st edition.
p.   cm.
"A Harvest Original."
1. Political consultants—Fiction.   2. Loss (Psychology)—Fiction.
3. Missing persons—Fiction.   4. Washington (D.C.)—Fiction.
5. New York (N.Y.)—Fiction.   I. Title.
PS3613.C38165E95   2005
813'.6—dc22   2004017422
ISBN 0-15-603058-6

Text set in Garamond MT
Designed by Cathy Riggs

Printed in the United States of America

First edition
K J I H G F E D C B A

12 May 2005

Dear Gerry,

To David,
Honor,
my parents,
and Fredrica Friedman

Sorry you couldn't
join us in New York—
I hope you enjoy
it!

Love,
Melissa

"We are not here to curse the darkness, but to light the candle that can guide us through that darkness to a safe and sane future."

—John F. Kennedy,
July 15, 1960

EVIDENCE
OF LOVE

PART I

Before

I

On a Saturday I have to abandon the office to cut down bamboo in my mother's backyard. I know she worries about me. She sits, troubled, in her house on the highest point in Washington, thinking about my springtime spent in a windowless office. Her thirty-three-year-old daughter talks on the telephone all day—as she did as a teenager—her job somehow spun, made up by these patchy, thick conversations, fueled by coffee and ticking clocks. She guesses that I am distracted by the problems of other people, swallowed by their plans, ruined on my blurry trips between the Old Executive Office Building and the West Wing basement, my late-night dashes into glaring power. We never discuss my job, though I can't help thinking she views me from afar as a certain kind of ferry in some ever-near typhoon, her daughter chugging back and forth, carrying messages from one sorry piece of land to the other. She reminds me about her "psychic feelings," and by her tone I know these must be ones of darkness and doom.

She tells me, too, that she respects journalists, believes in "integrity." And considering my job is to manage the media, herd them like a flock of sheep, she must be more concerned by this than my lack of fresh-air oxygen and my caffeinated complexion. Considering it was once my own vague ambition to be a journalist, she must fret about my own regrets. Plus, her daily view from her French doors over a long lawn to the lovely pines is being threatened by the bamboo.

So I stand in the blinding sunlight on Saturday in the backyard of the house I lived in for eighteen years. I know I am pale, skinny, and my eyes are blocked by the same kind of sunglasses I wore in college—many such pairs bought, lost, crushed—Ray-Bans, very black. I like my brightness filtered.

I walk down the sloping lawn and have forgotten how green the grass becomes in spring: sharp green even through camouflage glasses. The grass smells dark in the sunshine. It is the familiar damp scent of cool shadows, and it reminds me of the lawnmower buzz on late afternoons. The grass is flecked with violets, small purple spots woven across the endless green, but my feet crunch as I walk.

The bamboo sprouts hide everywhere, and I step on them like crackle-back insects. Adult bamboo stands tall, three feet deep against the fence, swaying patiently in the breezes. However, its offspring pop up unexpectedly, spread through the lawn and surprise me like so many rumors. I make my way: bending, grabbing the asparagus-like shoots, and tossing them toward the fence.

I haven't told my mother yet how much Harry has changed, slowly over two years and suddenly in the past two weeks. Maybe I am afraid of all sorts of psychic feelings. I will not tell her about the call on Thursday night, when the phone by our bedside sounded alarm at four A.M., the voice telling Harry something as he startled out of an already uneasy sleep. From the other side of the bed through the blue darkness, I watched Harry half-sitting with his head against the wall, his palm pressed against his forehead like a cool washcloth, listening and nodding. "Yes, of course I'll come now," he said simply and only. I knew his mind had already raced past me and was heading right back to the White House.

"They can't be serious," I said through a new panic that has taken me over, one that jolts me out of half sleep on these nights when he fumbles through his dark closet looking for the right suit. It's the same panic that sometimes makes me feel uneasy in our apartment, that makes me go to his closet and count his suits, feel each sleeve to be sure they are all still there before I cautiously open the top two drawers of our bureau to be certain that they are crowded with his socks and underwear. I have begun to have the same dream: the one where I am eight years old and I look at the waves on a strong summer day. I walk into the waves and they crash against my chest, low and harmless, great cool water on a hot day. But then a bigger one comes and I misjudge its arch; it crashes down on me and I cannot find my way back to the surface.

"Don't worry," he said on Thursday night as I followed him to the front door in a pale blue nightgown, "I'll see you tomorrow." But he was moving so quickly he forgot to kiss me or look back as he dove down the stairs.

I carry a pair of old, long hedge clippers; they have worn wooden handles, but I have never used them before. They are the ones I remember my father using, or at least I think they must have been his, because nothing has been moved in the garage for twenty-five years. I wear black jeans and a man's dress shirt; I figure at least Harry can help me with this task; his office shirt is now outside in a bigger world with me. And I wear black mules on my feet. Even though they are tough, nonparty mules, my mother still looks at them strangely. An alien sighting in her garden. She hands me the clippers and disarms me of my only useful tool: The cell phone lies mute on the kitchen counter; it keeps company with the strong iced tea my mother has brewed to brace me.

I weed the garden of the firm, stubborn shoots and shudder at the work of clearing them, the nasty disease growing in the sunshine. At least I keep them from spreading any farther and mutating into a jungle. I understand now why someone felt compelled to torch foreign landscapes, burn mean terrain, rid it of its ceaseless, concealing bamboo.

I have my own large trouble to address, grown high against the fence, and I face the immediate danger with my clippers. The bamboo looks taller up close, and I cannot even see the fence through its forest. The greenish stalks are thick and weatherproof like copper wire, like telephone cables meant to last through centuries of conversation. My clippers are dull. The blades have lost their edge; they have seen too many hedges to begin fighting bamboo now on this Saturday.

My mother stands on the brick patio, outside the French doors; she shields her green eyes, calls out encouragement, promises cold tea, air-conditioning, a warm bath, and movies. She laughs like she does when she is happy. Her husband, my stepfather, doesn't cut down bamboo. He reads quietly upstairs or tinkers with his train sets in the basement, which seems to please my mother, who loves him but sometimes likes him parked away. Her two beagles, Franklin and Eleanor, supervise me; they try to squeeze their puppy-plump bodies into the deep reeds; they try to help me plunge into the maze in front of me. I have known many other beagles—all belonging to my mother and named for presidents and their wives. These two are young and eager, hopeful, unlike the generations I have watched grow old until their dark patches have turned white and their eyes gloomy blue with cataracts.

My mother keeps the dead dogs in her lingerie drawer, brightly colored packages of ashes among her nightgowns. "For safekeeping," she says. But, I know, when she dies she wants to be buried with them (or them with her), a party of dogs. She will only hint at this. When she does, she raps quickly on something solid with her knuckles; she tap, taps on wood to keep her and the living ones safe.

On Friday I wouldn't see Harry in our federal anthill; he would spend the day huddled in our gated compound with his boss, the president, and his other advisers discussing, I imagined, whatever had called him out of our apartment at four A.M. in his navy blue suit. I guessed they would sit sequestered in a soundproof room that excluded their assistants, helpers, catering staff. They would evaluate risks, forecast damages, sketch control scenarios as, I think, they must do every day.

The honest fact is I don't know much about what Harry does in general or in specific in the West Wing basement. It makes me feel silly and afraid somehow that I don't. I should. I work in the White House, although in a less senior way than Harry does, and have a business card that says,

Public Affairs Officer for
the Vice President of the United States
Domestic Policy
Deputy Assistant Director of Communications,
Speeches, and Commentary

I also have a printed federal government job description that says exactly what I do, and has recently been amended to include the speechwriting duties.

Harry's business card says only, "Special Adviser to the President." And I should understand what Harry does. Alone at night he might tell me, but he doesn't; he can't or won't. Of course I have asked him, "What do you actually do?" I would laugh using a low, official-sounding voice to gently mock his title. At first when I asked, he would wink at me and smile. "Top secret, don't you know." He would kiss me and conclude, "Let's not talk about work; it's too boring."

I was very proud of him when he got this job even if I didn't know exactly its description. The first lady, Claire Wallace, had been his Ph.D. adviser at Stanford. He was her favorite student, and she was Stanford's favorite professor of American history, so they made a good team even back then. She took an immediate shine to his mastery of dates, trivia, declarations, and theory; she liked that Harry revered Thomas Jefferson and so carefully sorted through the troubled passage of the Civil War and the somber cavern of the Great Depression. And not only could Harry think big thoughts, he could write beautiful words, and his dissertation on the Civil War, "At the Heart of the Secession," became a book and led him to New York, to NYU, to me. When Claire Wallace's husband was elected president, she made the call herself to invite her favorite student to join her husband's staff at the White House. She called our apartment one concrete-cold night in December just before Christmas.

When I ask him now, he doesn't look at me. He turns away when I am so tired that I scream demandingly, "For God's sake, what does Special Adviser *mean*?" But sitting at my desk on Friday, I couldn't think about this hole that is growing wider around and deeper beneath us all the time. Instead I just wanted him to finish with his business and tell me where we might go on our honeymoon, to run away from all of this and maybe start things new, if only for a little while.

Sitting at my desk, I could not concentrate on the vice president's poll numbers in the Midwest or focus on the White House or wonder what Harry does every day inside of it. I could only worry about why he doesn't smile anymore or brush my hair back from my face or talk about the wedding that should be four months away, in boiling hot August because that is when Congress is in recess and the first family leaves Washington to sail along the coast of Maine. I want to know why we have turned into strangers who are at the loud, twenty-four-hour mercy of other people, we strangers with our unused pots in the kitchen and a drawer full of stained take-out menus, many that found their way from New York, trailing us like the crumbs of a morning-after bagel.

When Harry finally finished his Friday huddle, we didn't have time to talk about these things or anything.

Instead he called quickly to say he would have to work all night. "Call you tomorrow," I thought he said before a chorus of background voices took him over and away.

It suddenly seemed so strange to me that Harry and I can't speak of our difficulties, strange because I spend my life dealing with the successes and problems of other people with whom I share no fast bond. I talk to journalists all day long about the vice president. I talk into the night and over every time zone that defies good sense. I have things that I tell them and, mostly, things I don't. I am told what to say and to whom to say it. Sometimes, when language fails, I simply say, "No comment." I like that best, of course, because then I do not have to think of anything further than two words. For the moment those words are enough. But the discontented do not always walk away so easily; they linger, grumble, beg. So sometimes, when all else fails, the phone goes blank, dead, blame-it-on-the-White-House-switchboard: overloaded, you know. On Friday I realized this is what Harry is turning to. I realized that he has resorted to "No comment," that I, too, might be disconnected.

I am only able to cut a few of the stalks. Such grim progress. I stop and assess the situation, the trouble before me: As far as I can see, the bamboo stalks wave like victory flags. I continue in the strong sun heat though my mind circles to the silent phone. Since we moved to Washington, I have forced myself not to think about New York for fear of missing it too much and falling down the rabbit hole; but for the past few weeks I have thought of little else. I stare into bamboo.

I had already lived in New York for three years when I met Harry. I had migrated through the city, young with no money, working as an assistant at an old PR firm representing writers, with four overstuffed suitcases, a cardboard box, two pillows, and a striped cat named Josie. I went from staying with my mother's friends on Central Park West to subletting a strange, crooked apartment on Murray Hill, to house-sitting for a novelist on the Upper East Side in his well-heeled, book-lined "English basement," where to see any sunlight I had to stand on his concrete patio and stare upward between buildings that cast tall shadows down. Then there was an ill-fated share with a girl who had left the New York City Ballet due to sickness, which turned out to be something more like loud alcoholism as she sprawled on the floor each night, her legs spread into a clumsy split as if she were stretching for rehearsal instead of ranting and flipping through her scrapbook. I found an illegal sublet on West 72nd Street, a tiny box with big windows that made me feel as if I were living on a screened porch and, as bizarre Manhattan fate would have it, had me staring at the apartment building of an ex-boyfriend whom I still missed and who was already living with someone else.

I would move downtown, back uptown, then across town. I would stay with other friends and relatives of friends until I was promoted to senior publicist at the firm and finally managed to get a one-year lease, when a landlord could see that I could afford it, for a studio above an Italian restaurant on Macdougal Street. It was my very own 350 square feet on the cusp of Soho, and I loved looking out the window bars across the basketball court that edged Houston Street and Sixth Avenue; at night I would watch the rush of traffic on Sixth, the car lights rocketing uptown.

Each morning after I moved in, I loved opening the door of the little building onto the perfect narrow street with trees and pots of flowers on the doorsteps, starting my day with some other era's view of the city. I'd walk to work on these mornings, cool spring mornings bright and clean, up Macdougal Street, past my Italian landlord sweeping the sidewalk in front of his restaurant. "Buena mattina, bella!" he would say, wearing his long white apron and waving at me with a large, worn hand. I would pass other merchants hosing down their pavements, steel gates clattering up to reveal tiny storefronts, trucks unloading newspapers, pastries, bags of coffee. I'd cross Washington Square Park among dog walkers and sleepy students from NYU, arm in arm, carrying backpacks through flurries of cherry blossoms that littered the park benches, dusted the sidewalks.

I'd walk under the arch where Fifth Avenue begins its long, wide path uptown, and I would feel a giant thrill like being at the top of a Ferris wheel and swooping downwards. I would feel like I had finally arrived in the city as

I passed the grand old apartment buildings and quiet shops. I'd walk quickly in the fast tide of so many others swimming upstream toward nine o'clock. I'd count, 16th, 17th, 18th, dodging taxis on the cross streets, and would stride twenty-three blocks until I passed the Flatiron Building, always turning back to look at it as I continued up Fifth to my office on 42nd Street, across from the public library with its regal stone lions who wished me well each morning. I bought a few pieces of furniture: an oak table, a chest of drawers, and a blue rocking chair. I had found a home. And then I met Harry.

In May the weather remained unpredictable, but I still forgot my umbrella most mornings, and, anyway, when I left the building on that near-perfect day, the sun was shining down on the basketball court. As I walked beneath the arch, however, hatless in a thin silk jacket, little black skirt, and a pair of pumps, which were unfortunately suede, it began to rain, not in drops but in sheets. I made it to 8th Street, already soaked through in a sideways gale, clutching a wet manuscript I had brought home to read, when I had to take cover under the long awning of an apartment building. I remember that the wind still brought rain down the avenue and under the awning, so I moved closer to the stone entrance. I remember trying to wipe the water from my eyes with a wet hand, my eyes shut and briefly blind from the storm, when I heard, "Here, you might need this." I opened my eyes and saw him leaning against the entryway arch, a backpack slung over one shoulder, his thick, dark hair darker because it was wet through and trickling down his cheek. His eyes were such a bright blue and he was smiling, holding out a Kleenex to me. I looked at the ground, and I remember clearly that there was a large *3* carefully inlaid in mosaic tile. I looked down because I felt flushed, awkward with my clothes pasted to me. I was dripping on his shoes, but I knew if I stepped backward, I might slip, suddenly fumbling like a colt on ice.

"Thank you," is all I could say as I took the tissue with one hand and clutched the limp manuscript to me with the other.

"Here," he said again after digging into his backpack and producing a plastic deli bag. "That thing looks like it's about to fall apart." He carefully held the bag open, but my brain seemed to be drenched, too, so I clung to the pages and looked confused. He laughed and touched the manuscript. I can't remember exactly how, but it eventually found its way into the blue plastic bag.

"Where are you headed?" he asked after we both had stood for long moments watching the rain grow even harder, and I had counted fifteen taxis that splashed past us with their "Off Duty" lights on.

"To work," I managed, still overcome by some strange, drowning shyness that wasn't much like me at all. "Oh, uh, up to 42nd Street."

"Me, too." He smiled and went on brightly, "I'm doing some research at the public library." He looked at his watch, and I finally looked at him, brave enough for a second to notice how remarkable his face was, with a straight nose, long lashes, and a friendly smile. "Hey, wait here a minute, okay? I'll be right back," he said, and then dashed out into the storm, running north while I watched him disappear around the corner on 9th Street. I had no idea what I should do. I stood for what seemed like a very long time, holding the plastic bag, trying vainly to smooth my hair back into shape, wondering whether he would notice if I quickly put on some lipstick. For some reason I began to hum and stare at the huge drops of rain that looked like diamonds.

When he reappeared, he was carrying two small black umbrellas and shouted triumphantly, "Gotta love New York. Umbrellas on every street corner for three dollars. Four, if it's raining." He winked at me, and I realized his voice was quite low and warm, sounding vaguely South- ern, its gentleness somehow out of place amidst the tow- ering buildings and deafening sound of the downpour, jolts of traffic, sirens, construction hammers crashing pavement.

I felt in my wet purse and found a five-dollar bill that was balled up like it had been put through the washing machine. "Well, I don't have four exactly," I said, offering it to him.

He frowned just briefly, a small cloud crossing the bright face, and shooed away my sad five-dollar bill. "Treat me next time," he said, and then, "Okay, let's get ready." We stuck our little umbrellas outside the awning and opened them into the gale. We both laughed at their size: midgets that barely looked right for a child. "I guess," he yelled to me as we started out, each grabbing on to the rims so that the tiny umbrellas wouldn't turn inside out, my blue plastic bag dangling from my wrist and flapping in the wind, "for four dollars you don't get to keep your legs dry."

And we swam together uptown. My feet squished as my stockings slid through water in my shoes; I could feel the water splashing out with each step. We tried to talk but had to concentrate on fighting through the storm, forging our way over streams that flooded the curbs at every block, jumping away from Fifth Avenue when buses sent tidal waves of dirty water, weaving around others struggling with umbrellas that exploded inside out. I knew then I would have continued to walk the length of Manhattan in a hurricane next to this stranger that luck had brought me in a city filled with miles of other people trying to find someone.

"Catherine," he sputtered fifteen blocks later as a huge gust of wind caught us in front of the Empire State Building, "may I call you?"

I am tired of gardening with my worn-out clippers. I learned, when I first began this, that one snip wasn't going to do it, that the blades could not really handle the job. I tried to devise new tactics to compensate. I resorted to opening the clippers to their full, brave width and, with my arms pumping, hacking away at the impenetrable stalk. Like a little axe against a mighty redwood, I could only chip away, cutting and then twisting, breaking hard nature away from its roots, tiny bits at a time.

I feel like calling Harry, hoping his cell phone will be switched on wherever he is, to tell him that I love him, to tell him a light-hearted story so that I can make him laugh, deep and sweet. But maybe I'm afraid that his phone won't be on or he'll be curt with me, him so tired or busy; or maybe I just don't know light-hearted stories anymore. This worries me most of all. Harry once told me that I was the only person he knew who could make a ten-block subway journey sound eventful. And I used to love telling him things, little and small: how everyone sang Christmas carols on the 42nd Street platform; how a man bound for Wall Street, possibly with a briefcase, got off before his stop to help a woman whose child was in a wheelchair; how two elderly people whispered and kissed like newlyweds.

After conquering just a few full stalks, I stop. With Harry's shirt glued to my back and my sunglasses steamed, I look up. The sky is a startling shade of blue. It is an electric slice of height, dusted by whispering plane trails and dotted by black, low-flying birds. The flock of crows looks down at me, telling me something I won't quite understand. They warn me somehow in their wicked, loud caws, commanding me to move forward now with my eyes wide and my gaze straight ahead.

⌐

I was born just like my mother. I was born with the same large lips, in the same tiny hospital where nurses drawled and cooed to the babies under slow ceiling fans that cast blinking shadows on late afternoons. My mother went back to the town in Virginia to have her first child. She went back to the place where she grew up, a faded town that was buried deep in mud or choked in dusty tantrums. Men sat outside the hardware store, slouched and yawning, and ladies carried polite handbags down the main street. They greeted their neighbors with perfect Plush Pink smiles, planned exuberance, a kiss on two cheeks; they welcomed well-known faces as if they were foreign dignitaries. It was a town where evening spread over the yards in the smell of early supper and to the sound of radios murmuring, all tuned to the same station, all clicked off at the same bedtime. My mother packed a suitcase full of nightgowns and returned home.

She put her two beagle puppies in the backseat of the grand white Impala and left the nation's capital to weave through the sweltering back roads of Virginia. With the car windows down, the air came in waves of hot, heat-sick honeysuckle, pavement, and grass mowed sweetly in the cow fields. She was tired of waiting for the baby. She was tired of being in July and in the humidity that sucked every breeze out of Washington. She guided the big car down routes that looked familiar, and for long periods of time — sun dotting across the windshield and her stomach touching the steering wheel — she coasted as if she were lulled into sleep, swimming through the early afternoon. The puppies were restless in the backseat and, drawing long breaths through the window, they whined to the scent of rabbit and earth in the tailwinds.

My father was somewhere in the Far East. At dusk sometimes she would stand on the front porch of their house watching the street, remembering the car that took him away. She would sit until after dark trying to will the green Pentagon car to come back; she would flip through the *National Geographic Atlas* hoping to find him. Her finger would travel across the page over the wide blue areas to where the land and strange dotted cities began: Nha Trang, Binh Dinh, Dong Hoi, Da Nang, Hanoi.

And his voice would come in jagged spurts across the world to where she sat in the yellow kitchen in front of an electric fan set to the highest notch so it whirled like a helicopter. Waiting for his call, she'd stare at the bacon splatters above the stove and at the daisy-shaped clock, watching the arm jerk, plastic petal after petal. "It's 110 degrees in Ky Lam," he'd shout through a blanket of heat that swallowed her in the small, rented kitchen.

"It was 115 yesterday," he yelled, excited on the end of the telephone, boyish and laughing at the other end of the world.

"It's hotter here," she pouted back to him, so pregnant she stayed in a thin nightgown all day, padding through the house in bare feet.

"I've been thinking of names." His voice blurred in an echo. "I like John or Charles." She stretched her hand out to feel the choppy, warm air from the electric fan. "What do you think, darling?"

"Nothing," she screamed, but her high pitch was lost and unheard in the distant crackle.

"I'll be back in August," she thought he said.

"When?"

"I miss you," he yelled, but a flood of French washed his voice away and left her alone in midsummer, in a city where she knew no one except for the mailman and her doctor. She hung up the phone in the tiny kitchen knowing that her husband's voice had disappeared into a hotel lobby with potted palms and air-conditioning. She hung up the telephone and sat with her two dogs for all of June, half of July, waiting for me to be born.

2

The car waits outside their apartment building just after four on Friday morning. Harry gets in the back, nods to the driver in the rearview mirror, and knows that Catherine is watching him through the living room window as the car heads down the damp street toward Dupont Circle. Did it rain overnight, he wonders only vaguely as he pushes the knot of his tie tight, tighter, and does not look back up at the dark window with the curtains parted just enough for her to see the taillights. He has looked back before and it only makes him feel guilty, some strange stirring of guilt and loss that he has to cancel out as the car rounds Dupont Circle, heads down Embassy Row, and takes him away from the city toward Virginia.

It wasn't always like this. When they first moved to Washington, before the city intervened, Harry knows, they still had their hopes and their humor. He was proud of Catherine, the woman who talked to taxi drivers and the vice president with the same clear-eyed ease. In the conservative blandness of the bureaucracy she, with her long dark hair, long legs, and simple elegance, had immediately stood out like a sable among so many squirrels. He was sure she was the only one in the communications department who kept fashion magazines in a neat, tall pile next to her desk or who read French Vogue *cover to cover, studiously referring to her university dictionary every so often.*

Harry always enjoyed watching her walk toward him with her easy, sure gait, her head and back so straight, feet slightly turned out like a dancer. Sometimes when he would pick her up from her section in the Old Executive Office Building, he could hear the sound of her laughter as soon as he walked through the door. Most people don't laugh like she so easily could inside the White House. And he knows she doesn't laugh much anymore.

There is no place for emotions in Washington, he tells himself, trying to shake off the rest of sleep as he rolls down the window to feel a shock of cold spring air. This has become his chant when he leaves her like a child in her nightgown before dawn, a look of bewilderment pressed on her face like the mark of pillows. He will keep telling himself this all the way to Langley, where he will drive through the dark Virginia forests that surround the CIA like a fortress.

The Old Executive Office Building looks like a wedding cake. In a burst of turn-of-the-century enthusiasm someone decided to build a great work center, an opulent beehive ringed together with the throne itself, the White House. Postcards of the White House always carefully exclude the ornate, pompously carved mass of granite as if to keep the true power confined to the benevolent house, to the pristine marble quarters of the president. But most people work next door. Like in any other office building, thousands of people work together under fluorescent lights, live corralled into cubicles, and spend their days buzzing through nondescript hallways carrying nothing more presidential than a coffee mug or a pen or an entry pass. The interior of the grand building is decidedly shabby, dim environs beneath the glorious facade. Renovations are rumored every two decades, but it is complicated and, I have heard, even the carpet layers need security clearances. I suppose unsecured workers could plant listening devices, and someone in a hostile land could keep up with our chores, could decode what went on with whom at various happy hours, softball games, and employee beach weekends. I don't know if it's true, because people in Washington—even the sixteen-year-old congressional pages from out of town—believe that they need security clearance and that they are being listened to, observed, by a higher power.

During high school and college summers, I worked at the bookstore in the National Gallery of Art, and we had to be fingerprinted by the FBI. I felt thrilled and dangerous at the same time, as if the plotting bookstore workers, the postcard sellers, spent their lunchtimes masterminding the theft of the nation's great art treasures. Later I discovered that the fingerprinting routine was really done in case any of us touched a painting—so that they could track us to our greasy thumbprints.

On Monday I leave the subway and trudge in my new dread down 17th Street toward Pennsylvania Avenue and the office. In the first year of working there, I did feel a dazzled, sharp thrill as I approached the wedding-cake building. My stomach did the reverse of what it does now: It leaped in anticipation, like seeing a love who waits for you, like the ten minutes before you're allowed to wake up on Christmas morning. I felt brisk and light and patriotic. I even wore my laminated White House worker clearance card around my neck, out of the house, onto the subway, like a long string of lovely pearls. I would stand, holding the cool steel bar above me, and pretend to be oblivious to my fluttering laminated credentials. I would catch people glancing at them, and I felt pleased, even the tiniest bit powerful. Now, I keep the card and chain deep in my bag and yank it out, twisted in pens and a hairbrush, at the last moment possible. I put it over my head as I climb the worn limestone steps—flanked by two Civil War cannons, their copper a moldy green—and enter the building that smells of disinfectant, pass the guard point, clear the metal detector and the personal-effects X-ray conveyor belt that makes me wistfully think I might find an airplane on the other side.

I didn't see Harry until Sunday at almost noon. I had been lying in bed all morning waiting for him. I lay there with pillows stacked next to me where he should be sleeping until I had to get up and smoke a cigarette and look out the living room window down Swann Street.

When I first moved in with him in New York, I used to love staring out the big curved window of the Ansonia apartment building; I could watch the long parade of car lights on Broadway for hours. He would come up behind me, his shoes echoing in the odd dilapidated cavern of an apartment, and put his arms around me.

"See anyone down there you know?" He would kiss me and lean against the broad sill and look out at night lights with me, listen to the comforting horns that wound their way up to our perch seven stories high.

I moved in with him just two months after we met that morning in the storm downtown, and the first night at the Ansonia we sat in front of the large window, drank wine out of chipped teacups, and watched a thunderstorm rage through the Upper West Side. Harry, too, had lived in a small studio in the Village and had magically found this vast one for us to sublet from a professor who had to go to a nursing home but hoped to return someday to his high-ceiled perch in the wonderful Ansonia.

My belongings, which had filled my studio on Macdougal Street, looked quite meager in the two giant rooms, empty of the elderly man's one thousand books and a lifetime of objects in storage. We put Harry's two folding chairs in front of the window, propped our feet up against the sill, and watched lightning crash out of the sky and bounce off steel rods that stuck out of the tops of the grand buildings like hatpins. He held my hand as we counted the seconds between the flashes and the rumbling clatter of thunder.

On Sunday I watched him come slowly down Swann Street as it began to lightly rain, not wearing his suit jacket and carrying a plastic bag with a six-pack of beer in it.

"I was worried," I say too soon after he walks in the door and in a tone I know that sounds less worried than mad.

"Don't start, Catherine. I'm tired." He passes me and puts the bag on the dining room table and takes a beer right from it before going into the bedroom. He curls up on the bed with his shoes still on, and I spend Sunday afternoon lying behind him, holding on to him until his breathing turns to ragged snores, until he silences my mute questions with sleep, until I get up to take his shoes off and drink a beer by myself in the living room.

It is always at these times that I feel the sharpest pangs for New York, like remembering a long-ago love. I feel the sure pain of loss. Harry never seemed tired in New York. As an assistant professor of American history at New York University, he spent his weekdays in a quaint, snug office that overlooked Washington Square Park or in a classroom teaching young students things they didn't know about their country. He loved all of it. And I guessed that the girls must have had crushes on him, so good-looking even to strangers, and this made me feel more proud than jealous, because he and I spent our weekends with each other exploring every corner of New York City.

We never planned, we never rushed. We just set out late on Saturday mornings to wander north, south, east, west. We'd walk fifty blocks through the city's canyons down to the flea market set up in parking lots on 26th Street. We'd spend hours examining trays of old watches and jewelry; piles of dusty rugs; shelves of pottery and glass; row after row of furniture, beautiful or forgotten.

My favorite stalls were the ones of photographs: proud family scenes from another century; university class portraits, the graduates long dead; faded vacation snapshots with careful writing on the backs—"Myrtle Beach, 1936," "Vineyard Haven with the Rogers, August 1955." Each time we went to the flea market, Harry would buy me one or two of the pictures for five dollars, maybe ten, and we'd make up stories about them.

There was one of a fat, grand dame of a woman with ropes of pearls around her neck—peacock feathers shooting from her head like fireworks and a live parrot, blurred from flapping its wings in an ancient exposure time, perched on her shoulder—who we decided was an opera singer and we named Contessa Vanessa. There's another of a family picnic with twenty-six carefully posed people all wearing paper crowns—grandparents, little children—and, precisely in the center, a young man in an army uniform looking very serious on what must have been a bright day (even in black and white) because he squints like he is staring right into the sun. On the back of the picture, in neat ladylike script, it says, "Our Charles's Good-bye Party, Grand Sam's House, Pound Ridge, July 6, 1940." And this photo is particularly worn, as if repeatedly removed from its frame and lovingly fingered through the decades, so we decided that Charles never came home from the war, that he was caught forever at twenty in a paper crown sitting on a plaid picnic blanket next to his smiling mother, whose eyes must never again have looked as bright as they did that summer day in Pound Ridge.

I felt quite strange about these photographs, each one of a full life that had somehow found its way, abandoned, out in public, on a table at the 26th Street flea market. But Harry reasoned that we were giving them a home, and even if we felt strange, we were completely fascinated by them. One time, on a cloudless spring day, we discovered an entire photo album, perfectly bound in leather, the photographs inside precisely and exquisitely placed on thick black felt paper. Harry paid a hundred dollars for it, but we could never keep it. We stayed up late that Saturday night, almost to dawn on Sunday morning when pale light and birds washed over Broadway, looking through it. On Monday Harry carefully wrapped it in tissue paper and gave it to the NYU library. The album was filled with the life of an elegant family: a debonair father in a series of perfect hats, a mother with a penchant for earrings and silk-tasselled shawls, three daughters who frolicked and grew tall through the black felt pages. It chronicled their outings and birthdays and holidays. The dates beneath the photographs were the 1920s and '30s, the last one in 1939. The town pictured was Warsaw, and the holidays were holy days celebrated with the father wearing a yarmulke and full tables set out for seders. We, of course, never knew how the book came to 26th Street or about the long journey that brought it there.

The photographs we did keep we framed and hung together on our living room walls — the Ansonia and now Swann Street — a vast tableau of curious strangers who became so familiar to us. In each apartment we hung our favorite picture in the middle of the others: a large portrait of twin boys dressed in sailor suits who, even as toddlers, even though they are identical, could not be more different. The boy on the left looks like an angel with blond ringlets and a serene, otherworldly smile, but the brother on the right, with the same golden curls, is baring his teeth and his eyes are wide with an angry intensity. We decided that the twin on the left was clearly the good boy, while the one on the right must be evil, and Harry liked the idea that the opposites of human nature were so plainly illustrated in a portrait of twin boys wearing little sailor suits. It wasn't until the picture had hung on the wall for a while that we noticed that the cherubic twin actually had his hand on his brother's hand, and when we looked closer, we saw that the angel was, in fact, really the devil. While he smiled sweetly for the camera, he was obviously pinching his brother so hard that the child was gripped in pain.

On weekends when the weather was bad or we had been up too late the night before with friends and too much saki in the West Village or Indian beer in the East, we'd walk to Wolf's Delicatessen on Seventh Avenue. There we would eat corned beef sandwiches on rye, sandwiches so huge that we would just order one with extra rye on the side so that we could then make new, more manageable sandwiches from the mountainous one. I loved the bowls of pickles—crunchy, extra-sour dills swimming in onion-flecked brine—that the waiter, who moved as fast as an ant and must have been as old as Broadway itself, would slam down in front of us on the table crowded with tall menus, paper napkins, and three different pots of mustard. I loved the packed place that seemed to be one giant maze of large room after room, with its bustle and cramped red booths, humid breath and steam from the kitchen fogging the windows as the winter traffic roared by, with its huge papier-mâché bagels that decorated the walls and were dressed at Christmastime with circles of lights and red ribbons.

I loved going there, my feet numb after Christmas shopping, Harry holding our bags as we tried to cram in the door with so many other people, paper shopping bags crunching against legs and "I'm sorry's." Still now I can exactly remember the ovenlike warmth that met us after we had trooped up Central Park South, the winds whipping off the park across the long line of carriages with their patient horses wearing wool blankets and snorting, blowing steam into plastic buckets of feed. I remember the great relief of the warmth as Harry pushed the door open at Wolf's and the intense pleasure of the smell: pastrami and bread together with the scent of an enormous evergreen that seemed to take root by the entrance and was covered in lights, red balls, and tiny papier-mâché bagels. Walking in there, I always felt like I was an excited child or was visiting New York for the first time, or both. Waiting for a table, peeling off my mittens, holding Harry's hand, thinking of corned beef and the endless half-slices of rye, I felt completely content and like Christmas was right around the corner. Harry would put his face against mine as we watched others in the line ahead of us being seated. "Your cheek is so cold." He'd laugh, pulling away for a second before the kiss he'd give and the table we'd get in a crowded place from another time filled with warmth and families and pickles.

⌒

"She's just like her mother," Granddaddy said as my own mother sat with hers at the big comfortable table in my grandparents' Virginia kitchen. It was far from ours in Washington, reached by dark roads through ice storms. The house was large, safe, and in it my grandfather would build a fire for all the women, and he was happy to make us warm before supper. My mother and her mother laughed like girls and looked through fashion magazines. As excited as teenagers, they flipped through the glossy pages, imagining the perfect pocketbooks they could buy together. But my grandmother's sister, Aunt Sally Ann, did not imagine. She sat alone, across from them, rocking my baby brother as if he were her own. She whispered things to him, tangled yarns from her threadbare life; she told the baby her secrets in the drafty kitchen's night.

It was Christmastime and my father was in Vietnam. I learned this word, and my mother showed me where it was on the atlas. The place looked small and jagged. My mother told me that there were no Christmas trees there, "just jungle and some palm trees, maybe." I thought about this and wondered if they decorated the palm trees with lights, white ones high up on top of the thin windblown trunks.

"Do they have Santa Claus?" I had asked my mother, sitting on her bed as she packed her clothes for Virginia.

"I hope so," she told me, folding the nightgowns. Then she said something that I could not imagine. She looked out the window, black past bedtime, and said, "And I hope Santa's got some real firepower; that's what your daddy needs for Christmas."

On Monday while Harry is still asleep, I go to the office on autopilot. I know I need to focus on work, my day and week ahead. I need to learn to be the adult I am supposed to be: a committed one, a professional, one unchallenged by nostalgia, rewinds, regret. I need to remember what someone once said: "There is no place in Washington for emotions." But the walk to my office is a forced march. I feel like a foot soldier on the last leg of something or a cranky child trailing her parents in a furniture store or exactly what I am: sleepless, worried, and shaken. I don't think about the calls I have to make or return. I don't think about the speech I need to write for the vice president to give at the National Gallery on Tuesday night, the fourth one I will write for him. Instead I remember that the last time Harry and I went to Wolf's, a few short days before we left New York that December, it was completely boarded up, shut tight, closed down, a lonely blank corner of Manhattan. A handwritten note had been taped inside the familiar glass door, saying only, "Thanks to our loyal customers over the years, Merry Christmas." We couldn't remember when we had last been there, but it seemed as if it had disappeared overnight, and I tried to peer between the boards to see if the bagels were still hanging on the walls. Harry and I walked back to the Ansonia in silence, our own boxes packed and ready to go, and it bothers me now just as it did then.

I walk through a long and complicated maze to reach my sector inside the OEOB. It took me months to learn this route, memorize the right turns and the down-a-stairwell, up-a-ramp routine (something like the great wilderness of Hansel and Gretel without the bread crumbs), but now my feet just steer me there. I work in a once large room that has been divided into endless cubicles with partitions covered in brown, woolly carpeting to affect the efficient, economical look of an accounting firm or a travel agency—desk, computer, phone, chair, chair, phone, computer, desk. Each cubicle has its own bulletin board, which is the outpost of cubicle creativity, and most have bright family pictures pushpinned to the cork or helpful slogans, a basketball player here, a swimsuit model there.

Throughout the room there are boxes everywhere, as if the federal government needs every inch of its empire for storage. Many of the boxes are marked "Classified" and at first I timidly, ominously avoided them as if they contained nuclear waste. But I remembered all of the crated art in the dark, back hallways of the National Gallery with strict arrows dictating the direction of these forgotten crates, and mostly they were upside down or some other way than right. I used to shudder at a Titian standing on its head, but soon I got over it, as I would with the classified boxes, and now I have moved one under my desk to use as a footstool.

There is an office at each corner of the room carved out of drywall. They are small but have doors behind which sit the chief of staff, the deputy chief of staff, and two others who are high up on the food chain. The vice president has chosen them to lead or they have earned it or they have been plucked from somewhere else and plunked down here with us and the boxes, hidden in the belly of the Old Executive Office Building.

Fortunately my cubicle is nestled in the back of the room—a small measure of my two years of service and recent promotion—near enough to a corner so that I have only one partition, a luxury granted to me so I can have some quiet to concentrate on the vice president's speeches in between the hundreds of phone calls I make and take to discuss him with journalists. It is common for people to have more than one job description inside the White House. I like *speechwriter* better than *publicist* because at least I am making things up instead of being told what to say. I can imagine I'm writing a play, giving lines to the gentle and thoughtful vice president.

He looks younger than in his pictures, shorter, too, as I understand most actors do, unless they are airbrushed or standing next to women who have taken off their shoes, slumped slightly, barefoot, and foreshortened. His face, however, is genuine, not fixed somehow like the president's into that steel shark-grin, impenetrable, beaming or snarling (depending) with one slight twist of the lip. Often, the second-in-command is not camera ready. As publicists, we want to quiet his expression, we try to undo the crease he gets square between his eyes, a deep crevice that makes him look too worried, makes him seem like every trouble is doubled, magnified into public bas-relief. So we tell him funny stories, small ones with no punch lines that are meant to be distracting. He never really listens. He nods and furls, the crease turning gullies into ten-mile canyons. And then we say, "Sir, perhaps you should not, uh—"

"Frown?" he asks.

"Yes, sir," we answer, and then he eases a little, smiles gently to us, his audience, before he steps in front of the cameras to read his lines.

The first person I hear when I enter the sector is my partition mate, Jill. It is easy to hear her an entire room away because she is loud, manic, and shouts like a salesperson who wants you to buy her product or else. Every time she finishes with a journalist, she does not put down the phone but, rather, crashes it into the cradle. She snorts and mumbles postgame recaps to herself; she curses her opponent not under her breath. She has been lobbying hard to get herself phone gear to wear on her head like a travel agent. She claims bitterly that her shoulder and arm are wearing out.

She files a great deal of paperwork about this complaining request and has consulted an office environmental specialist. He has visited us, written careful notes about our windowless, airless plight and has shaken his head sadly at our crippled, slouched, carpal-tunnel-infested factory. And I for one hope her request is denied. I hope someone realizes that she will chatter into the headphone, swivel in her chair, crackle gum, and look like Lily Tomlin playing the mad switchboard operator. I hope someone can imagine what she will be like, day in and day out, yelling at the press as if she is a twitchy woman on the street screaming at trash cans. I wonder if they know it will only get worse. She started a month ago, and her pitch has grown steadily higher, creeping upward, the pitch launched from an already frazzled personality.

When she introduced herself to me — in an ill-fitting purple suit, matching high heels, earrings shaped like enormous gold starfish—she gripped my hand and pumped away. She said, "I'm Jill Amish and I've been hired as your equal. I just want to start out on the right foot!" I wasn't sure which one that might be, and she didn't give me a chance to ask. Beaming wildly, orange lipstick beaming, she finished off her introduction with, "You know Amish like *the* Amish: peace loving and old fashioned!" Helpless, I turned and left her. I left her standing with her newly sharpened fistful of first-day pencils, teetering next to the toxic boxes, laughing like a seagull.

My voice mailbox is filled, and I know this as I reach my darkened cubicle because the small flashing light blinks, quickened in panic. The messages are mostly uneventful: thirty-nine predictable monologues about quotes needed, deadlines approaching or missed, "Can you verify the spelling of the Deputy Assistant Secretary of Housing, Urban Development for Crime Policy's full name?" "When is the vice president's press conference on 'The

Crisis of Illegitimacy'? Is it in the same shitty place it always is?" "Where is he going this summer on vacation?" "How old is his daughter, Lucy? When is her birthday?" "Will he ever get remarried?" And then there are three messages from Yuri Cherpinov.

I have talked to journalists from all over the world. Sometimes I've talked to them in French, and I have learned how to say please fax your questions in twenty languages including Cantonese. Sometimes I speak English that I don't even understand, or rather, I don't comprehend what is being said to me in English. I have a hard time decoding the British most of all. When I speak with reporters from England, everything sounds so clean, assured, and delivered with "ever so many thanks." Then, what appears in print is often miraculously muddled, snide, written with a jolly twist of facts, and a whimsical contempt for the person who has served up the facts on a paper plate. I am relieved when the *New York Times* or most any local paper from some cranny, crevice of this country appears on my caller-ID box. At least then I am armed with a common language and a vague journalistic uniformity bound by the power of "no comment" and "off the record." At least I can appeal to an American spirit of cowboys and Indians, and at the very least, I can separate the tabloid writers from the serious reporters. I can gauge who is friend and who is not, because they can't be or don't want to be or just like grinding axes until the blades are sharp, gleaming, deadly. At least. But I feel very disadvantaged when "Unknown Number" flashes over my screen. When I see these words and pick up the phone, I know I might be challenged with Icelandic views or Japanese standards or British notions of "good show." And, of course, then there is Yuri Cherpinov.

We began our telephone relationship harmlessly enough with a few questions here and a couple of clarifications there. He had once been an editor at *Pravda* and recently started his own magazine, "for a new Russia," he liked to say. Strangely, it seemed to me, the magazine used an unusual amount of space covering American politicians as if they were celebrities. There were glossy spreads of Senator Simpson riding his horses in Wyoming, Elizabeth Dole addressing women veterans, Claire Wallace waving to schoolchildren, endless pages of Senator Kennedy doing almost anything, and it seemed as though Yuri had developed a special interest in the vice president. After I laughed politely at a few of Yuri's bad jokes, he announced to me that I was now his "favorite girl."

So he began to call every day, sometimes five, eight times, and as a day wore so thin I could see through it, he would begin to lose his carefully manicured manners and become belligerent. He would slur and shout at me over land and sea. I'd calculate the time difference between here and Russia and realize that somewhere before noon my time, he was already deep into the vodka. I remained polite, as trained, but I quickly knew too much about him: He had been married five times (twice to the same woman), his father was a famous general in the Soviet Army, he liked feminine women (like his mother), and he fancied himself as the entrepreneurial type. However, he pronounced this "inter-perennial" so I was left with my own interpretation of his free-market status.

In desperation I finally appealed to my immediate boss (he would say "mentor"), Al Johnson, the chief of staff. He is a rugged career publicist and never met a fracas he didn't like and also sees himself as the protector of his cubicled charges. I have grown fond of him, although he does remind me of the lawyers I once saw in Manhattan Housing Court; the ones who represent the rotten landlords, those bulldogs who win cases with mustard on their ties and who always see both the forest and the disposable trees. So Al quickly made a few phone calls to find out how important Mr. Former *Pravda* still was, and some fast hours later, he received a memo—brief and official—instructing me to be nice to Mr. Cherpinov. Of course, it didn't say so in those exact words, but again I had my own interpretation of the contents. Certain journalists have power and, well, since my stalker warranted a State Department memo, I imagined I should be pleasant to him. I imagined a kind of Russian publishing mob with tipsy Yuri as its kingpin.

The last two messages on the machine are from my close friend Laura and my mother. Laura's is somewhat muffled, and I can hear horns and traffic in the background as she walks across Times Square to the meeting she has flown from California to New York to attend. "This damn phone," she yells. "Can you hear me? Can you? How are you, sweetie?" The message cuts off and I imagine Laura under the billboards cursing and laughing on the dirty, paved triangle that splinters through Broadway.

My mother says simply, "I just wanted to wish you a happy Monday, honey." And I feel, as I stand in my cubicle hunching over the phone and a pad of paper, both sweetened and guilty. I still haven't told her about Harry's behavior, his odd indifference, and she might understand. She would know about my night wandering, the waking dreams of his disappearances and reappearance, the rewinded words, unsaid words, the endless loop of words. She would certainly be sympathetic, but I worry that I would trigger her own shocks and memories. So I just haven't told her, and I let her blame my job for my sure need to lie down in the backyard and stare up at the sky when I should have been chopping bamboo. Plus, I can't imagine how those particular words would come out to my mother, how they would sound to me, and if I could even form them. She, too, has known him for four years. She laughs at the way he butters his bread and then pours salt on it. She likes his bashful moments, his funny speed talk and rapid walk, his stubborn mix of Southern deflection and plain ambition. She likes him in general, and in specific, she likes him because he loves me.

⌒ *Harry pretends to be asleep when she kisses him good-bye. Catherine struggles with the front door, warped and tilted from a century of Washington summers, and he gets up only after he hears her go down the stairs and then waits a few minutes longer. I will have to fix the door for her somehow, soon, he decides in the shower. He doesn't want her to always have to wrestle with that door. He also wants to repair the air conditioner, which they brought with them from New York, the ancient filter now clogged with the dirt of two cities. He never talks about New York, and he guesses that's because he can't. It is hard for him to remember teaching American history to eager, open twenty-year-olds, him with his backpack and eagerness, too. It is hard for him to think of her then, her head tipped back and laughing one night when they rode the Staten Island Ferry three times, swinging around the Statue of Liberty after midnight. He cannot think of her now still planning their wedding that seems more than a lifetime away. He starts to write her a letter, sitting at the dining room table with a bag of empty beer bottles next to him. He writes two paragraphs, cancels them out, and then, for good measure, takes a cigarette lighter to the scribbled page and watches it burn slowly on the windowsill.*

The phone rings before I can come up for air from my voice-message pond, mired thoughts, and it is Yuri Cherpinov, so I sit down with my coat still on. I turn on my metal desk lamp, which seems to have been working for the government since World War II and shines on through peacetime.

"You never call me back, Katerina," he says through a fierce echo, dressing up my name for the reprimand. I begin to stammer an apology but he doesn't care because he quickly announces that he is on his car phone; he is driving through Saint Petersburg, and I do the math in my head and realize it is after lunch there. He probably has a toothpick in his mouth as he steers his heavy Mercedes through ancient streets, looking for lovely girls who don't remember much of Leningrad and want to disco with him.

"I saw you on CNN," he enthuses, forgiving me my trespasses at a stoplight. And I don't have the heart to correct him and tell him that it was C-SPAN. I can't bring myself to tell him that while I was answering questions last week in Buffalo about the vice president's proposed elementary school plans to journalists more interested in the free doughnuts, I was thinking of how the trees were already beginning to flower in Riverside Park. Harry and I had so often walked along the paths there lined with cherry trees, apple trees, the blossoms falling around us like confetti.

Anyway, Yuri would not let me correct him if I tried, and he continues, "You are so beautiful, so young to be important. Your boyfriend is lucky but he better teach you some Russian, no?" He always says this despite the fact that I have explained to him countless times that

Harry does not speak Russian. Today I don't repeat my-self, and he goes on but I lose what he's saying because Jill is talking at full volume. She rants about the Secret Service to me, no one, to herself. And as she and Yuri talk into both of my ears, I look at my blistered hands from cutting the bamboo and think of Scarlett O'Hara. I re-member when she visits Rhett Butler in prison. She is wearing her ghastly curtain dress and pretends that she is still a lady until Rhett grabs her hand and sees her cal-luses. I wonder what would happen if Yuri could see my own bumpy calluses, my bitten nails and pale, dry skin. He'd know I was really a field hand, a common laborer, and maybe, just maybe, he'd stop calling.

But he goes on and on. He jabbers in the illusion that I have all the time in the world to talk to him, that my other phone lights aren't blinking like a crowded railway crossing, and that I have become the special Yuri Cher-pinov Desk at the White House. He wants to talk about the president even though I have explained—over and over—that I am not qualified to do so. He persists. He is obsessed with our president and will only put him in his magazine looking angry or tired. As much as he likes the vice president, he despises the first in command. He wants him impeached, although he pronounces it "imparched" and his reasoning is as unclear as his speech. He keeps insisting that the president is pro-Communist because he has publicly said (as so many others have) that, at least when it was the Soviet Union, the nuclear weapons were accounted for, as opposed to now when they are stolen and sold to the highest bidder. Perhaps in Yuri's shocking logic, he finds this practice simply part of any good free market.

In my delirium, still wearing my coat in the airless cubicle, I can't help thinking of the desert when he says it. I am parched. I am inter-perennially imparched. At any rate, he does not see why a man who has done less than he has can be the president of the United States. "He has no *real* power with us anyway." He shouts "real" and goes on, "He does not even know what power is, hah."

When I try to humor him and explain that President Wallace was elected by the largest majority in history, he just snorts. "Big deal!" It makes no difference to him because my president is on a mission to hold his president accountable for all of Russia's nuclear weapons. After Yuri lectures, yells, pontificates, he abruptly asks me if the president has ever asked me out on a date.

"Certainly this guy has eyes," he tells me, laughing in a rather jarring way. And I imagine that Yuri believes that the White House is like some federal harem where the sultan can pick any woman he wants from her cubicle. Again, I don't have the chance to disappoint him and tell him that I rarely see the president and on the few times I have had to deliver a piece of paper to him or have been in the same room with him, that he has been extremely businesslike, hurried, completely uninterested in me, an employee in a city of his employees.

Before I can explain, he concludes, "He should just resign. I know people who could help." I know, post-lunch, he wants to sound sinister, but fortunately his car phone is losing the energy to transmit him to me from the beautiful streets of Saint Petersburg. And I am glad that he is fading and that I don't have the chance to counter him and tell him that the president would never resign, no matter what. I do not have the authority to argue with drunken Yuri Cherpinov. But I know that President Wallace is a ruthless, fierce fighter, and I cannot say this to the Russian man on his car phone. I cannot say that the president's ancestors were pioneers who crawled, clawed their way across this vast, mean country to California; that he comes from people who endured three thousand miles and its cruelty, who bled, lost one another, suffered, and survived. It wouldn't matter to Yuri anyway because he just believes that movie stars and presidents automatically come from California, and I know he has never considered how hard they had to fight to get there — or here, for that matter.

And here is universes away from the president's California, from his tattered childhood in Los Angeles, in a worn-out, state-built house that caught asbestos chunks from the Hollywood sign when the wind blew too hard. He crawled and clawed, for sure. So many millions of voters need a special breed, an über-pioneer for another century. He survived the perilous journey to the other side, to set up house of a different kind. I wish I could speak to Yuri in his own language and tell him that our president understands cold blood and the ultimate reach of power. That the president of the United States believes, all too well, in the steeliness of what Stalin said to his Red Army troops as the Germans advanced on them: "Not one step backward."

3

⸺ *Harry puts five suits in a suit bag and then searches for as many clean holeless socks as he can find in his top drawer. He tries to remember when they last did laundry or, rather, carted it down to Dupont Circle to the Chinese man who already calls Catherine Mrs. Bellum and seems to feel sad that the two of them have so many lone, stray socks between them. Harry looks at the top of the bureau crowded with photos, and he wants to take one—Catherine laughing on Houston Street in front of a street vendor selling yellow, stuffed ducks; the two of them kissing on a beach in South Carolina, his father behind the camera; Harry in front of the White House on his first day. He wants to take just one but he knows it will upset Catherine. Instead he searches beneath the rejected socks*

*and finds an old packet of photographs, the only ones he has
of his life before Catherine, and takes out the one of him
when he was at Stanford, young and riding the Tiburon
Ferry from Sausalito to San Francisco, standing on the deck
and looking toward shore.*

I have turned on the tiny plastic fan near my computer to
try to pump air into my square space. My day on the telephone has sucked out what little oxygen existed in my
corner of the universe, but the fan only recirculates the
fumes of Jill's Lilac Pleasure perfume, the backwind of
her furtive squirting. Harry's picture is posted at the center of my bulletin board. He smiles broadly in it; he grins
so happily and squints into the sun on a late Paris afternoon two years ago in the gardens of the Louvre. Behind
him stands a little glimpse of the giant, towering Ferris
wheel. The night before the photo was taken, we rode
it three times; we held each other in the swaying car
high above the city. We circled—down, back around,
up—memorizing the landscape that swept by our feet:
one bridge, two bridges, a slow boat on the dark pink
light of the Seine.

While I should be working on the vice president's
speech, I think of what to say to Harry to remind him of
the Ferris wheel. Maybe we need to take another trip to
Paris, maybe just have a weekend in New York. He has
worked on either Saturday or Sunday for nearly a year,
even when the president is on vacation. He has traveled

eight times overseas without me. All of a sudden I feel a kind of resolute jolt of enthusiasm when I think that this might be the answer: We simply need to go away somewhere, anywhere, together. It sounds so simple, but then I remember recently even the simplest of plans have become complicated.

I plot how to approach Harry with my plan, but the phone rings and I have the newspaper open on my desk covering the caller-ID screen. I answer the phone without even a warning signal on this half-safe Monday, and a woman's voice tells me, "The vice president wants to see you upstairs." I do not recognize the woman's voice that startles me out of my Lilac Pleasure daze. I shuffle papers as if there were something I could bring, contribute, to a meeting with the vice president at this very moment.

"Now?" I ask the voice still waiting for my quick, efficient confirmation.

"Yes, now." She sounds surprised by me and my surprise. "Are you all right?" she continues, and then hangs up, impatient that I am not up six floors already.

The vice president sits at the very top of the Old Executive Office Building. He is king of the wedding cake, and the window behind his desk looks over the White House. The vice president can swivel in his high-back chair and look down at the gleaming white marble high above the West Wing. And he is looking out the window when I enter his office. I timidly approach his open door, after it has been opened for me and I have been announced, my name relayed by three different people upon my arrival on his floor. I feel nervous today as I pad across the plush carpet like a child entering the intimidating, quiet vastness of a library or facing the doom of the principal's office.

"Catherine," he says as I walk through the door with a rumpled notepad in my hand. He says my name still staring out the windows, looking at the White House and the fresh, tiny buds on all the trees below.

"Yes, sir?" My voice chokes slightly into a question.

He swivels back around to face me, and he looks tired. "Close the door and take a seat, please. Thanks for coming on such short notice."

I am always surprised by his manners. Most people in Washington, I've discovered, reserve their manners for higher-ups, people they need favors from or voters, FBI investigators, the IRS. He is naturally polite and a gentle man, a sharp contrast to his own bold, backslapping boss. The president and he are opposites in every way and that worked well in the campaign. While the president is a large man who lurches over six feet with the broad, beefy shoulders of a linebacker and has to have his suits specially made, the vice president is slight and may be shorter than I am, but since I always slump slightly when I'm close enough to measure, I can't be quite sure. The president has more than a full head of hair, a mass of curls he tries vainly to tame into shape, his dark eyes look as loud as his voice, a rasping boom that barely needs a microphone, and he usually winks his right eye for cunning emphasis as in "Gotcha." The vice president is nearly bald and his eyes are a watery, wide blue. He looks like someone who thinks before he speaks, and when he finally does, his voice has a calm lilt, twinges of the South combined with the flat "ahs" of his transplanted Boston. If the voters fell in love with the president, then they must have figured they could trust his less glamorous sidekick, the studious younger brother, the reliable accountant, the dutiful civil servant who has had his share of personal tragedy and responsibility: a dead sister, the dead wife, a young daughter he is raising himself.

"I'd like to talk to you off the record if we could, Catherine." His brow is caught in the frown, and I try to find a comfortable position in the slippery leather chair. His eyes are fixed on me, serious, and I think for a moment he might know that rather than working on his speech I've been fantasizing about a romantic weekend in a hotel with Harry, thinking about wandering the crooked streets of Saint-Germain looking for little shops that sell photographs. He may know that I cannot neatly cut off my emotions and go about business as usual. I think he may know that I really don't belong in the White House with its relentless chores and duties, that this big job is wasted on me and I'd rather be back in New York worrying about whether a writer is too drunk to read his novel in public, and then laughing later and drinking with my friends. Maybe he understands that I prefer limited responsibility and weekends in bed with Harry and the newspapers (that I can read the Style section first without ever lighting on news of the White House) with Broadway humming beneath us, the whole city ready to bring Chinese food to our bed.

Instead the vice president tells me, "No doubt you know that the Libyan government is finally paying restitution money to the victims of Lockerbie." He tells me in his measured way, now staring at his desk, tracing patterns on it with the top of a fountain pen.

"Yes," I answer, and feel the heavy weight of hearing the word *Lockerbie*. My frivolous thoughts have to vanish as I sit in the vice president's office talking about terrorists.

"And you know my feelings about Lockerbie." He goes on in a tight, cracking voice, and I stare at my hands, realizing sharply that my own self-absorption has blinded me to the importance of other things. My throat catches as I know I've turned as selfish as the rest of Washington. Of course I know how he feels about Lockerbie; his sister, just married, was on that plane, had happily boarded it in Frankfurt with her new husband.

"I trust your instincts, Catherine, and your sensitivity with the press." He looks up at me and this kind man who's paid me a compliment cannot know how poignant these words are to me right now and how completely undeserving of them I am. I need to stare out the window, over his shoulder, because if I have mastered the myopic motives of Washington, I haven't yet perfected the blind-lie gaze.

"I'd like you to think of some story placement ideas; how we can remind the public of the tragedy without making it personal to me. This is not my tragedy, but you know people tend to focus certain issues on those in office." He says this in an almost quizzical way, as if he, too, has not conquered some of the bitter truths of Washington. "So many people died on that plane and on the ground, I just think we need to remind people what evil things . . ." His voice trails off, and he swivels his chair back around, mercifully leaving me to stare at his back.

We are quiet for a long while, and I imagine he is thinking of his sister. He is looking at the White House but he is thinking of her smiling on that plane, holding her husband's hand on takeoff. Perhaps they were going to order champagne from the drink cart and waited excitedly to reach the right altitude, to hear the big metal cart creak down the aisle and toward them. Maybe they would tell the stewardess (we know there were nine attending the flight that early morning) that they had been married. They were probably bursting with the news that had only just happened, in a small judge's room in Vienna. Perhaps he remembers his own long flight to Heathrow, his drive to Lockerbie, a town he had never heard of before it became central to him, a daily word in the rest of his complicated vocabulary. He cannot forget what he saw when he got there. I don't know this for sure but I imagine it as I look at the back of his chair. I do know that the bodies fell. Like some kind of hideous hail, each one landed in a garden, a shop, someone's kitchen. I read this. Before, I thought that they had just gone instantly with the explosion, that the passengers did not know what had hit them, that they had stayed in the sky with the flash and the fire and smoke. Yet they found each one of them on the ground, and I know, too, that the vice president still corresponds with the Scottish policeman who found his sister tangled beneath some rosebushes.

Suddenly the vice president swings back around to me, faces me, as I go close to tears. "Think about it, Catherine, and let me know what you come up with."

"Yes, sir," I say, thinking what a gentleman he is for not mentioning the speech I should have finished by now.

"Okay?" He looks at me like the concerned father of a six-year-old and etches out a smile.

"Yes, sir," I say before leaving him behind with his memories and long view of the White House.

⌒ *As the train pulls out of Union Station, Harry fingers the Saint Christopher medal in his pocket. He does this on airplanes, in cars, taxis, subways. He forgets his wallet, his keys, but never the medal that Catherine gave him, which is supposed to keep him safe on all of his journeys. As the train picks up speed and clatters through the charred outskirts of D.C., he remembers when she presented it to him wrapped in a blue Tiffany's box. It wasn't from Tiffany; it had been her grandfather's in World War II, but she liked the idea of gifts in those perfect blue boxes. And he imagined her asking the serious man behind the counter for an empty box. Harry was sure that she chatted with him and told him her plan for the box, and no doubt, after she was finished he even polished the medal for her and wrapped it neatly inside, carefully tying the white satin ribbon.*

Harry has always marveled at Catherine's ability to talk to journalists on the telephone as if she were meeting them at a party. She gives each one equal time and remembers if they have children or have just returned from vacation. She has had great success with journalists, but he also knows that her trusting approach could get her into trouble. He worries especially about the Russians. KGB agents used to pretend to be journalists, which seems benign compared to the people who pretend to be them now. Harry wishes he could tell her how much he worries. He fingers the Saint Christopher medal as the train rockets north.

I leave the OEOB at just after seven, which is early by White House standards, but I have finished writing the first draft of the vice president's speech and am even a little bit pleased with it because I think that the vice president actually knows something about twentieth-century American art. So his speaking at the opening of a major exhibit at the National Gallery's East Wing won't be a stretch for him, like, say, the first speech I had to write, when he addressed the audience at the twenty-fifth anniversary of the Indianapolis 500. I had only thirty minutes to compose it with him in the car that drove us from the airport to the speedway.

"I think we can use a lot of speed metaphors," I had said to him hopefully.

"But I campaigned for national speed *limits*," he said to me quite worriedly.

"Okay, then maybe we can just recycle some of the romance-of-the-car speech you gave last month in Detroit." I knew he liked that speech and probably could remember most of it by heart.

He smiled slightly, loosened his tie, and peered through the tinted window at the passing scenery. "God, I always forget how flat Indiana is."

"Maybe we shouldn't use that, sir," I said, which made him laugh on a very bleak stretch of highway.

With the art speech finished, I hope that Harry will get back to the apartment before midnight. I stop at a little Italian grocery store on Dupont Circle and buy his favorite hard salami, artichoke hearts soaked in wine and lovely spices, fresh pasta, and four different kinds of olives. I will clear all of the newspapers and bills off the dining room table. I will find our silver candlesticks and chill some crisp white wine. Inspired, I go to Kramer Books next door to the grocery and buy three travel guides to Italy. I head home thinking of the hidden, narrow streets of Venice, with the comforting sound of water echoing through them.

There were nights when I would walk up Broadway, shivering as January winds gusted through the city's canyon, and I would count up the side of the Ansonia to where our apartment window was, and when the light was on, glowing bright, I would suddenly have the warm feeling of being petted, my back stroked lovingly like a cat. But as I walk down Swann Street, I can see that there are no lights on in the top-floor windows. It is too soon for Harry to be home, but I feel a sudden emptiness nonetheless.

As I climb the three flights of worn stairs, I feel some kind of inexplicable fear, nothing rational but still it grows sharper as I climb. I put my key in the lock, and maybe I imagine it but tonight I do not have to wrestle with the door; it opens so easily. The apartment is entirely dark, the only glow comes from the streetlight outside left bare by the winter trees that still don't know that it is spring.

My cat, Josie, greets me with an incessant yowl as if she hasn't been fed in days, and I pour a thoughtless clatter of dry food into her bowl. That is when I see the note. It sits on our empty, crooked kitchen table that we bought at the flea market on 26th Street. I leave my coat buttoned when I take the piece of paper to hold it up in the vague streetlight. I put the bags of food and books carefully on the floor. I cannot breathe, really I am not able to fill my lungs; they just stop pumping in and out. For some reason I think I might know what it says. I cannot turn on any of the lamps or lights because, like breathing, it might make the moment real and illuminated. If I can suck in the hot air of our overheated apartment, I might be alive, holding the note with my name written on it in Harry's careful hand as if, by mistake, it might have been discovered by someone else. I open the note and read it in the darkness. Harry always uses black, heavy marker to write notes, even letters, and so I have no trouble making out the words in the silent dim of our living room with all of our photographs on the walls, the twins in their sailor suits and Contessa Vanessa and her parrot staring down at me.

I read and reread the simple sentences but cannot figure out their meaning. I know he is gone; I don't know why exactly, can't imagine precisely why and how now. I feel breathless and crazy as if I have wandered into the middle of an important conversation and have no benefit of its beginning or end to help me understand what is being said: "Catherine, I will be gone on business for a week or longer. I will not be coming back here afterward. We will talk, of course, but you cannot change my mind on this & I feel it will be for the best. I am very sorry. Harry"

I put down the piece of paper and go into the bedroom; perhaps with distance the note will turn other shades, grow new colors like magic. *I will be gone on business.* I turn on the small bedside lamp and look at the bed, which has all of its pillows there and tossed about, some with his deep head print still intact. Superficially everything looks just the same as I left it when I walked out the door this morning. On top of the bureau there is my hairbrush, flowered jewelry box, perfume bottles, our framed photographs and stray buttons, a dried rose that Harry gave me a month before when I had to work through the night. I open his two, deep drawers and close my eyes hoping. When I open them they are nearly empty, most of the underwear and socks have vanished from the bureau that I brought with me to the Ansonia from Macdougal Street. A few old socks are left, lie in the bottom of the drawer like litter on a pond, and I wonder why he didn't just throw them out, why he didn't save me from these last stragglers, dirty and toes worn out from all our walks together. I look underneath a torn gym sock, a faded dress one, and find his envelope filled with photographs. I have looked at these pictures hundreds of times; in secret I have flipped through them to see how the man I love was when he was younger, to see him smiling toothless in front of a Dairy Queen, blowing birthday candles out with eyes closed in concentration as if he is wishing for something really big, wearing a Boy Scout uniform with his right hand across the badges. He has forgotten these in his haste, I think. I hold them to me as I slide open his closet door; the thick row of suits has thinned down by a half. I know by feeling their arms which ones are missing. I can tell that the best suits have gone into the night with Harry and away.

He stands under the familiar cement overhang at Penn Station; he waits with everyone else for a taxi. Harry watches each cab, the long line like some kind of dance, a passenger leaves, a passenger boards, the cab moves forward. When Harry gets in the backseat, he looks through the Plexiglas partition at the driver's ID card; he always does this. It reassures him to know the name of the person who's driving, a bit of a superstition like on an airplane when he introduces himself to the pilot and the person sitting next to him. The driver tonight is named Igor Ventushenka, and his Russian accent is thick as he asks Harry where he is going.

"The Waldorf Astoria Hotel."

"My English no too good," he offers, and Harry looks out the window at the city he used to love, the rush of Eighth Avenue pushing him backward into his seat.

"I try to study," the driver continues as they turn onto 44th Street and pass one of Catherine's favorite restaurants. "It so hard—like that!" He points at a huge theater marquee that announces Les Misérables, *which had been showing since Harry first arrived in Manhattan, so long he hadn't noticed it since. "I no understand what that mean, 'less miserable.' What that mean, 'more happy'? He says the word as "hoppy" but Harry does, in fact, understand what he means.*

"Nyet, znachit, Byednie Lyudi. Ets muzykal 'ni spektakl' o frantsuzskoi revolyotsil." Harry explains to him in perfect Russian that it means "the miserable people" and it is a musical about the French Revolution.

"Poyut i tantsuyut o revolyutsil?" The driver sounds incredulous that people could sing and dance about a revolution. Perhaps he is also shocked that an American is speaking to him in Russian from the back of his cab.

"Nu, pochemo nyet," Harry tells him, "go figure," as he rolls down the window to smell the city like a perfume worn long ago.

⌒

When I was six, when I was seven, I could not sleep. My father knew this, and he would come to me down the varnished hallway in his slippers and open my door. He would lead me downstairs, get my coat from the closet, and put on his overcoat to cover his pajamas. "Be quiet," he would tell me, "your mother is trying to sleep." She stayed in their room most of the time, pregnant with my brother. She would be in bed before I came home from school. My father and I continued into the garage that smelled like cold gasoline, and he'd open the passenger seat door for me. "Catherine, this is the last time absolutely," he would always say, tired behind the steering wheel.

We drove in the dim night; we drove between flashing traffic signals; we rode around circles; we passed embassies, monuments where the white buildings illuminated the black sky like fireworks. On the long curves of lawn between the memorials were hundreds of bodies, sleeping, huddled together for warmth and comfort. "They want peace," my father told me. I had seen them awake on TV, when they would stand and shout things at the cameras, but at night they lay quietly under flag shadows that dotted the wide marble buildings, grew large like bats from the spotlights.

My father, excited by spring and temporarily forgetting inconvenience and the world, would point to the Reflecting Pool and at the gusts of cherry blossoms that iced the dark pavement in front of the car. He sang songs that hummed, soft and old, over the radio. I rarely saw my father as he traveled by himself through the day city, wearing his uniform with medals shining. On these trips, his striped pajama cuffs sticking out of his coat, he'd steer slowly by the White House. We would wave to the guards who stood out front smoking cigarettes, leaning against the tall wrought-iron fence. He would show me the Rose Garden and point to the still upstairs windows of the residence and say, "You should sleep, too." And I, comfortable in the deserted night city with my driver, could fall asleep in the passenger seat with the car taking me home.

PART II

He Leaves

4

Of course I do not sleep. I
pace the apartment and cannot face putting Harry's favorite salami and olives away, so I leave the bags on the
kitchen floor. I pour a glass of wine and drink it in a few
long swallows, but it makes me feel lonelier to be drinking alone out of a wineglass that Harry and I bought
together. At first I feel numb and strange and try to re-
arrange the cat's two bowls as she runs away from me.
Then I am angry with Harry. I am angry as I watch the
clock tick toward an acceptable hour to go to work. I
don't know what else to do. I compose a letter to him that
I will e-mail across the White House server. It begins:
"Your curt note doesn't even sound like you. What has
happened to you? Are you even Harry Bellum?" I stop

writing because that thought scares me in my blur: Maybe the aliens have come down and replaced my lovely Harry with someone who just looks like him. I can't think of a better explanation.

Some time before midnight I search his suit pockets in the bedroom closet, his coat pockets in the front hall one, looking for a stray scrap of paper or perhaps a matchbook with a telephone number on it. I search for anything that might give me some small sort of explanation. But I do not find any scraps or numbers, just a few sticks of Harry's favorite gum, a button, a handkerchief. I always found it sweet and old-fashioned that Harry uses handkerchiefs and this one I unfold and it smells like him, like oatmeal soap and warmth, and I carefully refold it.

I call Laura on her cell phone because I know she will give me good advice. She has been my best friend since our freshman year at Brown, when we discovered each other in our dormitory otherwise filled with women swimmers who wore thick flannel nightgowns and made popcorn every night in loud air poppers they had each brought with them from small towns or sprawling suburbs. Laura and I both read *Vogue,* spoke French, and knew the names of clubs in New York. And she was, even then, an odd mix of wild, red-lipsticked beauty and total seriousness. She wanted to be a film director but chose to major in religious studies. She is the only person I have had martinis with, and the four she guzzled, with extra olives, left her light and giddy, fully in command the next day, singing in the dorm halls as she often did, while I was too sick to go to the library and lay in my room all day watching the ceiling for menacing spiders.

"I'm sure it's just temporary," she says to my relief, she says with her usual practical tone when I reach her in a restaurant that we both like in New York. I can hear the familiar noises of the place, loud laughter, clattering plates, and she goes outside to focus on our conversation and I listen to the occasional cars rumble along Prince Street. It makes me feel both comforted and aching, a far-off horn, a fire truck in the distance.

"The note does sound weird though," she goes on, lighting a cigarette as I light mine. "God, he really has changed, hasn't he? It could be a phase, maybe he's just really overwhelmed."

At about four A.M., after I have stared out the window for an hour, I realize that it does, in fact, get darker before it gets lighter. Predawn is the blackest time of night. Other random and useless thoughts that go through my muddled mind are about the astronauts' wives: I wonder how they felt when their husbands left, soared upward, away from them, and into the unreachable, pitch black. I can imagine a young wife in the sixties, in a Texas suburb, putting her children to bed in a newly convenient home where she is supposed to keep busy all day. After dark, after the babies' bedtime, I can imagine the silence of the rooms. She would sit, just her and the golden retriever, listening to the numbing sound of crickets outside mingling with the occasional laughter and TV cackling from the neighbors. The husband next door probably returns home from work every night at the expected time, safe from his short drive in the clean Chevy. And there she'd sit alone, on through the blackness, the still house, her own husband circling somewhere, once, twice behind the moon that she can see from her picture window. I imagine that after a while, with the dinner dishes done, she'd wander out into the backyard and look up toward the stars, brightness like diamonds, flickers, him; she'd stand by herself staring skyward. Maybe he wouldn't come back at all. The pain in her stomach must worry, and she'd be left as she was then, down here, alone on earth, anchored to the ground.

At five A.M. I wonder if I should take off my engagement ring but even the wondering hurts. Harry asked me to marry him in the Central Park Zoo. It was the October before we moved—before our lives turned a different color—on one of those vivid autumn days when everything looks crisp and sharp and the air smells like apples, leaves, and fires. We were standing in front of the seal pond when he suddenly said, "I have something for you." Out of his coat pocket he took an envelope and inside was a photograph of a proud-looking black bride and groom, the bride beaming in a long lace veil, the groom wearing a white rose in his buttonhole. On the back were the words in Harry's bold handwriting, "Will you marry me?" The seals splashed, the leaves swirled, children laughed, and when I, speechless for once, looked up at Harry he had a nervous, wide smile and he was holding a small brown velvet box. "I'm sorry." He grinned. "It's not from Tiffany's."

∿

My father helped me memorize my lines for our second-grade play, *Winnie the Pooh and the Honey Jar.* I was cast as Kanga and given a costume of a dyed-brown suit made out of old long johns; it smelled of mildew and had been fitted with safety pins, dressed up with felt ears, a long tail stuffed with newspaper, and a pouch, a place to put my toy squirrel who would play the part of Little Roo. "You have to listen," my father said to me gently after I had thrown myself in my pajamas onto the dining room floor in stage fright, agony, a memory blackout of what to say to whom.

"You have to listen to Piglet and then you'll know what to say back to him," my father reasoned, holding the script bound in purple construction paper, standing above me still wearing his daytime uniform. "Piglet says, 'Hello, Kanga! It's a perfect day in the forest.'" He tried giving Piglet the affected air of an English gentleman. I hid my instant giggle in the carpet, my hot, wet cheeks sticking to the wool. He was a very good Piglet and much better than the boy who was cast in the part, Randy Smith, who always hung his head so low he swallowed his words. My father repeated the line to my silence, and with a flourish he spoke to the whole house in his booming, deep voice.

"Now what do you say, Kanga?" he asked me, lying under the table, stubborn and fingering the carpet tassels.

"It's a fine enough day for Little Roo." I tried, my petulance now fading from actual into acting.

"Excellent," my father shouted, still in character as he pounded the tabletop theatrically above me. "Now try it standing up."

⌒

By six A.M. I get ready for work. I do not have patience for the shower, for the slow mixing that the knobs require to produce a comfortable, mild stream. I plunge in cold. The drain hasn't been working recently so the water quickly collects around my ankles and I am standing in a leaky boat, trying to shampoo my hair in icy water. Under the freezing water, I remember the note that now sits with the empty wineglass. *We will talk, of course, but you cannot change my mind.* Why had he never asked what might change *my* mind about this situation? I douse my head in cold water and the shampoo stream just keeps pouring into my eyes, streaming down my face like stinging tears. *I am very sorry.*

The taxi pulls up to 17th and Pennsylvania slowly. "Do you really work here, miss?" the nice driver from Nairobi asks me as I try to count the dollar bills that are crushed into balls in my big black bag that Harry used to call "the black hole" because that's the one area of my life I never organize. "Why," he goes on in the rearview mirror, the bright whites of his patient eyes on me as I attempt to assemble the fare from my cluttered bag, "do so many people hate Americans and want to blow them up?" I know he expects me to give him the short answer, but I can barely concentrate on counting the sticky quarters covered in tobacco flakes.

"Lots of reasons," I say lamely when I finally dump the money into his outstretched hands, struggle with the door, and climb out into the quiet, clear morning.

On Monday night Harry sat up late in his room at the Waldorf Astoria Hotel. He is staying on one of the two secure floors owned by the federal government that can only be ascended to by an elevator linked to a computer housed deep beneath the ornate lobby. He drank three beers by the window and looked up the East Side, all the way up the straight, lighted path to East Harlem and to a bright little bridge beyond that flickers like fireflies in the distance. After the first beer, he had been thinking about how much Catherine likes hotels, ordering room service and lying in a big, clean bathtub, singing like a happy child. He smiled and caught himself, opened another beer.

He knew he should not think about her anymore. He knew he had left things in order. He had even asked Sam O'Connor to watch out for her. He trusted very few people now, but he gambled that he could trust this particular Secret Service agent, a man who stood next to the president but could never repeat anything the president says, not one word, not one sneeze, not one utter. Harry was hoping he could trust a man whose whole life is about protecting other people's lives with his own.

Everything had changed for them when Harry got that first call from Washington on a bitterly cold December night when they lived just across the park but so far away from these secure floors of the Waldorf Astoria. He opened the third beer quickly. Catherine had been sitting on their couch watching him as he was offered the job over the phone. She was wearing his socks that were much too big for her, and she was hugging her knees, looking at him with wide, trusting eyes as his conversation sealed their fate. When he hung up the phone she leaped off the couch and started hopping around, excited for him, "Was it her? Was it her?" she kept asking, believing that Claire Wallace had offered him a job in the White House. "Yes," he had said as she kept hugging him, and that was the first lie of so many he would have to tell her.

I have left my sunglasses in my office, and I remember this in the glare of the granite building. If I was only half-concentrating on work yesterday, today will certainly be worse. I have worn some of my favorite clothes to make myself feel better, the perfect cashmere sweater, Prada trousers that I told Harry were half price, which wasn't quite the truth, and a beautiful spring coat I got in Paris at a shop that looked like a little gilded box. I even put on my lipstick so carefully with a lip brush and did a double, triple squirt of Chanel No. 19 as a final attempt at confidence. But my stomach flutters when I face the building. I need coffee, water, no questions asked.

The questions begin as soon as I enter the building. "Could you please put on your credentials, Miss Porter?" the first guard asks as I step in the door. I dig in the bag again, groping for laminate. "What don't you have in here?" the second guard quips as he takes his turn looking into the dark depth of my bag. "They working you too hard?" the third guard ventures as I trip over the cord of the metal detector. And I will have to face the walk, the maze without coffee, but I stop at a tired, government-issue water fountain. I bend over it, push down on the creaky button, feel the cool water against my lips, and I close my eyes so that I will not have to look at the sad piece of chewed gum that cowers in the drain. I slurp in the trickling arch that tastes like rust.

When I reach my cubicle, the message light on the phone blinks like the signals at a crowded railway crossing. Before I do anything else, I pick up the phone and dial Harry's extension; it rings and keeps on ringing. It usually gets picked up by his assistant, Rebecca, or rolls over to the monotonal operators who answer, "The White House," as if bored. My phone rings right back and Harry's name, his extension, slides across my caller-ID screen, and I stare at it paralyzed, jolted somehow by the ringing sight of "Bellum, H."

I snatch up the phone. "Harry?"

"No, ma'am," an unfamiliar voice tells me, and goes on robotically, "I'm afraid Mr. Bellum is not in the office right now."

"May I speak to Rebecca, please?"

"Sorry, ma'am, Miss Fisher is on vacation."

"Well, this is actually Catherine Porter," I try. "Do you know how I can reach Harry?"

"I'm sorry, ma'am." The monotone continues, unmoved. "He is not in the office right now." She repeats this because it is the only information she is allowed to give out about a special adviser to the president.

I quickly dial Harry's mobile phone, and I finally hear his voice, with a strange sense of relief. It is his usual message saying, "If it is an emergency, my beeper number is . . ." I hang up and know he will not think this is an emergency. He has left his note and that must be that to him. He will think that I should no doubt give him "space," "time." He will think I have gone crazy, and as I sit at my desk with the busy business of Washington swirling around me, imagining that "Bellum, H" has rung back from someplace other than the White House, I am beginning to think so myself.

⁓

My father bought roses for my mother on beautiful bright Saturdays when I would trail behind him to the florist wearing my new sneakers, red or blue. Back at our large stucco house with its wide porch waiting, my brother, just barely born and tiny, welcomed us. He had a special coo just for me, and I would bury my head in his round belly that was nearly covered by a doll-sized white T-shirt. He'd sit on the shady porch in a little plastic chair, a kind of space capsule; he would bounce back and forth, arms flying.

My father would put the baby, for safe measure, on top of the big porch table. The table was firm, steady for the baby's weight and rocking, and it caught the gentle breezes that came from pines and apple blossoms. I would play with my brother's miniature hands and feet, his nails so small like pink seashells, and I would watch my father roll up the sleeves of his denim blue shirt. He was serious in his work. He would spread newspapers across the solid table and unwrap the roses. He'd carefully lay them across the sports pages and comics that grew damp underneath the flowers. I knew how to read but the comic strips still seemed alien to me: Snoopy slept with a sound like *ZZZZZ,* and I couldn't understand who talked and who thought with bubbles coming out of their heads.

I would kneel on one of the green chairs that always stayed on the large, wrapping porch. Once they had been kitchen chairs; the two of them had been breakfast seats and yellow, but my mother grew tired of them inside, I guessed. She put on my father's old denim blue shirt, roomy but not quite enough over her huge belly that kept my brother inside until he was big and loud enough to come out. She painted the chairs in the driveway; she painted them green like new spring leaves, the tender ones that burst suddenly on the apple tree, near us on the porch.

The baby and I would watch my father work. I'd plant my elbows on the comics and the table, my face near my brother's chunky legs churning, sunlight threading through the trees, bright golden. My brother made chirping noises and sounds like grunting or like the seals I had heard in the zoo when they barked for their fish, clapping wet flippers at the fish lady in her tall yellow boots. My father's face was focused as he stood over the roses, damp papers, and us. He picked up each rose, long stem with bloom on top; he held each in the morning air that had turned fragrant with sweet roses. Using a toenail clipper, large and silver, from the medicine cabinet upstairs, he would work his way down each stem. He would tell the baby, say to me watching closely, "Your mother doesn't like the thorns."

5

By eight thirty I have opened
my e-mail to write to Harry. He checks his e-mail wherever he goes; he checks it twenty, thirty times a day. I have
to write him something so that he knows I do not accept
his behavior, do not accept a note that might as well have
said, "I've gone out for a pack of cigarettes and am never
coming back." I will have to be careful not to say too
much on e-mail as everything is closely monitored on the
White House server, but right now I don't even care too
much about that, about the invisible people who are
watching us, regulating our relationship, monitoring our
breakdown.

As I write, I do not hear Al coming up behind me; on
better days I have radar.

"Catherine?" he says my name as if it really is a question, and I realize, fumbling to close the e-mail screen, that I am not, in fact, who he thinks I am or wants me to be. "Will you join me in my office, please?"

Al sits down behind his large mahogany desk and folds his hands in front of him; he looks at his short fingers. "Is everything okay, Catherine?" he begins, and continues without my answer to guide him. Before I can answer, the phone rings; he ignores the first ring, the second, and then scoops it up on the third, barking, "What?" He leans back, way back in the tall, black chair, and I can hear it creak and resist. "Well, fuck him! You know this is the last fucking thing I wanna worry about." He listens briefly but shuts whomever up with, "Just fuck him. Yeah, I'll call him back. And he's not the fucking bureau chief. He's the asshole managing editor." He rolls his eyes at me and points to the mouthpiece. "Get it straight, honey, okay?" He slams down the phone and resumes his prayer position.

"Good," he says to me as if I have answered that everything is okay, as if I don't know what time the night is blackest. I focus my eyes on his, which are half hidden by half glasses that, I think, he wears to seem goodly, sympathetic. There is a partially eaten bagel on his desk, resting in a greasy piece of waxed paper and piled high with cream cheese and butter. He takes a bite out of it, and I have to turn my eyes away; I look at a patch of brown carpeting instead. I imagine that he's been chewing on this bagel since before six A.M., and I feel like my stomach is turning into compost.

"I think"—he sputters bagel crumbs at the desk—"that you've done a really fine job on the vice president's speech tonight." He holds my stapled pages together and peers at them through the half glasses like a librarian. "Yeah, I especially like how you open it with the Jackson Pollock flag thing."

"Jasper Johns," I say before I can stop myself from correcting a man who is always right.

"Whatever," he says, because I'm sure he didn't much care in the first place. "Today you've got to plan the VP's appearances with Mrs. Wallace. We're going to put them out there together to show 'em all this big house is one happy family."

"I saw the vice president yesterday," I say, trying to seem serious and focused, indeed, glued together by effort and fear. "And we discussed some ideas about Lockerbie and—"

"Fuck Lockerbie," he shouts with such great strength that I feel the winds and crumbs fly across the table. "He has got to get off that fucking flight." He shakes his head and looks at me with a kind of squint-eyed contempt. "Of course that is purely off the record. But it is not your job to deal with a decade-old news story, so forget about it. It's over, done. I just need to know now if you can handle everything."

His eyes have widened, he has taken off his benevolent half glasses, and he stares directly at me. He wants to excite me into action, rouse me from the sidelines, get my sorry ass off the bench, make me run down the field with the big boys. I know that he used to coach his son's Little League team, and I can only imagine that he got the fat kids, the bespectacled, slow kids to play their untalented little hearts out. They probably damn well learned to hit a ball or, at least, learned how to look peppy enough on the field. I nod my head at him, fake some spirit, and say, "Sure, I can handle everything."

When I return to my desk, I look for Will Bennett, who sits three cubicles away from me in a tiny, drywalled cave that he got when he was promoted to deputy assistant chief of staff. He is my best friend at work, maybe the only one there right now as Harry is moving fast away from all of his previous positions with me. I want to take Will outside, and he will come with me patiently, even though he doesn't smoke and doesn't like me to but understands that sometimes I can only think when I smoke. Tie flapping, he'll dance in front of me trying to dodge the exhaled fumes. Will is the only person at work whom I confide in, tell personal details to, ask for advice. It's his natural personality to be confided in. And he will listen carefully with his head down, with his thin arms unconsciously hugging his slight body in concentration. He knows the vice president well and he knows me. He knows that Lockerbie will haunt me now. And Will understands boyfriend trouble because he has had much of his own; he knows about heartache, desertion, the male ego, and loneliness that creeps into places it does not belong.

Will is not in his little office, it is dark. I know he sometimes worries about me and how I deal with all the pressures, and he would worry now if he knew that Harry has officially retreated from my life. Even in the best of times, Will often tries to tempt me to eat more by bringing in bread he bakes himself ("When I can't sleep," he says and shrugs) and, in desperation, with a big bowl of Gummy Bears he keeps on his desk. I worry about him, too, because he has been disappearing lately. It is easy to disappear at the White House, to get swallowed in the maze, but it has been different with him, and friends share a certain telepathy where absences are charted.

I pass his empty office with my cigarette and lighter in hand, the cigarette growing soggy in my palm because it is too much of a security production to carry a bag out and back into this building. Especially today. I do not want to face so many people and detectors; I do not want to smile and pass inspection. The west door is the closest outside escape hatch to my sector, and it's where I usually go to smoke, but it also faces the West Wing back entrance to the White House, and I don't feel like facing the White House right now.

So I decide to smoke outside the east door instead. I make my way through the maze, across the giant building to the entrance where I can look out on an anonymous street. Two guards, smokers, too, man the big door. They smile and let me pass when I wave my concealed weapon, my limp cigarette, as if it were the most crucial of all credentials.

It is bright outside. Washington light is different in the spring. It is elated, weightless, different from the solemn gray shades of January, February. I squint into it as I take the first drag of my cigarette and wish that I had remembered to bring my sunglasses out into the day with me. People walk past on 17th Street; they wear baseball caps and carry video cameras; they stop and look at me through the high wrought-iron fencing and hope that I am someone important enough to film and show to the excited folks back home; they stare at me through the black bars as if I am a bear in a cage. I know they cannot imagine that I care more about my boyfriend than about my White House job. Admittedly, I do care for their vice president but not because he is my superior, important to the country, but because he is, seems, like a real person who still has emotions and is caught so off guard by his own sadness. And they do not imagine one of their leaders as he really is: a slumped man sitting in his office looking at framed pictures of his dead family members, praying that the president will do his job well so that he doesn't have to assume any bigger, more ominous responsibilities, so that he will not have to forget about Lockerbie, his sister, personal matters. I close my eyes and inhale.

When I open them again, the tourists have moved along toward the monuments, the food trucks, and the cherry blossoms. I look to my left and someone approaches me from a distance, from my side of the gates. I know the figure is Secret Service because only Secret Service personnel can walk on the grounds the way he does: circling the great building around the side, over the grass, sidestepping tulips, and ducking his head under trees as if he is strolling through a public park. I know, when he is still far away, before he waves to me, who he is. From a distance he looks enough like the president to be confused with him. And that's the point. He is special guard for the president, protecting him with a similar head of dark, gray-flecked curly hair. He stands close enough to the president to shield him—curl for curl—from a bullet. And Sam O'Connor waves a long, fiercely built arm at me as he makes his way, more leisurely than purposefully, around the perimeter.

Sam looks little like the president up close, from the front. The back of their heads, their tall, solid frames could be identical, but Sam's face is distinctly his own. As he nears, he smiles at me with his broad Hollywood smile. He wears mirrored aviator glasses that are flashy and more fighter pilot than standard issue Secret Service. And while most Secret Service men are recruited, trained to blend in, in a kind of clean-cut, average-guy way, Sam stands out. That, too, is the point, I suppose, because so does the president. If the president's face is a reassuring mixture of ideal American faces, then Sam's is most certainly Irish. His nose is strangely tiny for his big boy face; it is crooked and rearranged like a boxer's. I wouldn't be surprised if he had been a boxer but, I think, the nose developed somewhere in the DNA, somewhere seas ago in Galway.

I guess he's what they call Black Irish, with dark, wicked eyes—sharp brows arching above them—that dart constantly, survey the world and its crowds, its loners; he always looks many steps ahead. The filing staff, who frequent the cafeteria, the loud girls who eat nothing but Jell-O and Tic Tacs, call him a "triple S." Confused, I mentioned this to Will, and he laughed at me for not being able to decode their mysterious phrase. "Just try," he begged me, he wanted to hear me translate secret staff speak. I did come up with numerous inventions, much to Will's handclapping delight, but nothing that matched the simplicity of the truth: Secret Service Stud.

He approaches me with an unlit cigarette flopping in his lips. "How's tricks, Soho?" He uses my Secret Service code name, which is really only used when I ride on the vice president's airplane, which I have only started to do in the past year. I would like to witness the Secret Service naming process. I asked Sam once why I was called "Soho" and he answered matter-of-factly, "Because you're tall and wear a lot of black."

I imagine the Secret Service men, sitting around their own cafeteria, trading war stories and naming us like pets. Will is called "Prof," which makes sense because he's extremely smart, neat, and gentle, as you'd hope a professor would be. Al is "Bull," which is also appropriate because he can be fierce like one, a charging, stubborn force of nature. But it also may be a little tongue-in-cheek Secret Service humor and short for Bullshit, which they must believe that publicists are responsible for when they refer to our sector as the "Spin Cycle."

Jill is unnamed still, and of course, this is her new sore, her latest complaint, a nagging exclusion that she just won't stand for. I shudder to guess what they would call her. She treats them like nuisances, hired help, over-built nonthinkers who shield her from her own boss and make trouble for her.

"Who do they think they are?" she yelled at me after one man had to physically stop her from barreling into the vice president. "Don't they know who I am?"

"They're just trying to do their job," I ventured diplomatically, keeping my back to her outrage, to her head stuck above the partition.

"Well, they'd better let me do mine!" she snapped as she flapped back down into her chair, and I heard "fucking bastards" muffled in the brown, woolly partition. She then pounded at the buttons on her phone to file a formal complaint with some bored branch of the government, which probably had its own code name for her already.

"Beautiful day," Sam continues, lighting his cigarette, and reflexively offers me another when he sees that I am stamping my finished butt into the pavement.

"Thanks," I say, and I take one of his king-sized Winstons from the pack he holds out. He had expertly tapped the package so that one popped out for me, and then he lights it with his silver Zippo that wafts butane before he snaps it shut.

"You okay, Soho? You look kind of worn-out." He actually waits for my response, one concerned eyebrow arched upward to the limestone tier of the wedding cake that we stand underneath. I know he comes all the way around to this side of the building to smoke, to avoid the White House like I am trying to do. Except, in his case, he's hiding from the president. I guess the first lady, too. Sam doesn't want his boss to catch him smoking, so he comes over here as if he is sneaking away from his parents to take a quick puff. I find this slightly amusing, his ducking the president, because it is his job, his duty, to forever shadow the man. But I understand. It is my job to be nice to people, to make up clean truths and present a positive image of this world, and right now it is the last thing I feel like doing. I need a break and so, I suppose, does the shadow of the president.

"Sure, I'm okay," I lie.

"Yeah, they're probably just working you too fast in the Spin Cycle." He inhales deeply, an extra long intake of smoke, and watches the street in front of us. His eyes move fast through the gate and follow the traffic, the pedestrians, businessmen; he is looking, always looking. And I'm glad he's not focusing on me with my eyes bare, me the tall girl in black who is not focused on her job moment to moment the way he is.

"Uh-huh," I respond, though vaguely enough. I know Sam won't prod, poke any deeper, because even—maybe especially—the Secret Service has secrets of its own. Besides smoking, Sam, I know, wears a huge gold wedding ring that has two snake heads intertwined. I met his wife, Tammy, at a company softball game, and I can imagine that this petite, very blond woman in a halter top designed such a thing, such a monstrous token of love. Sam is devoted to his tough, coiled wife, and he thumps his heart with his fist when he speaks of her. But when he's working, he keeps the ring twisted around on his large finger so that only a wide gold band shows. He winked when he demonstrated this trick for me. It reminds me of what I used to do in New York when Harry first gave me the engagement ring: I would turn the lovely sapphire and two diamonds inward, my secret, just a slim silver glimmer on the subway.

Sam hides the wedding snake ("Sam and Tam Forever!") and tap, taps the two twined heads against the wrought-iron handrail as he smokes.

"You got plans later?" he asks, genuinely interested, and I shake my head. I think he knows that even in better times I don't rush home to cook a three-course dinner. "If your boyfriend is working late again, maybe we could grab a couple of drinks. Tammy's in New Jersey with one of her sisters."

I shiver. Harry works very late, and of course Sam knows this from the West Wing log, from standing in midnight rooms with him and the president. What, I guess, he couldn't know is that I now have a note telling me Harry won't be coming back to Swann Street again.

"Sure, I can meet at about nine, after the vice president's speech at the National Gallery," I say, stamping on the tan filter of the borrowed, strong cigarette, because I can't imagine sitting in my dark apartment tonight looking at the framed photographs on the walls. And before I can stop myself, I add, "You probably know Harry's comings and goings better than I do right now."

He laughs bigheartedly as he inhales the last cloud of smoke but doesn't comment on my remark or newly minted paranoia.

⌒ Harry walks down Fifth Avenue on a crisp day when tides of women are trying out color; after a long winter they glide up the avenue in blue, tulip pink, soft yellow. He would never have tried to steer Catherine to such colors: She knew what she liked; she preferred to wear black and muted shades.

"They're so simple," she would tell him, "easy to wear like a school uniform and then you can always add dashes if you feel like it."

After much deliberation, he did buy her a red shirt for their first Christmas together, and maybe it was his own small attempt at a dash. He laughs at the memory as he passes the Plaza Hotel, where a tall man plays something old and familiar on the saxophone. She unwrapped the shirt and smiled at him sweetly. She even wore it once, which he loved her for, and it didn't matter that she put a dark gray sweater over it so that only a glimpse of red showed at the collar and cuffs. Harry had to admit that it looked much better that way. He crosses Fifth Avenue to glance in the window of Tiffany's. He is quite certain she would have liked a simple platinum ring as her wedding band.

I will have to venture into the West Wing basement today, down a long soulless corridor near to where Harry's office sits, which I'm sure is dark and locked. And I will have to represent the vice president today in a room filled with people speaking loudly for the first lady; we will construct a public scenario for the vice president and the first lady to be seen together. We will put a lot of effort into creating an effortless photo opportunity of the two smiling, looking to all the world as if they might even spend weekends together, as if the president and the first lady might actually invite the widower up to their big family house in Maine. The reality is that the president and vice president have nothing in common but these politics and the blocked-off car passageway between the White House and the Old Executive Office Building.

It is everyone's opinion, however, that the public does not feel comfortable with this actual arrangement— poll numbers tell us so—one that has probably existed throughout history or so Harry would tell me. Today I will help get the vice president out of his office, away from his Lockerbie websites and photos of his dead wife and sister. We will put the vice president on display, dust him off, trot him out in public. Everyone, here inside at least, believes it will be "magical" for the vice president to be around Claire Wallace because the first lady, at first suspected to be "a cold intellectual," is now loved for her Minnesota roots, cherry pie recipe, easy smile, and careless hair. Her poll numbers are even higher than those of the popular president, and they are highest with women. Perhaps women know that to get to the White House with her ambitious husband, the first lady has been across a bleak frontier and back, over one mountain, two mountains, three, and that she has weathered an unspeakably lonely landscape, pulling the wagon behind her. All the way.

My mother always liked the ocean best. She liked it better than landlocked views. "The ocean has reach," she would say. And I imagined its long arms stretching out with her hopeful gaze, millions of sunlit miles reaching before her toward England.

She had never been there, but she read about England as if she were still in school and studying. She read my baby brother and me bits of history—some about forgotten kings, some of crowns and ships and horses—and things from fashion magazines. She listened to the English people on the radio, and she would dance in our yellow kitchen when a song came on that she liked. "My British boys." She would smile, and chant, "Ob-La-Di,

Ob-La-Da," to us until I knew all the words and could sing them for my father. She made us tea at four o'clock each day and would serve us "biscuits" that were really Chips Ahoy! cookies from a cardboard box, but they turned into biscuits on her china plate covered in pink roses. My small, fat brother pounded on his highchair tray when he saw them coming; he'd pound his greedy fists against the plastic, screaming from his throne. My mother framed a black-and-white picture of her favorite Beatle and put it with our family photographs, in a special place, so that he smiled between us like our own. I'd look at his familiar face with its crooked teeth as if he were my cousin Paul, my distant cousin from across the sea.

One summer we went to the beach for my mother. We drove past farms to Delaware, where we stayed near enough to the ocean and my mother was able to sleep if she could hear the waves. She never went swimming but my father did; tall and tan he would emerge from the sea smiling at my mother in her bikini, at her lying on the beach nearly naked for my father's eyes. I'd watch her doze gently on the sand with her eyes closed, her arm draped over her face to cool her eyes from the midday sun. And she would wake up, rub my back, and tell me, "I must have paddled away."

6

As the meeting with the first lady's staff gets close, close enough that my stomach makes it hard to breathe, I think about putting on lipstick, coloring myself into calm, bracing myself with the powers of Red Confidence. I should be preparing ideas instead, filling my computer with bright, snappy plans to transform the vice president's image inside the pages of *USA Today.* Instead I look for Will, whose office remains dark and empty. Instead I sneak outside again to smoke and compose a letter to Harry in my head.

I try to think of ways to quiet myself, to steady my callused, sweaty hands, to organize my thoughts so they aren't spilling over like the piles of paper on my desk. I drink lukewarm water with drops of a British potion in it called Dr. Bach's Rescue Remedy that looks soothing enough in its sturdy brown bottle with an eyedropper top. It claims to be made of flower extracts and promises to "comfort and reassure." However, I notice as I look at the label that these mysterious flower essences are mixed "in a grape alcohol solution," and I feel confident that this must be the key ingredient. I even feel vaguely reassured.

I tidy my desk. I begin to make notes for the meeting but the phrases just wander and tangle. I can't imagine what the vice president and the first lady will do together that will seem natural and less like stiff, stuffed lions in a museum, so I stop writing notes and instead write, "Dear Harry." There must be a letter in me, and it might be helpful to describe my helplessness to the man who, long ago, used to seem so helpful. Unfortunately, my mind cannot make a sentence come through my hand. I cannot form any kind of sentence that would make him read to the next one. For no reason, I remember reading something once about the fact that Marilyn Monroe's psychotherapist used to keep a small rowboat in the backyard swimming pool of his Beverly Hills home. He liked to lie in it, looking up at the sky, rocking back and forth, floating away from the telephone and his patients. On this odd, blurred day, I somehow enjoy thinking of the little doctor bobbing around in his lifeboat, sipping a martini in the aqua blue water.

Harry once told me that when his mother died his father drove him, then maybe eight (for some reason Harry could never quite remember), all over the state of South Carolina to any movie theater that was playing *Some Like It Hot* because that was the movie he and his wife had seen on their honeymoon. When Harry said this, we were sitting on a rock in Central Park, a cool fall day when the buildings looked even taller against a faultless blue sky. He put his arm around me in a cascade of leaves and told me that the louder people laughed (usually only a handful in any audience), the more his father wept. Harry would stare hard at the screen so he wouldn't see the tears streaming down his father's face.

Yuri Cherpinov calls at exactly three o'clock and shakes me from my airless half sleep that tastes like flower extracts. It is night in Saint Petersburg, and I can tell by the jagged static that he is once again on his car phone; I can tell by his own kind of static that he has finished his cocktail hours and must be on his way to a late dinner. Music plays in the car and I can hear it before I can hear him, and I can tell it is, in fact, him because the music has a thumping dance-floor beat and sounds something like the Bee Gees singing in Russian.

"Katerina," he bellows, seeming pleased that he has included me in his evening plans. "I am here with a young lady who wants to come to America."

I hang on to the phone as I twist, bend, and dig into my bag for my lipstick. "For school?" I shout back, knowing perfectly well that the girl sitting next to Yuri Cherpinov in his new Mercedes is not interested in studying in the United States.

"Oh, Katerina," he laughs as the Slavic Bee Gees hit a full choral high. "She wants a job, maybe like yours, maybe she work with the bad president and you."

Perhaps it is the president and me in the same sentence that I find funny, and so, abruptly, I laugh for the first time in days and I am surprised by the meanness of the cackle. "How is her English?" I ask, although I hardly think it matters how well she speaks English.

"It is good! Here, I show you." I hear a muffled exchange in Russian, some teasing laughter, endearments, more disco music, and finally Yuri resurfaces from somewhere between the girl and the road. "I'm sorry, she is, how you say? Not brave."

"Shy," I offer as I pull my lipstick from the dark tornado of my bag.

"What?" he screams, and then the circuits click. He vanishes into the night with the young Russian girl in his passenger seat.

To get to the office of the first lady's director of communications, it is necessary to enter the West Wing at the front of the White House. My laminated credentials allow me to roam free in most of the building, except for the Oval Office, which you have to be invited into, and the private quarters upstairs. However, in an unspoken rule, to show respect for the first lady's office and her staff, I will wait in the special appointment waiting area with its embossed presidential seal on the parquet entrance floor, Oriental carpets, and plushly rigid sofas. Marine guards in dress uniform and white gloves stand aside as I walk through the double doors that are covered in the thickest of bulletproof glass. I walk slowly with legs that don't bend right, even in my Prada pants; I clutch my writing pad and date book, which is bare and neglected inside. I have started jotting things down only after they've passed by, and April begins with the single notation: "Harry Away Again." I have carefully avoided writing about the future. A few weeks ago I had even erased the August date we had sort-of-decided-on for the wedding.

The waiting area always has a feel of tense excitement. People greet each other on the sofas as if they all have been chosen for the same secret mission. They don't quite know what to do with their eager hands, and some carry small china coffee cups, rattling. The cups are filled with a beverage of choice, served by an elderly black man in a white jacket and bow tie, and the cups are decorated with a tiny White House etched in gold. The visitors fumble with their nerves, laugh too giddily, and admire the central display of freshly cut flowers. At Christmastime, a towering evergreen gives them a better diversion and they ooh, ah over the standard decorations as if the plain glass balls were far more magical than the ones at home.

Brenda, dressed in a red power suit, sits behind the round, wooden table buried deep in telephones, guest passes, and scheduling books. She smiles at me. "Catherine, hey, what a hell day! How y'all been doing over there?"

"Great," I manage in the buzz, drone of the waiting.

"Super. I just love those pants! You always look perfect, damn you!"

"Thanks. Uh, Brenda," I say. Before I can control myself, I blurt out, "You don't know by any chance where Harry is on business today, do you?"

"Honey"—she waves a manicured finger at me—"you gotta keep better track of your man!"

I'm sure she is right, but she can't know that her advice has come much too late.

"Anyway," she tells me while looking at a book that, upside down, looks as if it's been written in code, "maybe he's in Maryland today in preparation for the meeting at Camp David with the Russian president." She pronounces Maryland as "Merry Land" and I feel moronic that I didn't know that the Russian president will be meeting with President Wallace over the weekend. Even a few months ago I was sharp enough to know such White House basics, and now people who read the *New York Times* every day must know more than I do. My emotions have turned me into a fraud.

"I'll call down to Sylvia and tell her you're ready now." She hefts her heavy black receiver. And I don't feel ready; I am not ready for a serious meeting today (or yesterday or the day before).

I, too, begin to mill around, look at the carpet patterns, and smile vaguely at the strangers who all have some business in the president's house. I smell the flowers that are gathered in a spring mix of daffodils, pale tulips, and tall, yellow lilies. I imagine the federal flower collectors, people who have been hired to pick and arrange these vast displays, and I know there must be someone with a general service ranking, with a title and seniority, who has flower management on his or her mind all of the time. A deputy assistant secretary of something must know what's appropriate for a Wednesday, for Thanksgiving, what's nonoffensive to the Greeks, spunky enough to recycle for the children's Easter-egg roll, and maybe even what's fresh enough for the president's mistress. This person is armed with a cell phone, a beeper, and budget slips; I guess this person manages a great staff, has protégés and minions who really know their flowers.

Sylvia, the perky assistant from the press office, suddenly emerges from the back stairwell door behind Brenda's command center. She bursts through the door in a panting hurry, catching me with my face inside the flowers. She is ready to lead me past Harry's deserted office and the basement below. The stairwell that we go into is not formal or marble like the front stairways nor does it have any painted portraits of the presidents, red velvet ropes for looking (DO NOT TOUCH). Instead it is a narrow two flights that turns sharply like regular, back fire stairs except for the reminder of two framed photographs of the president and the first lady looking Kodak happy, waving to the workers as they travel to the basement.

The long hall leading to the communications center has thick blue carpeting, and the pile is luxurious but the sheen and pattern are all business. The hall smells of damp dog and I see Huby, the president's skinny Irish setter, lying on his back, paws up, against the wall near the first lady's communications room. He is an erratic, slow-witted dog who has the run of the West Wing. He barks at nothing in particular, steals the interns' lunches from their desks, and plays endless games of fetch with the Secret Service members who throw tennis balls in the blue-carpeted corridors. Huby is short for Hubris and I know this from Harry. However, a lot was made before the election about the origin of the dog's name. So his real name was covered up, changed in the press because it is doubtful that the public would have accepted the president's inside joke. Instead the dog's name was said to be short for Huberman and a tribute to the president's mentor at Harvard, Leonard John Huberman, the ancient political scientist who had famously dined with Stalin and infamously wrote that he found him "surprisingly witty."

Emmett Strong, the first lady's deputy assistant chief of staff for communications, is seated behind his desk, which looks much like Al's, large and wooden, a higher grade of government issue, and he has his jacket off and tie undone. The sleeves of his white oxford shirt are rolled up, and he is wearing the bulky, black scuba watch, which every time I've met him he's pointed to and said, "This is for swimming with the *real* sharks, baby." Elsewhere the "baby" part of the stupid joke might bring to mind work-place sexual harassment, but here Emmett is just another of the many press officers who speak with all the patter of a drive-time disc jockey.

He has the phone sandwiched between his cheek and shoulder; he doodles with a pencil on a scrap of paper in front of him, and he does not look up when I enter. Sylvia motions me to one of the chairs before the mammoth desk, a burgundy, high-backed leather chair that looks as though it belongs in someone's library with hunting tapestries and a fireplace. There are framed photographs on the walls, of Emmett in scuba-diving gear, a posed wedding shot, and many of the first lady by herself: She addresses a crowd, her fist in the air triumphant; she throws the first pitch at the World Series; and she hugs two refugee children with open arms. Harry has similar pictures of the president and her on his walls, a kind of shrine to the first family, but it suddenly occurs to me that Harry never had any personal photos along with them, not even a little one on his desk. For some reason my throat catches at this absence, as if he never really had a private life, no me, no New York street corners or beaches with our eyes squinting in the sun and our hair undone by the wind.

Emmett continues to talk, doodle, and his part of the conversation, his contribution to the phone call, is "Uh-huh, uh-huh" and the occasional "Right you are." He holds the pencil up to me, pausing it midair like a baton to an orchestra ready—it's a time indicator, I think—and he looks at me finally, hangs up the phone, and says, "Hey, babe, you look fantastic. Life must be treating you well."

When the office fills with people, I start to feel hot and panic suddenly, feeling trapped, tied down to the burgundy chair. Sylvia stands behind Emmett with a notebook, and I think she glances at me strangely, as if she knows I have nothing prepared to contribute. The room laughs at everything Emmett says, but I cannot hear any of what he's actually saying. I am too worried about the fact that I am seated and can't leave without making a scene; maybe I should just go ahead and make a scene; I could bolt, run, just get out, no more pretending to be businesslike. Instead I just look at the worn patch on Emmett's shoe that is wagging at me, his big feet rudely on the desk, him tipped back in his chair, hands locked behind his head showing the sweat stains underneath his arms.

Everyone around me works for the first lady, seven people who are all members of her fleet; they crowd near me, perch on furniture like lizards. I alone speak for the vice president, and this is particularly unfortunate right now because I do not think I can speak at all.

The conversation turns to ferries. This, after all, is a brainstorming meeting and someone in the fluorescent room has brainstormed that the first lady and the vice president should ride a ferry together. The idea started as a boat but then the democratic question was voiced,

"What kind of boat?" Sailing looks too elitist, too Kennedyish, and much too recreational with sunglasses with hair blowing, and so after an hour of much discussion, the boat becomes a ferry. Emmett announces, "Good show!" I go along, too. Sherrie Meager, Emmett's colleague, asks me what I think when they have all agreed that this will happen anyway, and I nod as in "okay." I know I am supposed to go along and that no one really cares what I think of any of it.

"That just leaves us with where," Sherrie says, making notes. She balances against Emmett's desk on the farthest side from me. She presses one speed-dial button on her cell phone, and in clipped, kindless speak she commands her assistant to search and find every ferry that floats in U.S. waters.

"Off the top of my head," Ralph Bauer, squirming in the chair next to me, injects, "I know that Staten Island and Martha's Vineyard both have daily ferries."

"There's a Wall Street to Weehawken one," someone says helpfully, and I have trouble imagining what the public's full vision of Weehawken might be.

"Martha's Vineyard! That's it." Emmett sits upright and pumps his fists in the air as if he has saved the game just in time. "Mrs. Wallace will be in Boston at the end of the week, so it's perfect." The room agrees and Sherrie applauds with her pen flipping against her palm. I think of her poor assistant still scrambling to find every last ferry in the United States.

"The vice president can't do that," I say, and it escapes so quickly that the office is silent before I know it's out or where it's going. My face turns hot, Emmett's turns sharp, and he frowns.

"Why not, Catherine?" Sherrie hisses, glancing at Emmett with a snap of her head. She straightens her back and her high heel raps against the desk like a pointed gavel.

And I think of the vice president, and the strange look he gets when he talks about his wife, the pained shroud that unrolls across him. I've seen it happen twice. I've watched him take his reading glasses off and hide his eyes beneath his thumbs in the second before tears. She was thirty-eight when she died of cancer; after surgery, radiation, chemotherapy, she died a pale reed after they gave her enough morphine for the pain. She was sick in the hospital two years ago when he was elected, when he and the big boy president were landslided into office. There is a picture of the vice president and his wife, Susan, in that gray hospital room on the night it was confirmed that he had four years in office, that he was given a time guarantee for his own life. He looks excited, kissing her fragile cheek that is mostly high bone covered with a thin veil of skin. Perhaps he saw the election as a sign, a hopeful validation, a stay to the sentence they'd been handed. And their daughter, Lucy, just turned four then, is in bed, too; nestled under her mother's crooked shadow arm, she smiles at her mother, who wears a stocking cap on her head, a tassel that night for the celebration.

I think of another photo I've seen in his office of them right after they were married. They both look serene and indestructible, hugging each other on the top deck of a ferry leaving Wood's Hole. Her hair is long, blond, swept back by the wind, and her head tips upward toward him. Eyes shut against the sun, in the warmth of the day and the future and in happiness, she smiles large for him, her husband.

"Because," I say after an awkward pause of time, trying to sound firm and steady, looking at no one, just the polished desk ahead, "the vice president and his wife went to Martha's Vineyard for their honeymoon."

⁓ *Harry had always planned to take Catherine to San Francisco, but like so many destinations, they hadn't quite made it. He wanted her to see the fog as it rolled across the sunny, steep hills and feel the wind on the bay from the deck of the Tiburon Ferry. He leaves Tiffany's, after he had gone inside and spent thirty minutes looking through the glass cases marveling at the diamonds big and bright. He tucks his purchase in the inside pocket of his suit jacket and walks to the Plaza Hotel.*

When he enters the lobby, he remembers that when Catherine first moved to New York and was looking for a job she told him that she used the Plaza as something of an office. When she had a midtown interview, she would leave the apartment she was staying at on Central Park West with her mother's friends and walk down the long slope of Central Park South. She would stop in the ladies' room in the Plaza to freshen up, reapply her powder and lipstick in the comfort of marble and grand mirrors. She would wash her hands with rose-scented soap and tip fifty cents to the woman who handed her a towel. Before she went back to Central Park West, she would stop in the Plaza again and make telephone calls from a cozy wooden booth nestled across from the Oak Room. He likes to think of her in those days, using the Plaza as her clubhouse.

Harry takes off his dark glasses as he walks into the Oak Room, lets his eyes adjust to the sudden darkness on this spring day, and looks around the near-empty place to find the man who will give him another clue to his future.

I keep a spare change of clothes in the bottom, deep drawer of my filing cabinet. I learned early on that I would never have time to go home and change for sudden evening obligations, so I rotate a few simple pieces that I can jump into easily in the ladies' room, transform myself from daytime into night. The National Gallery opening is black tie, and even though I will not be staying for the fund-raising dinner, even though I will be there only to make sure the vice president is comfortable at his podium with a glass of water and that the few invited press in attendance have a digest of his words, I choose a formal option in my metal drawer. I have wrapped the clothes carefully in blue tissue paper because I once read that Coco Chanel did this on all her trips, her voyages, to avoid wrinkling. I keep packages of new stockings in various colors, a pair of lovely black shoes encrusted with jet beads to dress up any outfit, and a choker of pearls with a blue glass stone in the center that Harry and I found at the jewelry booth in the flea market and that I think looks vaguely Romanov.

In the large, cold bathroom, I slip into the long narrow skirt I have chosen, a midnight blue satin one that goes well with the fitted black cashmere sweater and necklace, and is the perfect length to show off the pointed night shoes. I have always loved the skirt because from the front it looks rather plain, but at the back it has a small kick pleat that, when you walk, shows a glimmer of a different, brighter blue shade. I put my hair up, fold it into a fast chignon, and put on lipstick and mascara. My transformation takes less than ten minutes, and I am ready to go over to the National Gallery.

I exit the grand West Gate at a few minutes after six o'clock and decide to do the ten-minute walk instead of catching a cab. On Pennsylvania Avenue the sidewalk and street itself are sealed off from pedestrians and cars; the wide avenue in front of the White House is fortified against gawkers, extremists, terrorists both citizen and alien; it is lined with huge cement-block barricades that would certainly stop tanks and have been tested to do so. I want to walk, to smoke a cigarette, and see the twilight, the last shreds of day, some light before night falls outside the walls of our fortress. I pass people in suits and jogging shoes who walk quickly home and carry briefcases. I stroll down 18th Street in my party shoes, turn away from the White House in the direction of Constitution Avenue.

I bought the shoes for the inauguration balls two years before and have kept them carefully in two felt shoe bags I got from a hotel in Paris. Harry and I had gone to six of the many official balls held on that cold January night. We went from a dinner at the White House in the Blue Room, where I barely ate and nervously sat two tables away from the president and first lady, to the vast, red-carpeted hall of the Kennedy Center, where Harry danced with Mrs. Wallace. I watched him proudly, him perfect in his new tuxedo, his bright blue eyes shining as cameras flashed and recorded his waltz with the president's wife. We went to hotel after hotel, our special gold tickets getting us in wherever we wanted to go; we danced and laughed; we drank champagne with other presidential appointees, each one with the same giddy expression of holding gold tickets on a historic night.

At four in the morning we sat on the marble steps of the Lincoln Memorial. Harry put his coat around me because I hadn't wanted to spoil my outfit with one. I hadn't wanted to cover my pride and joy, a shimmering gray Lanvin gown. Harry held me tightly in the empty monument, President Lincoln staring down at us like a giant, benevolent dinosaur, the mall stretching in front of us in its long, regal parade of buildings.

"Can you believe it?" Harry asked over and over on that night I wore my dancing shoes.

⌒ *Harry leaves the Oak Room at dusk and knows he will have to stay in New York waiting. He will have to wait to see what happens between President Wallace and President Regov at Camp David over the weekend. At least three times a day Harry wishes he had never met the two Russians who had so altered his life, had complete power over his future. When he met them, an odd couple for sure, one very skinny and the other very fat, a kind of Laurel and Hardy pair of arrogant businessmen, they were selling ex-Soviet computer hardware and software. It was the software that was most worrisome, highly secured programs that contained endless names of people who had turned on each other through long Moscow winters. There were American names, there were English names, there were Saudi and French names on these vast lists. And each name had a story with it. Some were simply embarrassing moments in history, duplicitous tales of superpowers, but some of the stories were more than that; some of them were evil, deadly, global. There were names of people who still roamed the world somewhere, probably in the Middle East, probably in Manhattan or Detroit, Albany, Santa Fe, names long since changed with their faces, fingerprints, duffel bags filled with plutonium, chemicals, bomb codes, dusty glass jars of plague germs, smallpox, mutant viruses. And everything is for sale. Everything finds its way to the highest bidder.*

Harry will wait to be told what to do next. He will spend his days wandering through the city, uptown, downtown; he will find himself tracing many of the routes he took with Catherine as they roamed through the city, finding their way to Chinatown for lunch, sitting outside Saint John the Divine on Sundays listening to the music trickle through the giant doors.

His cell phone rings as he stands in front of the fountain outside the Plaza, its water just turned on after a long, frozen winter, the offices in midtown letting out workers into long floods moving up Fifth Avenue, and Catherine's work number flashes on the cell phone screen. He doesn't answer. He waits until he is halfway up Central Park South, heading to a favorite bar near the Ansonia, before he listens to the message. It says, "Please don't do this to us, Harry. I love you."

7

Whenever I walk into the Na-
tional Gallery, I have a flash of the optimism I possessed
at sixteen, eighteen, nineteen. Working in the bookshops
there—stationed at the one perched so high up in the
East Wing like a tree house or in the bustling central one
on the main floor of the regal West Wing—was menial
labor. I punched into the cash register countless ten-cent
postcards of paintings that the tourists hadn't even gone
to look at and rolled endless poster-sized versions of the
same, but I loved the setting. To me it was a bit like that
story of the two children who get locked in the Metro-
politan Museum and spend the night roaming the vast
building and sleep in Napoleon's bed, because un-
escorted I could walk through the galleries as they were

closing for the evening. I sat with the blue Picassos all alone, listening to the sound of far-off vacuum cleaners. I wandered through the darkened marble hallways, hearing my footsteps echo, heels click-clicking on the varnished floors of the Delacroix room.

I had made some friends there, Walter, John, and Tim, three young gay men who had left small, Southern towns and gone north to the closest big city. They worked in the bookshops year round, and I, like a migrant worker, would drop in each summer for the tourist season. We all thought of the jobs as temporary, and during our breaks we'd eat sandwiches out on the blazing hot Mall or smoke cigarettes in the guards' lounge, which was heavily air-conditioned and usually empty, and talk about our plans. We all dreamed of New York. Washington was already too small for us, and none of us dreamed of a life measured out in general service ranking numbers or employee pension schemes in the federal government. Maybe it was like living in Los Angeles and wanting nothing to do with the entertainment industry; perhaps it was just that we thought of Washington as glamourless, the inverse of the L.A. analogy. I remember that Walter wanted to open a nightclub, Jerry wanted to get his Ph.D. in classics at Columbia, and Tim wanted to be in love. I planned on running my own gallery or writing or becoming a photographer, depending on the summer I was dreaming.

I stopped working in the bookshops when I was a sophomore at Brown University and got a summer internship, through the friend of a friend, at *Mademoiselle* magazine in New York. It, too, was a menial job. I brought the editors their iced coffees, fat-free yogurts, and dairyless chocolate bars; I ferried proofs between departments, wheeled clothing racks down crowded corridors. But I loved the setting. I loved arriving at Grand Central Station every morning from Laura's home in Connecticut, after her father dropped us off in Greenwich with the words, "Get 'em girls." And Laura and I would waltz through the grand terminal, skip up the wide stairway in our carefully bought sandals, and scoot down the hot, teeming sidewalks to our first jobs on Madison Avenue.

My grandfather and I rode to the hilltop. We creaked along the back, winding road slowly in his old truck, the tires following the narrow ruts of one that had gone before, one that had braved the snow to look for Christmas trees on top of the ancient hill, almost a mountain to me. Light flurries dusted the windshield. I could count each of the pale flakes and my grandfather whistled carols; he sang one about silver bells and Christmastime in the city. We were alone in the forest on the first Christmas that I was old enough to go with him, winding high, higher in the coughing red truck, me petting his big arm, covered in plaid wool, that would steer us to the perfect tree. I could see smoke rising in the distance, and I knew it came from unseen chimneys, houses where people baked turkey filled with stuffing and laughed like my mother and hers.

"Just you and me, Catie," Granddaddy said, and he seemed pleased that I was along to help him find the biggest tree in Virginia, big enough for ropes of lights, and glass balls, icicles, candy canes, and the many dancing bears who played instruments and hung parading from all the bows and needles.

"Your mother used to climb trees out here when she was a little girl," he told me as we inched along the slippery road, cold air coming through the window cracks. "She'd climb highest in the wind." He wiped the inside of the window as it steamed over with our breath and carols. "There she'd sit, looking far away. I think she could see all the way to the city!" He stated this as fact, and I laughed knowing that she could never see into that kind of distance. I imagined her way up in the top of a tree, the wind bending it, rocking it and her back, forth like a boat on high seas; I thought of her looking toward the horizon and dreaming of her life, the city, my father, the ocean, and me.

⌒

The airy East Wing lobby, with its giant Calder mobile gently spinning three stories above, is filled with people racing around in pre-event activity. Some of them re-arrange rows of golden chairs; some of them bark orders into little black microphones attached to their heads; a few of them rush toward me as I emerge from the metal detector. And this nervous little flock chirps at me and guides me to the podium set up in the center of the vast foyer.

"We've got a pitcher of ice water all ready for the vice president!" they shout.

"He doesn't like ice; he'll need it room temperature," I say.

There are frowns and a chorus of orders as the pitcher is whisked away.

"We've got the teleprompter all set up!"

"The vice president doesn't use a teleprompter for this kind of speech."

"He doesn't?"

"No," I say calmly, hoping some of my calmness will soothe the agitated nerves that jangle all around me. "This speech is very short. He'll have it memorized."

I stand behind the podium and squint up into the spotlights that beam down from the glass ceiling above. "We'll have to lower the lights so he can look into the audience."

"Dim the lights!"

"And we'll have to move the podium slightly so that it is closer to the painting he will be referring to," I say, pointing toward the enormous white flag painting by Jasper Johns.

"Movers! Movers needed in main lobby!"

And with that my job is done until the vice president arrives, and I will speak quietly to him, whisper that so-and-so is sitting in the front row, tell him that so-and-so lent *White Flag* to the exhibit, tell him something funny about the assembled guests to make him laugh and feel at ease. My job is done until I will stand in this vast foyer where I used to sell postcards, where tonight there are glimpses of stars through the enormous glass roof, and listen to the vice president of the United States give a speech that I wrote for him. I will listen to him describe the importance of the exhibit, the significance of twentieth-century American art; I will hear him say, "Even in white paint the brightness of the stars and stripes shows through; even in white paint the emblem of the flag is filled with color, that of our imagination. Freedom is never invisible, whatever color it is painted in."

"You're not staying for dinner?" the vice president asks me politely after the loud applause finishes and people move down to the gallery below where tables are set and candles flicker.

"No, sir, I never sit at these things. Valuable table space, if you know what I mean." And, of course, he does. He knows that his presence here tonight has filled each table at one thousand dollars per diner, and he winks while other handlers steer him over to the director of the National Gallery.

As I make my way through the lobby toward the main entrance where I will meet Sam, I run into Kendall Stein, who is holding a glass of champagne and wearing a tuxedo. I have known him since Brown, when he was the editor of the newspaper, the *Brown Daily Herald*. In those days he was cocky and sure; now he is slightly rumpled and balding and has watched his journalism career head southward from White House correspondent at the *Washington Post*. He cannot know that I have a Rolodex card for him filled with crossed-off numbers and titles that trace the downward trajectory of his time at the *Post,* ending with his current, shared extension at the Metro Desk.

"Don't worry, Catherine, I'm here tonight as a civilian." And I know his father is a very wealthy art dealer. I also know that he wouldn't be covering a vice presidential speech for the *Post,* because now he reports on house fires outside the Beltway and bike path repaving plans in Rock Creek Park. What I'm not exactly sure of is why he fell out of favor at the paper. The press corps rumor is that he became obsessed with certain cabinet members and had tried to publish an exposé proving that they had actually been placed by the CIA instead of chosen by the president and congress. Such myths are made and shattered by the hour in Washington.

"So how's Harry?" Kendall asks with a strange wink, and for some reason, standing in my beloved lobby of the National Gallery of Art, I feel a cold, new surge of panic.

⁓

At my grandparents' house, I slept in my mother's own baby brother's room that looked like it was still decorated for a little boy. The walls were dark blue, deep blue like in an aquarium, and there were wooden bunk beds covered in spreads that had baseball players on them. I chose to sleep up top and climb a small ladder, because it felt new to fall into sleep high above the room that smelled old and familiar.

Uncle Teddy was no longer a boy. He had grown very tall and shaggy; he had disappeared one night, run away; he went up north, to another country, because of the war, my granddaddy said. "He doesn't want to fight," my mother told me, and she missed her younger brother who could not come home for Christmas to see us. I don't think he knew about my little brother, so tiny, or much about me, much bigger than when he had seen me last, at my third birthday party with balloons, a clown, and my father.

"He's a criminal," Aunt Sally Ann blurted out in the garden. She was trying to dig through the rock-hard ground, frozen on the day before Christmas Eve. She wanted to bury a squirrel she had found in the forest that morning before breakfast; she had brought him back in the pocket of her coat and whistled as she laid him out for his last rites. I ran out to her, slammed the creaky porch door when I saw her from the kitchen window clearing a patch of garden for her newest grave. She grew herbs in that patch, too, but mostly it kept things safe: dead birds, rabbits, squirrels, and the odd gopher. She assessed the job, returned to the kitchen, and came back carrying a boiling teakettle, using a garden glove for a pot holder. Then Aunt Sally Ann poured the scalding water over the frosted dirt, trying to thaw the earth. She bent over in a flannel nightgown, rubber boots, and a goose-down parka that used to belong to Teddy, and chiseled away at the ground with a rusty ice-cream scooper. "He's a criminal and he can never, ever come back here," she shouted between other things that she told just to herself.

When I repeated this to my grandmother, her face turned tight. She suddenly looked tired over the turkey she was stuffing, she was filling with large spoonfuls of warm bread and cooked onions. It smelled like butter and seasoning, and the kitchen had already absorbed the scent and held it, full and delicious like pepper and sage. After many spoonfuls she finally stopped, wiped her hands on her apron, and said, "He just wants peace is all."

I thought of the bodies who slept in the long lawns stretching between monuments, on the grass knitting the white buildings together. My father had told me, on one of our night-drive wanderings, that they wanted peace, too. "Why didn't Uncle Teddy just go to Washington?" I asked, and pinched off a bit of the sticky stuffing to taste it, a bite of supper so early in the morning. My grandmother put her soft hand on my cheek and smiled. "Because, sugar, those are the people who want him to fight."

And I went to sleep in the bunk bed and thought about my mother's brother up north, the cold snow falling on him without his blue goose-down jacket, so close to Christmas, so far away. The boy's room was extra quiet that night; his guitar was propped up against a basket filled with playing balls—basket, football, tennis, too—a bank in the shape of an elephant sat on the bookshelf next to rows and rows of toy soldiers, carefully dusted, standing strong and ready in the darkness, gleaming.

It is just warm enough for people to sit outside the Dubliner, and they huddle in jackets and trench coats, around tables that sit in a corralled section of pavement in front of the cranky old restaurant nestled behind the Capitol that boasts, "Est. 1805." I know that Sam loves this place with its green-and-white-checked tablecloths, long sooty bar, so much so that he even had his wedding reception here. I adjust my eyes to the darkness within the dank joy of the Dubliner. Sam is greeted—by the bartender, by the other patrons, by a nervous waiter who clutches a stack of tall menus in his hands—as if he is a celebrity, as if he is the prince of this small, friendly country.

"Set 'em up, Joe." Sam waves to the bartender, and then, realizing this line is an irresistible introduction, he begins to sing "One More for the Road" like a sad, young Frank Sinatra.

He laughs, half bows to enthusiastic applause from six men hunched around tables, five men lined up along the bar. "See, I still got it!" he tells me, referring to some distant crooner past that I know nothing about, as he leads me to the big center table and pulls out a wooden chair, scrapes it across the nearly mopped floor for me. The rushing man with the menus pays urgent and full attention to us; he reassures Sam that there is plenty of shepherd's pie tonight; he leaves for a blink, returns just as fast with a dark pint of beer for Sam and a full-to-the-rim glass of yellowish white wine for me.

I drink two glasses of the sweet wine and eat two bites of my shepherd's pie. Sam switches to Scotch, polishes off his meal, and chides me about my dinner. "Eat up, Soho, you're all bones." Like an obedient child, I chew and swallow a few more mouthfuls of mushy potatoes, finely ground beef mashed together with the cold potatoes. I am proud of this big effort and Sam nods approvingly and asks me how I find my life inside the White House.

"Challenging."

He laughs in his big Irish boom. "Very diplomatic answer. That's why you're a publicist!"

"And you?" I ask somewhat coyly because I know that under no circumstances do the Secret Service discuss their jobs.

"It's a great honor to work there. It is for all of us." He looks so serious and I feel ashamed for my diplomatic answer.

"And what did you do before?" I ask just to say something, because I already know that he was a highly decorated officer in the army.

"Army Rangers," he says modestly and only. "Not like that low-account boyfriend of yours"—he winks—"who could only make it into the Marines."

And I always found Harry's Marine Corps past so incongruous with his gentle personality. He told me on our second date, in a tiny Italian place on Bleeker Street where the ancient waiter called me "bella," about his time in the Marines. He had been both animated and wistful as he told me, a time of pure boy glory before he went on to get his Ph.D. at Stanford. He loved officer's training; he loved sailing on the huge battleship to Korea with his best friends, Sammy and Phil, both still in the Corps, with arms like steel beams and hair cropped into harsh triangles. Once when we were walking around South Street Seaport, we passed a navy ship anchored at the dock. It was evening and they were lowering the flag on deck, each man nearby standing at attention, a whistle blowing to mark this nightly ritual. Harry stopped, he stood quietly, and looking up at the ship, he saluted.

"Did you ever fight?" I ask Sam.

"Sure. Somalia, Iraq."

"Why would you want to?" I ask because of the wine and because I wonder why anyone would want to.

"Fear." He laughs a ragged sort of half laugh and lights a cigarette with a snap of the Zippo lighter, which I notice has the army seal etched on it.

"Did you ever kill anyone?"

"Yes."

"Did you see them?"

"Still do."

He surveys the room and leans closer to me for a moment. He does not look at me or wink; instead his face suddenly looks deflated as he says, "Soho, the truth is that Tammy's left me. She's not visiting her sister; she wants to move back up to New Jersey."

"Sam, I'm . . ." I try but my voice, my lips freeze parted.

"Lots of people find Washington"—he smiles at me weakly as he searches for the right word and borrows mine—"uh, challenging." I look at the smoke that curls up from my cigarette and blurs with his, and I wonder if he knows that I suddenly understand tough Tammy and her need to flee.

"At first Tam liked the idea of the White House. But you know Secret Service wives aren't really included in much; they're pretty invisible like we're all supposed to be." He leans back in his chair and looks at me; his eyes narrow and seem very black. "I guess it's hard for your love to know you have to be more loyal to someone else. You know that it's your job to take a bullet from some crazy bastard." He slaps the table and laughs in a grim, tired way.

"I'm sorry," is what I finally come up with, and I know it sounds weak, shallow in the loud darkness.

"Hell, Soho, what I need is a girl like you." He winks and pats my hand. I smile because I'm sure he must be joking; the two snake heads of his ring go on shining in the dim.

After another glass of wine, I suddenly feel the need to ask him what Harry's security name is, one of the many things I need to know about Harry, but instead we are quiet. The room is crowded by the time an old man sings; at first he does so in a whisper and then a deep tone comes out of his fragile frame like thunder. It seems fitting, expected, to hear this song, "Danny Boy," in such a cliché of an Irish bar, but even so, my throat begins to tighten as the patient, sure voice forms heartbroken words, the longing phrases of the missed and missing. I want to cry for many reasons. I am tired on the final leg of this Tuesday. I am bewildered as my wine-soaked mind ricochets from war to Harry, to Lockerbie, to love, to the vice president. Sam can sense, from across the table, that I am fading into trouble, and he says gently, "I'd better get you home."

8

That night I dream about a plane crash. I am standing on a beach and I see the plane explode above me in a giant blaze, parts of it fly toward the sand, me, and I run. When I wake up in the dark, I am no longer on the beach; I am lying on the edge of my bed, pillows stacked where Harry used to be. The TV is still on and loud; its glow makes the room a flickering purple; and it takes me a while to recognize the characters' voices in a late, late night rerun of *Mission Impossible*. Someone has poisoned a king, I think. Certainly the spies will save the kind king and the world from destruction between commercials for the Psychic Hotline and bankruptcy lawyers. As I emerge from the sleeping panic, my run across the sand, I pick up the small, black, Braun clock and put it close to my eyes. The milky fluorescent green hands say it is after four, and I am relieved that I can sleep in front of the TV for two more hours.

Instead I think about the Staten Island Ferry. It was decided, after two and a half hours, that the first lady and the vice president will ride the Staten Island Ferry together. It will be good for them to be seen with the commuters, the secretaries and salesmen, riding across the New York harbor, the ferry swinging majestically around the Statue of Liberty. It will be an American image: the working civil servants with the people. I don't think either one of them has ever visited Staten Island or been on the inside of the ferry that is more like a crowded, sour-smelling bus than a floating, romantic vehicle of transport. I don't think they'll eat the greasy doughnuts at the snack bar or get a plastic cup filled high with weak yellow beer. And I will be somewhere on the ferry or, more likely, on the dock, managing the reporters and photographers that I will have to be nice to even though I will only be thinking of when Harry and I used to ride the same ferry before the tide shifted and we hit hard on dry ground.

⌒ Harry takes the elevator to the top of the World Trade Center to have breakfast with a Russian professor who has helped him understand history, who has helped him understand where the men he is involved with come from, what made them turn as deadly as winter in a gulag. He rubs the

Saint Christopher medal when his ears pop as he rockets past the ninetieth floor. Catherine has always been frightened of heights and even got nervous in the Rainbow Room at the top of Rockefeller Center. He took her there on an early date before he knew better or had seen panic in her eyes. It was a clear summer evening, and they could see down the Hudson, across Manhattan, the most romantic view of her beloved city. He remembers that she barely spoke; she gulped her wine.

"Is everything all right?" he had asked.

She nodded and then shook her head. "I feel too much like Icarus."

I am trying to feel the freshness of the day. It looks as if it has rained overnight. Swann Street is ringed by puddles and washed clean. Leaving the apartment building, I try to feel confident that I have at least slept a little, washed my hair of the smoke from the Dubliner and for a moment silenced the pained, nagging voices in my head. I walk to work, cross over Dupont Circle, turn onto 17th Street, and continue past office buildings, both new and grandly old. I try to trick myself into brightness like the morning. The city sounds of birds, low flying in front of me in the morning clear of the nation's capital.

The bomb squad is crowded outside the Old Executive Office Building when I enter the black wrought-iron gates. It is only seven thirty, but I wear another favorite outfit, a dark blue shift dress, and carry a cup of coffee that I bought at Abe's Coffeemill on Farragut Square.

The bomb squad looks ominous as I approach the White House. There are at least ten steel-reinforced trucks that look like they belong to some futuristic bank, slate gray machines that are wide and armored. Men hover and wander; some wear bulky, lead-plated vests and plastic masks with metal hoods. My fake confidence starts to evaporate as I cross the blue sawhorse police stops and make my way to the main front entrance. No one tries to stop me so I take out my credentials as if the full federal bomb squad were not there to greet me. At least, I think, I'm not late.

"Catherine!" A man in plastic headgear waves at me, and even through his blurry mask, I can see that it is a squad member, Tom, who tried to teach me to play pool at the office Christmas party. "Nothing to worry about. We're just here to do a little housekeeping." He seems to want to reassure me that I can proceed safely, go to work as usual, and for a moment as I put the chain over my head and straighten the photo ID against my chest, I am disappointed. A bomb scare might close down my sector for a few hours, and then I could sit on the limestone steps between the copper cannons, drinking my coffee and wondering if Harry is drinking his coffee, too, black, very sweet.

"Thanks," I say to the armored man. He must imagine that I am eager to get to work and that I won't let mere explosives stop me. He smiles broadly as if he has somehow helped the nation, as if ridding the government of bombs before breakfast had ceased to be challenging enough.

The cubicles are all empty, but I can hear Al on the telephone as I enter the sector, and he is shouting. I know it is not the vice president he is talking to because he has a special, soothingly enthusiastic voice he puts on for those conversations. I walk to his open door and wave in at him; he widens his eyes, salutes me as if I am indeed a good enough employee at seven thirty A.M., with my coffee and nicely applied lipstick.

The truth is, I am glad that I have pleased him because now I can hide in my cubicle and feel like I have accomplished something already. My day ahead will be long, longer still because it will be slowed and complicated by many other people. I will have to write a draft of a press release—one page, no longer—about the vice president and the first lady riding the Staten Island Ferry this coming Friday. The official reason for the ride, they decided in the meeting, will be to celebrate the newly reapproved quarterly budget of the Department of Transportation. Never mind that the budget was approved two months ago, because no one wrote about it at the time so it was like the tree falling in the forest: No one heard a sound so it must still have a news value, somehow. There is new money for public works and the restoration of national treasures, and this is reason enough for the vice president and the first lady to take their turn on the ferry. I'm not sure that the Staten Island Ferry qualifies as any kind of treasure but certainly the point can be stretched with the photo op of the two of them smiling, framed by the Statue of Liberty.

The press release will have to be read by at least twenty people, including Emmett, Sherrie Meager, senior White House staff writers, internal editors, fact-checkers, copy editors, proofreaders, and Al. Each person will inevitably keep the one page with them, buried on their desks, for much longer than necessary and will ignore my polite begging for urgency. Each will read it after they have finished their own telephone calls, lunch, the crossword puzzle, and they will make their corrections, suggestions, and general unsolicited comments as to its merit. One reader will contradict the reader before him, and I will have to show the newest editions to all the past people. I will try to move forward by paddling backward. The readers will argue with each other through me, so I will have to diplomatically explain to the fact-checker that, yes, a senior writer is trying to make up the facts and that we have to figure out some way to be factually accurate without offending anyone with the truth. Skip Greene, the head fact-checker, will give me a long, slow lecture on his art and how he has saved the White House many, many times with his careful work.

As I input all of these revisions on the computer, I will be rushed and will misspell, invert, and skip words, and so I will show each new draft to a copy editor before it goes to anyone else on the assembly line. No semiofficial sign-off person wants to read such a flawed thing, a one-page draft with mistakes. And this whole process will draw out until evening. It will gather importance during the day and will take on the crucial nature of a State of

the Union speech; tempers will ignite over my press release, and I will feel the pressure of perfection and ap-
peasement. When it is finished, it will sound nothing like
it did when it started, and I know this as I sit down to
begin.

I turn on my metal lamp, my computer, and check my
e-mail; of course, I am hoping, as one would hope for
rain in a drought, that Harry might have e-mailed from
wherever he is to explain himself more carefully, somehow elaborate on his cryptic but certain note. I press
"send" on the one I drafted on Monday night. I have
carefully edited it, and it now reads, "I'll pack your things.
Let me know when you'll be getting them." I feel a little
bit defiant when the screen announces, "Your mail has
been sent!" but then I wonder why I didn't just remain in-
dignant, cool, and somewhat rational.

I wonder why I chose instead to launch a missile.

I save but do not open most of the messages that are
there: six interoffice memos reminding all staff to do
something different, better, more economically sensible.
There is one that I open from OfficeofVP, thinking it
must be a publicity update, a mild reminder about something I've forgotten. Instead it is from the vice president
himself, and it says simply, "Thanks, Catherine, for your
efforts on Lockerbie. However, I realize it is inappropriate at this time to pursue that issue."

I am sure that Al did not tell the vice president "Fuck
Lockerbie" as he had bellowed at me, but I imagine the

message got through nonetheless. I feel a huge stab of pity for the vice president, and momentarily I genuinely feel for someone other than myself; I feel bad that his whole life, behind these walls and outside, is dictated for him.

The next interoffice message I open is from Sam, and I am embarrassed that he sounds apologetic for the night at the Dubliner. He sounds so stiff, unlike himself; he just says, "Thanks for listening to me although I'm sure I said too much."

I am left with the rest of my day ahead and surely a couple of trips to the West Wing, dashes across the great divide of the blocked-off car passageway that separates me from Harry's impersonal, empty office. The anger rises again, hits me in an unexpected stab. As I open a new file and name it "VP-Staten Island," I feel the curse of Harry's behavior, his refusal to deal with me and his actions, his refusal to tell me why he isn't coming back to our apartment, that he will be buying new clothes and underwear rather than telling me something even half close to the truth.

There were a lot of stories about Aunt Sally Ann. There were stories about the time before she wore her rubber boots with her flannel nightgown, about her life before she stood in the backyard of her sister's house trying to catch snow with a frying pan. "For the houseplants," she told me. To me, at seven years old, it seemed to make sense that the African violet plants would want to drink the water from thawed mountain snow.

She was beautiful once and I had seen the pictures; I had studied all of the photographs that covered the piano, and I especially liked the one of her with my grandmother and Aunt Beatrice, three young sisters wearing hats and smiling, squinting into the sun behind the large family house in Richmond. Sally Ann wanted to be an actress, and she went off to New York City to become one. She lived in a tall building just for women and she took lessons on how to speak loud and clear. "Then she met a man," Granny said, "whose name was Tennessee Williams." He was a young man from the South, too, and he wrote things for actresses to say on the stage, magical words that made people cry. But I thought that he had a funny sounding name; it was strange for someone to be named after a state, and I said it over and over like a chant. Granny told me that he liked Aunt Sally's acting very much. He liked her spirit and their conversations about back home, too, the talks they had over bourbon in paper cups through late nights when her eyes grew even greener. He wanted her to be in one of his plays. He wanted her to take the part of a person with another queer name, Maggie the Cat. And when Granny and my mother talked about this, I imagined Aunt Sally Ann wearing a cat costume, a furry white one with ears and a long tail filled with wire so that it stuck straight out and turned up at the end. But there wasn't any costume. Any at all, I guess, and that is why Sally Ann wouldn't be this lady for the man named Tennessee.

Plays in those days opened in Richmond, Granny explained. "And God bless her heart, Sally Ann didn't think it was right to stand up there in front of all of Mommy and Papa's friends just wearing a slip." "A slip," Granny said, as if the very word was naughty. I didn't understand why someone could not be an actress just because she didn't want to get up on stage in her underwear. But this was the case for Sally Ann, and she left all her clothes behind in New York, in the tall, female building. It wasn't even the play that she had cared so much for, but rather something she found out about the man, why he would never be able to love her. He had told her the truth, "I like men, Sally Ann."

She went home to Richmond without even her suitcases; she got on the train with only her pocketbook, and later she moved here. She moved into this house to live with her sister and her young husband. Everyone looked sad when they talked about Maggie the Cat. They shook their heads and said, "Bad luck." No one ever mentioned that name to her. No one said New York or Tennessee in front of her, standing in the backyard with her frying pan, chasing snow on the morning before Christmas Eve.

⌒

The press release is hard enough to write. It seems extra difficult for me this morning to write something that is convincing, something factual that really is mostly fiction or facts woven to make people believe in our smoke and mirrors. Jill stomps in noisily behind me, it is eight fifteen and she is carrying the clippings pack that has not been distributed yet. I know that she must have yanked it off the wire-mesh cart in the hallway, manned and pushed by Edgar, the sixty-year-old mail boy. I'm sure she took it knowing that she was disrupting poor Edgar's count and his painstaking rhythm of distribution.

"Catherine, I can't believe that those pricks in the bomb squad had the gall to stop me," Jill yells so that the entire sector can hear. She slams down her packet on her desk and the motion starts an avalanche of her large plastic purse, her keys, newspapers, which tumble and crash onto the desk and floor.

"Maybe they thought you looked especially dangerous today," I say as I review the first paragraph of the release on my computer screen.

"Don't even joke about security issues," she snaps, and I know that the bomb-sniffing dogs probably alerted their handlers to something that only dogs and children know for sure about Jill Amish.

I have decided to let all of my calls go directly to voice mail, and I have turned down my phone volume so that I will not hear it ring although the names and numbers—or lack of known names, unblocked numbers—still flash mutely across the caller-ID box in front of me. I stop typing when I see "Dr. Milt Avery" pop up, because I know it is my mother calling and I haven't spoken with her since I hacked away at the bamboo on Saturday.

Even though it is my stepfather's name, I am sure it is my mother because my stepfather has never called me in the twenty-four years that my mother's telephone has been under his name. It is not out of lack of friendliness or genuine feeling that he doesn't call. He is a patient, generous man who listens to people and knows emotional things like the psychiatrist that he is should know. He just does not want to intrude on my life and I appreciate him for that. I pick up the phone because it seems easier to get it out of the way quickly, rather than drag it out and on and have to call her back.

"Catherine, honey," she begins. "I had a strange dream about you last night and just wanted to make sure you were all right."

"I'm totally fine, Mama," I say, adjusting my tone to attempt to fool her as I type in "the proud vessel that has been ferrying workers across the harbor since 19TK." I don't feel like looking into the exact date of the ferry's maiden voyage and leave it for Skip Greene, who will undoubtedly research every other detail and factoid and then spend an hour telling me about all of his ferry findings.

"How's Harry?" She never asks this question so early in a conversation and I feel a rush of panic about her telepathic powers and a queasiness at the weight of what I am hiding.

"He's good, busy," I say, racing to, "I am, too, and I've got to go to New York tomorrow so I have to finish this press release."

"Oh, that's just great," she chimes. "Why don't you spend the weekend with Paul? I'm very worried about him." And I know she is not worried in specific about my brother even if she does fret in general about his Wall Street bravado and the "peculiar" woman he's married to, who has spent the past two years decorating their co-op on Park Avenue with an obsession that is tilting toward insanity. Rather, I know my mother feels some unnamed concern about me, and I'm sure that she wants another family opinion to give a name to this problem.

"I'll try," I manage, and think that I actually might try. The thought of a Sunday alone in my apartment seems to depress me even in passing, the slightest thought makes me feel grimly hungover and tired. "I'll talk to you soon," I tell her fast and hang up in proof of how busy I am. I really want to avoid any prying, and I am too frightened to ask her if she saw a plane crash down in her dream.

"Will won't be in again today," Jill smugly announces over the partition when she knows I've hung up the phone.

"Where is he?" I ask automatically, and I feel strange suddenly about his absence.

"I thought at least *you'd* know that much," she says, proudly stabbing me back for my dangerous comment.

I quickly dial his home phone number and get his recording; the calm, reassuring voice I have missed for days. "Call me, sweetie," I tell the machine. "I'm wondering where you are and what you're doing. I hope at least you're having fun somewhere."

By midmorning I think my press release is good enough to be rewritten by a staff writer down the hall. I take it, marked "Draft 1," to the writers' sector. I survey the cubicles to see which of the eleven writers looks the least busy and which is the one who won't treat the press release as if it were a thesis dissertation. I choose Charlie Singer, who is slumped over his desk reading a newspaper and eating an Egg McMuffin; he is a practical kid from Illinois, has a poster of Michael Jordan pinned to his partition, and seems to be the least fussy of the group. He waves at me with a handful of little white McDonald's napkins crunched in his fist. He wipes off his breakfast grease, takes the page from me, and quickly scans it.

"The Staten Island Fucking Ferry?" He laughs, swallows Egg McMuffin, and shakes his head.

I shrug my shoulders and lean against his desk. "That probably shouldn't be the headline."

"Okay, I can do it but plea-se! The whole thing seems like kind of a stretch if you ask me, but I guess nobody asked me."

I'm glad that Charlie Singer sees today's absurdity. I am comforted that this solid, corn-fed American boy has been in the White House long enough to see its irregular nuances and not long enough to have caved in to them, succumbed to the machinery.

Edgar has carefully placed the clippings pack on my chair, and I flip through the pages, of Senate votes, the vice president's plans for literacy—Read Early, Read Now!—to see if I can find any news of where the president traveled yesterday and where Harry might have been with him. He visited a veterans' home in Boise and a car plant in Lansing, but there is no mention of his special adviser.

Charlie appears after only fifteen minutes, a record time in my experience with hundreds of rounds of press releases. He brings the page to me himself, which is surprisingly democratic and which is not done here; everyone else on my list will dial my extension when they have decided to finish. They will tell me to come over, pick up the changes. Or, worse, I will have to call them, track them down, stalk an editor or proofreader at the other end of the building and extract the work from them.

"It's fine," Charlie says, puts the paper in front of me, and then he presses it down on my desk as if he is trying to close a suitcase that is too full. "Only a couple of changes." He points to a squiggled phrase he has injected and a sentence he has circled and flung downward with an arrow. "It's probably better not to lead with the 'reapproved quarterly budget thing.'" He rolls his eyes, his tie is already loosened by eleven. "I mean, that's a real square peg, you know?"

Of course I do know, and I thank him for his efforts.

"Sure," he says as he is leaving. "I think it's good enough that the VP and Mrs. Wallace will be up in New

York anyway and that riding the damned ferry is just part of their schedule."

"Yeah." I halt, trying to give him the whole truth so that he can help me conceal it. "But they're going to New York *just* to ride the ferry."

He stops and shrugs; he lazily makes his tie even looser so soon in the day. "We know that, but we can imply otherwise."

I stand outside the west side exit wearing my dark glasses and holding my piece of paper. I look over at the West Wing as I smoke. I stare across the passageway to the White House. I can combine my trip to Emmett with a cigarette and know that I am safe enough out here because he is trapped in the building for a meeting and will not pop out the door unexpectedly, surprise me across the canyon, and yell, "Hey, babe, didn't know you smoked!" As I stand and inhale, exhale, I know I am avoiding all sorts of things. I am using the press release as my excuse not to return fifty calls to the press, respond to hundreds of e-mails, write a briefing paper to the vice president's staff on his trip to New York, and everything else that sits untouched on my electronic to-do list.

A perky intern recited Emmett's schedule to me and warned me that I only had about a ten-minute window to get him to look at my press release. "It'll only take five," I assured her, knowing that I won't be invited into his office at all, not for a simple press release. The cigarette makes me dizzy, and I inhale through the feeling as I watch the last of the bomb squad trucks pull slowly off the compound.

When I get to the special appointment area, Brenda greets me with her relentless Southern enthusiasm as if I were exactly the person she had hoped to see today from behind her ground control desk. She is wearing a faux Chanel jacket with gold medallions on the sleeves; her blond hair is precisely bobbed.

"What can I do for you, my dear?" She smiles at me as I hold on to my piece of paper and lighter, which I quickly try to conceal in the presidential waiting area. The place isn't completely full today. The president is out of town, so the crowd is thinner than usual. Sherrie Meager sits on a sofa with a manly looking woman, listening with unbroken attention to whatever the very tall woman in aviator glasses is telling her. A group of anxious men huddle around the flower display—all peonies today, white and red—and I can tell by their appearance that they are a foreign group, perhaps Eastern European, a tight flock of jittery men wearing mouse gray shoes and every credential they've ever been given draped around their necks like Mardi Gras beads.

"I need Emmett to sign off on this," I tell Brenda, displaying my press release like I'm offering her a dead rat, holding it between two fingers as if I'm dangling it by the tail. "So maybe I can just give it to Sylvia or her intern."

"Sure, honey." Brenda blinks back at me, her eyes dabbed with carefully applied mascara. "Listen, I have a little news bulletin for you." She brings her voice down into a sorority-type whisper. "My friend in the Human Resources Department, Office of Employee Travel Services, told me that Harry is staying in one of the rooms at the Waldorf Astoria."

"I knew that," I blurt out, and wish immediately I had just nodded, instead. My voice sounds exactly like I feel. Hearing that he is in New York, I sense my heart losing two beats, neither of which any machine would detect, but still I can feel my heart in its entirety, beat, boom, beat, boom boom.

Brenda keeps smiling in a placid, noncommittal way, perhaps registering my obvious ignorance as if it were just part of the parade she orchestrates each day from behind her gleaming desk. It's then that I notice that Huby is lying underneath her desk, at her feet, and he begins to twitch and kick as if he is running in a dream. Brenda bends over, speaks down at him, cooing sweetly, "Watch my stockings, big boy." She dials a number and whispers into the phone, "Hi, I think it's time for him to take a shit!" She says "shit" as if she is saying "bubble bath," her tone all filled with vanilla and honey, her smile not fading as she hangs up the phone.

"How's 'bout I call down to the intern who's holding the fort today, and you can leave your document with me?" She wants to keep coordinating this day smoothly. "Post-it?" She helpfully holds out a pad of white Post-its with the presidential seal faintly printed on them like a watermark.

I do not have a pen and I timidly take one off of her organized desk. I fumble with my lighter and lay it down near her regal, glass green shaded lamp. I write, "Please let me know if this is what you want."

"Okeydokey!" Brenda smacks her Fresh Frosty lips and takes my Post-ited piece of paper that now is withered and wrinkled from my clutching. "Let's just give it the old stamp!" She takes a little machine that looks like a snout-nosed gun with a digital, red-light display of the exact time to the second, and she pounds it onto the paper. She grins widely like a pleased and perfect librarian.

The sector smells like Jill's cabbage soup, and I catch my breath as I walk back to my cubicle knowing that it will only get worse as I proceed. She eats this soup every day as part of a diet she read about in *Glamour.* I pass her, hunched over her soup, and without glancing away from the steaming vat she is stirring, she says, "Al has been looking all over for you."

The door to his drywall island is shut, and I debate whether I should knock on it or slip away, and when I am half turned around in my decision, the door swings open.

"Catherine. Just the person I need. You've saved me a trip, come on in." He stands aside in a mock gallant gesture, and I enter with the fear of land mine, treading carefully over the carpet.

"Sit, why don't you?" He waves to the chair as if I don't know where it is, and he shuts the door. He likes to say that he believes firmly in an open-door policy, and this means that, most of the time, the sector can hear his conversations, deals, bluffs, accusations, staff admonishments, at full volume.

"How's New York coming along?" He walks around his desk but does not sit down; instead he looms in front of me with his belly touching the mahogany.

"Fine. The release is with Emmett Strong now." I look at him, but then I stare at a towering stack of folders in the middle of his desk.

"Good. Give me a draft later on, okay?" He delivers it as an offhanded comment, and I am surprised by this because Al is the ultimate sign-off—and stumbling block— for any press release concerning the vice president.

"I won't be sending you on this one though. Jill should do more traveling," he goes on, still standing. "Mint?" He offers me a peppermint Life Saver, holds out the roll that has its paper and foil unwound like streamers. I take one but hold it in my hand, keep it between my fingertips. I cannot absorb the fact that Harry is in New York and that I will not be now. I do not know yet if I am relieved; I just feel cold and hot, somehow the sensation of fever.

"I do want you to go up to Observatory Circle tonight to brief the vice president," Al continues, crunching three Life Savers at once. "Take him the final release, explain the tone we're trying to set. Make him feel good about the trip, you know."

His voice is unusually paced and quiet, and I cannot tell what is behind it as he swallows his candy and inserts a few more in his mouth. I have never been to the vice president's home to brief him, and no one else I know has either. We only go up to Observatory Circle when he is hosting a public event, a charity, a dinner where press are invited. I wait for Al to elaborate as my Life Saver is melting, getting sticky between my fingers. He must see the confusion on my face because, instead of elaborating, he laughs. "You don't have something else planned for tonight, do you?"

"No, it's just that—"

"Well, then, back to work," he says abruptly, and I stand. He puts his chubby hand on my back as he opens the door and says, "He'll expect you at eight.

"And, Catherine?" he calls as I head to my cubicle. "Maybe you should put some lipstick on; you're looking kind of tired."

The afternoon disappears, and Will has not called me back or come into the building. I really need to talk to him about Harry and my trip to the vice president's house. All afternoon I run from office to office trying to track down sign-offs on the press release, or I sit in the stifling cubicle waiting for people to come to me, and I can't keep my mind from pressing rewind, from playing past scenes, and I cannot stop from falling down the rabbit hole. I remember one of the last days we were in New

York, most of our belongings in boxes, the U-Haul van rented, the photographs taken off the wall and wrapped in bubble plastic. It was New Year's Eve, and snow covered Fifth Avenue, a thick, white flood spread in front of us, Harry and me, all the way downtown to the party. The taxi windshield wipers worked hard against the blizzard, and the driver leaned forward on the steering wheel to peer out on the situation and our chances of progress ahead. He looked like he was from a warm climate, used to burning sunshine and dry seasons, and he watched the snow falling through the headlights with wonder.

Harry had his arm around me, and I opened the window to hear the city's hush of snow. "Slowly we make it," the driver called back to us like the leader of an explorer team. He would get us there through the dark and treacherous terrain. By the Plaza, decorated for Christmas almost in another year, Harry kissed me on the ear. The taxi wheels weren't gripping and we slid, back and forth, in a slippery sidestep. "Let's get out," Harry said suddenly, grabbing my hand. We left the taxi behind and he spun me around in the snow. I looked up into the night, the thick flakes tumbling over the buildings like beautiful white water, the streetlights turning each flake into a diamond.

"We've never danced in the snow before." He laughed as we waltzed our way down the center of Fifth Avenue.

The vice president lives at Observatory Circle and so does the national time. Someone once described the function of the place as "the Greenwich of the United States," which made only passing sense to me at the time, because I lived in Greenwich Village and Observatory Circle seemed as far away from my mindset as any distant timekeeping mecca. But here in the United States, our time is indeed kept and regulated at the Naval Observatory, which is set on a grassy hill next door to the Victorian, turreted white house of the vice president, high above the embassies and downtown D.C. The compound, which is sprawling and ringed with tall iron gates, is only blocks from my mother's house, my childhood home in Cleveland Park, the neighborhood that surrounds the National Cathedral like a medieval village. And Observatory Circle is one of the few places in the nation's capital that is not on the tourist map: The vice president's house and time-watching towers are not for public observation, camcorder sightings, loud buses, or tour packages.

The press release, "Draft 32," was finally approved at five o'clock, and I presented it cleanly and with the headline, "The First Lady and Vice President See New York with Its Commuters," to the fax department along with a list of two hundred names and numbers to send it to: news desks, photo editors, Manhattan-based political writers. At seven o'clock Edgar brought me the list back with a long series of red check marks beside the names or the small notation "N/A" for no answer, as well as a few random comments and queries made in ledger-perfect, tiny red writing: "Someone answered" or "Area code has changed." I don't know what life would be like for a federal faxer, for someone who mans a machine all day and hopes, more than anything, for a successful, shrill beep that means he can use the check mark and move on.

The one good piece of news about this trip is that I know the vice president actually loves to talk about commuting. He had been a lawyer in Boston before he changed into a politician, and he often reminisces about his commute on the T from Cambridge into Boston. He recalls the burst of energy he got when the train passed over the Charles River and stopped just after the bridge. He hasn't used this personal memory in public for a while, and, I think, maybe it would work at the ferry landing; he might be able to convey the rituals of commuting, show the world that, yes by golly, America really knows how to move its workers! At least I have this half idea to discuss with him in my briefing. I brush my hair, put on some lipstick, and try to douse my grinding stomach with two long swigs of Pepto-Bismol.

By seven thirty the area around the White House is nearly deserted, except for the homeless people who live in cardboard shanties in Lafayette Park, but a white and green taxi quickly finds me. The driver, with a backward-turned military cap on, is American and tells me so; he rattles off national origin statistics on cab drivers as I close the door, and it turns out that only 4 percent of New York drivers, for example, were born in the United

States. "I don't know about D.C.," he says. "Probably even less; it's kind of a West African trade here."

I tell him where I'm headed and he looks in the rearview mirror. "Delivering something to the VP?" he asks me, and seems to enjoy that he's guessed my mission and tells me, by way of explanation, that he goes to law school during the day and just drives at night. And he takes me around Dupont Circle and along embassy row. He names all of the embassies as we pass them. "That used to be the Iranian one," he lectures. "Before, you know, they were booted out." He gets a little foggy with the new Russian flags, and jokes, "I guess they're really starting to run out of color combinations." We cross a small thin bridge and only a few cars speed underneath, down Rock Creek Parkway. They rush like the sound of a brook below. The giant mosque looms on my right, and it is heavily gated, barely lit, dim and armed against the arguing factions that want it for their own, one Muslim group worshipping, alone. "Never been there," the driver says, and I don't tell him that I have, that I went into it with a grade-school history class, with the daughter of a Middle Eastern king, that we went in without our shoes on, more than twenty years ago.

We ride up the hill. Massachusetts Avenue climbs steadily on an angle, turns, and curves as we pass the Japanese embassy, Brazilian, and then the English one; a statue of Winston Churchill stands slouched but regal in the darkness; he straddles American and British soil both, one foot on each place, and he gestures to the long grass slope of the Observatory compound. My driver and I pull off the wide avenue and up to the gatehouse that looks like a tollbooth with its tollgate flashing. The guard opens his sliding window when he sees me rolling down my taxi one. He is watching television, a small black-and-white set that flickers from some other era inside the booth.

"Miss Porter," he says, giving me back my White House ID. "You'll have to go on foot up to the residence."

I walk ahead and away from the guard, his glowing booth, and my taxi driver backs up, recedes onto Massachusetts Avenue with my story to tell his next passenger. A Secret Service agent leads me up the long path that is lighted by an endless procession of small, square lamps, stuck in the ground like waxed bags holding candles for a summer party. I carry my heavy, paper bundle—a package from Al, my press release, the thick xeroxed stack of today's press clippings—following my guide, who is silent. We pass through a wide rose garden that separates the grounds from the immediate yard with its swing set, and we continue on, climb the hill to the large white Victorian.

The man takes me to the side entrance. It's like any porch-side entrance of an old country house, with a screened door opening onto a wooden one, and through the bright leaded windows, I can see the vice president, alone in the family kitchen. It looks warm inside; the room is centered by an enormous farm table, old and rough-hewn, and it is covered with a child's drawings, open storybooks, and a pair of reading glasses. The vice president stands at the sink with his back to us; he is drying his hands with a cotton dish towel and is wearing a gray T-shirt, faded jeans, and moccasins without socks. Before I enter, I put my bundle down on the ground for a second so I can quickly put on some more lipstick.

I'm escorted into the kitchen and it smells of soup, coffee; it smells like a kitchen on those quiet nights when rain pours steady against the windows. The vice president turns around, still holding the towel, and smiles at me. He looks younger than forty-four: Unsuited and leaning at his own kitchen counter, he seems young, not aged like in front of the cameras and with his big job glaring.

"Hi, Catherine. Thanks, Jim," he says, and the Secret Service man vanishes. I do not have time to see where he goes; he just evaporates. I stand in front of the door, planted firmly, clutching the papers. I cannot think of where to go next.

"Here, let me take all of that." He comes to me without the towel and with his hands outstretched, a wedding ring shining on his left. "Leave it to Al to clutter up my house with more paper." He laughs and winks as he takes my burden away. I smile, but with my hands empty and unprotected, I feel useless and twist my engagement ring from outside in, twirling it five, ten times around.

"Sit, sit," he says, and quickly pulls a chair out. "I've just put on a pot of soup. Vegetable. Will you join me?"

After we have discussed the Staten Island Ferry voyage, which, much to my relief, he takes with humor and light, he tells me to call him Mark instead of sir. I have eaten two bowls of soup and had wine. We have finished a bottle and have started another. We have talked about work, ourselves a little, even laughed, and then he asks me about Harry.

"I don't know him very well, but I'm sure he's a very capable man," he says diplomatically.

"I suppose," is all I can think to say. I can taste my new resentment and it surprises me.

"So, when is the wedding?"

"That's, uh, a bit complicated."

"Like most Washington love affairs!"

I'm embarrassed hearing "love affair" come out of my boss's mouth, and for some reason, with quite a bit of wine, I feel it is time to correct him, "No, sir—"

"Mark."

"We actually aren't together anymore."

"Catherine, I'm sorry. I honestly didn't mean to pry." He puts his hand just briefly on my back, brushes it quickly, and I suddenly feel like I might tell him more and maybe too much.

"He changed a lot when we came here. In New York he seemed, I don't know . . . open."

"This is a pretty serious town."

"I guess." And I am relieved when he pours me another glass of wine. "It's all the secrets that I don't like."

It is probably my imagination but the vice president shifts his weight and suddenly looks uncomfortable, somehow, in his chair. He gets up and crosses over to the brick fireplace and mantelpiece that is lined with Susan's photographs: She smiles with her new baby, Lucy; decorates a Christmas tree with her husband; poses on the sunlit steps of the Lincoln Memorial.

"I don't know if grief ever really ends," he says after what seems like a very long time looking at those images. "It does get better though," he adds quickly, in a camera-ready tone.

He comes back to the big table but does not look at me. He puts his hands to his face, and his thumbs hide his eyes. Instinctively, I reach my hand across the table; when he opens his eyes again, he takes it; and we sit quietly for long minutes, thinking perhaps of the kiss that will follow just after midnight.

⌒ *He thinks about calling her as he walks through Greenwich Village, stands on Sixth Avenue and sees the lighted windows of her old apartment on Macdougal Street. He knows he can't call her, so he just looks at the windows and knows she was happy there, hopes she will be happy again.*

9

I should make follow-up calls to some of the fax recipients of the press release, give the press members a compelling reason to join our little party at the ferry landing at five thirty to watch the Friday evening Staten Island Ferry, but I can't. As I sit in my cubicle on Thursday morning, I am paralyzed. I sit in the dark without the heavy metal lamp on. I arrived back at my apartment at two A.M. in a strange state of excitement. There had been one short, startled kiss; a talk about the kiss; another kiss as Mark walked me to the black Secret Service car he had called to drive me home. He held my hand as we walked through the dark rose garden.

I did not feel guilty when I walked into the apartment; Harry's note still crowded among some empty wine bottles. I did not stack the pillows on his side of the bed as I had done the past two nights and all the many nights he didn't come home when he still lived here. I spread out across the bed but didn't sleep. I smoked in the living room, petted Josie, and thought much too far ahead with wine and two kisses.

By the time I reached the office, the morning light and the grand building reminded me that I have kissed my boss, have kissed the vice president of the United States. I wish I could have called in sick. I am, must be, but then someone might ask why. Someone, I think, in growing paranoia, would surely find out what I have done. I sit in my cubicle and wait to be reprimanded. By ten o'clock I turn on my computer; I scan the long list of my in-box, race past Strong, E. and Meager, S., three from the *New York Times,* countless others from newspapers and radio stations in the tristate area, and land on VP/MS. As I open it, my fear quickens, and I know he will say how inappropriate I am, that I am strange and needy and no wonder Harry left me. Instead it says, "See in-house mail." Edgar has delivered two large bundles of mail this morning that I have ignored, one from the outside and one from in here, both tightly wrapped in plastic cords like the ones that bind together stacks of newspapers. I wrestle with the smaller one, my hands so shaky that I can't grip the scissors enough to cut through the stubborn plastic.

The bundle finally spills across my desk, and I sift through it as if I'm digging in the sand until I find a plain brown envelope with a large red stamp bearing a government seal that says, "Confidential, Penalty of Trespass and Prosecution." I rip it open quickly like tearing off a Band-Aid, and inside there is a small white envelope. It is his personal stationery and on it in neat, sure script it says, "Dearest Catherine, History dictates that I don't say too much electronically, with posterity comes precious little privacy. Thank you for the lovely evening. Would you be my guest at dinner on Saturday evening? I can send a car at 7:00. I will wave at the Statue of Liberty for you. Best wishes, Mark"

Will finally calls me late in the day after I have read Mark's note close to fifty times. I have hidden it in my top, locked drawer, and for extra security I put it back in the envelope that threatens prosecution. Will sounds tired and is calling from home, and I blurt out, sounding like a teenager, "I have *so* much to tell you."

"So do I," he says, but my own loud roller coaster of the past few days drowns him out, and since I can't tell him anything personal over a White House phone, we agree to meet for drinks tonight.

The Hotel Washington looks like all others on the inside, in the lobby, which is standard hotel decor, heavily patterned, palm fronded, and spotlessly housekept. However, when I take the elevator to the twelfth and top floor to the terrace, it is like no other place in the world. The large terrace, although filled with its average-looking drinks tables and coupled chairs, is the most exquisite platform; a magical observation deck that surveys the sprawling city, lighted and spectacular, nearly close enough to imagine being in it but still, far away from its surreal architecture, powerful monuments. The White House sits just beneath, almost at your feet.

I am early, ten minutes before nine, but Will is already sitting at a table against the edge of the terrace. The place is empty in the April chill, but it is the clearest night I have ever seen. There is a glass of white wine waiting for me across the little metal table from Will, and somehow it looks more inviting than my friend, who is wildly picking in a snack bowl that sits in the middle of the table. I know he is looking for peanuts, and he seems like a hungry bird, pecking. He stands when he sees me, and he is dressed immaculately as always — jacket, cashmere turtleneck, charcoal wool trousers sharply pressed — but his face is pale, nearly as white as his floppy blond hair. I think he is about five foot seven, but he always claims to be five foot eight and a half inches and stands up ballet-straight whenever he says this. Tonight he looks very small, as if he has been shrunken, tumbled too long in the drier since I saw him last week. I kiss his cheek before I sit down, and it feels so cold, dry, and suddenly I feel as if he is a stranger, as if someone has switched places with my buoyant young friend.

"Okay, you go first, Cat." He always says this to me instead of hello, eager for our gossip to begin.

"Harry left," I tell him before I sit down, and suddenly the simplicity of it makes it seems true and very sad.

"I'm sorry, Cat." He really does look sorry and he takes my available hand as I use the other to sip my wine. He looks into his martini and asks the question only he would, knowing as much as he does about Harry and me, "Were you surprised?"

"I guess not. He's been so weird and cold for months."

"Many months. What did he say?"

"He left a note."

"Brave guy. Have you spoken to him?"

"Nope. He's away on business. New York, so I hear."

"Great timing. Now he doesn't have to deal with you until he's ready." Will shakes his head, and his words make the wine catch in my throat. I feel like I might finally cry. I feel crazy and deflated and quite lost sitting on the terrace in a city that I don't want to be in, having kissed a man I shouldn't have kissed, in his kitchen when I was supposed to be talking about a business that I don't even like.

Will smiles weakly, and his sweet eyes try to look into mine. I stare inside my almost empty glass with great determination. Tears have welled; they escape downward, and they run along my chin, draining toward my neck. "I can't believe any of this." My voice and brain are not wired to the same frequency and I cannot express what I am thinking because I do not really know.

"Well, honey, there are worse things." Will grips my hand. "Just think, you could be ugly."

I laugh a little, grimly. I try to please him but I know he knows that all I really want is another glass of wine, which he orders. I rest my elbow on the table and put my face into my hand; I look over the terrace edge at the glorious city beneath. Everything is set at odd angles from this vantage point; it is a crazy postcard shot, as if the nation's capital were caught unguarded in its sleep, as if unwatched the teapot buildings had begun to dance and change places.

Will is also looking down at the city. "You know, it looks almost harmless from up here."

"Harmless," I echo, but don't mean it.

He smiles. It is large and sunny; his whole face looks like it is smiling, reflecting the glow beneath us. "Actually, you know I love this city, I just do. I really love it."

"Will," I say after I can think again. "Do you know what Harry actually does for the president?"

"What?"

"No, I'm asking you."

"Didn't you ever talk about his job?"

Suddenly I feel embarrassed in front of my friend about how little Harry and I have spoken about anything in two long years. "Sure," I say, "I just thought you might know more details."

"Cat, you know how segregated the White House is." He looks at me in a quizzical way. "There are reasons that the vice president's office doesn't know everything that goes on with the president," he offers as if he is giving a civics lesson to a tourist rather than to me, someone who should know better.

"I guess I'm just being paranoid."

"Everyone in this city is. Some just have more reason than others."

"Now it's your turn," I say, because I feel so tired of me and my uncertainties.

"Okay, I might as well get it over with." He takes in a deep breath as I blow smoke away from him and down toward the fully lighted White House. "I've had a lot of doctors' appointments lately, and only Al knows this so far. Sorry, I had to let him know first."

My mind shuts off, and I look at Will who has now focused on the tall, straight-backed Washington Monument.

"Cat, I've got cancer." He laughs strangely, a bleak chuckle that just happens. "You know I always worried about HIV. I mean, I've had my share of loser boyfriends." He arches an eyebrow at me. "And now, when things are so great with Peter and all, I go and get leukemia."

"Will," I begin but do not know where to take it. He, as usual, comes to my rescue; he squeezes my hand and says, "Let's get really drunk and then we can talk about your Staten Island Ferry thing, which I'm now referring to as Operation Gilligan's Island. Don't the two of them kind of remind you of the Professor and Mary Ann?" I laugh and it is real this time, and his clouded eyes twinkle somehow.

He eats an olive out of his empty martini glass. "And

I guess that leaves us with what for the president? Gilligan?" I wipe my face with both hands and smile at him.

"You know what really stinks though?" he asks me, and I cannot imagine what might stink more than his news. "No matter what I say to people, they'll just think I'm lying and that I really have AIDS." He shakes his head over and over; he looks out to the black sky that is high above the city and pounded bright with stars. "Kind of ironic, don't you think?"

~

On Christmas Eve every year there was a pageant in my grandparents' town, after dark and in the frost-touched cold. I called it the pony parade and that is what it was: people dressed like angels, elves, biblical characters. They wore red and green, some had antlers on their heads, and all of them rode horses down the main street, children first on their proud ponies. I would ride Tilly that Christmas when I was seven; I would ride the pony I loved best. She was small boned, fine; she was black and white, tall for a pony, and she greeted me by whinnying when she saw me coming through the cold stallways of Granddaddy's barn.

I brushed her for two hours on the day before Christmas. I rubbed oil on her, shoulders downward like my mother taught me. I worked the oil into her coat until it gleamed glossy in the still light of the barn in winter. Tilly's mother, Finch, had died the summer before. By that time she was very old and gray around her muzzle; her back had sunken like a sofa that has lost the stuffing in its seat. Finch had been my mother's pony, and they went around Virginia together when they were both young and before either had children. They went across the state jumping jumps and winning ribbons, mostly blue, that hung on my grandfather's workshop wall like grand banners.

Tilly had turned old, too, like her brown brother, Trigger, who belonged to Uncle Teddy before he grew too big and ran away. But unlike Trigger, who looked worn as a sullen mule, Tilly was pretty with her back fine and straight. She tossed and shook her mane when I entered her stall and I was proud as I brushed her. I liked to kiss the velvet spot, soft and prickly, between her nostrils. "Besides," my mother said to me that Christmas Eve day when the sky was white and the air smelled like fires, "she belongs to you now."

I spend the next afternoon on the Internet, ignoring my phone and e-mail, researching leukemia. There is limitless cyber information on the disease: basic facts, survival statistics, medical journal entries, new treatments, bone marrow transplant descriptions, chat rooms, and "the holistic way of living with leukemia." The word *living* coupled with this kind of cancer seems to be a Pollyanna oxymoron. It seems that many people suffering from it do not live very long at all. I try to bolster myself with the most scientific and medical information, official jargon, prognoses, but my background is notably scienceless, limited entirely to eleventh-grade biology and the study of Mendel's pea plant genetics, a few random facts remembered about photosynthesis, reproduction, and some vague recollection of Darwin and his birds. So I turn away from the complexities of bone marrow harvest and go to the chat rooms.

Last night Will told me that his boyfriend, Peter, is taking the next week off to be with him at the oncology center. I had instantly liked Peter when I met him last summer, but did not think I would when Will told me, bashfully, that he was a United States Attorney in the Justice Department. I imagined that he could only be tense, combative, dismissive in a high-strung arrogance. But in person, at the restaurant where Will proudly introduced us, he was calm; he had a soft, open laugh that made his eyes light up and his nose crinkle. I tried to picture him as the pit bull he must be in the courtroom, but Will told me that his trial style was not much different from what I had seen and, Will said, "The juries all love him." And I knew immediately that Will did, too, and that, finally, in his life Will had everything he wanted.

I pick Gummy Bears out of a bowl as I read. They cling to each other in clumps, multicolored jelly bears lumped together. I keep reading the exchanges until I have to stop for a few minutes at a time when I feel like

I might not be able come up for air again, when I feel like I am drowning. The people discuss their treatments, naming drugs and durations; the procedures are all painful and some are designed to kill the body with the inspiration that powerful drugs will be able to bring it back to life again. I learn that there is no way to isolate leukemia. It cannot be radiated, amputated, removed, and some people in these chat rooms discuss philosophy, theology, and the bad luck of getting a cancer that is not an island or even a continent but the whole damned globe; a cancer of the blood, a disease that becomes its own ruthless universe. There are angry chatters and also humorous ones; there are natural leaders and helpers who try to make the others feel better. Sometimes they succeed. But I am left with little hope in the leukemia chat room, for there is the pervading sense, even with jokes and verse, that the dialogue is between those who have learned to speak in some special language of the condemned.

I feel like I am intruding. I cannot face this computer screen, this radar screen, and imagine that Will now belongs more in there than outside with me. A woman from Tacoma, Washington, writes that she is putting together memory boxes for her children, Susie, age two, and Dale, age eight, who is now a champion in the state's Pee Wee Soccer League. She types a careful description of everything that she is putting in his box—pictures, a trophy he gave her of "World's Greatest Mom," poems she has loved, cartoons, a medal she won for running track in college — and she begins to tell about the box for Susie. Her phrases become shortened and they jumble as she tries to describe what she is putting together, leaving behind for her baby. She stops and pleads to the chat room, "How will she even remember me?"

A woman from Needles, Arizona, jumps in and gives Tacoma pleasantries for the ages, from the feel-good world of self-helpers, greeting cards, the Bible: Needles lectures her on acceptance, peace, and *coming to terms;* she concludes with, "Tell dear little Susie that she should be proud that her mommy will be safe with God." Tacoma is silent, reading perhaps. And I wait for Tacoma's reply; anxiously I sit and watch the screen; I hope that Needles's words have somehow helped, comforted, have made her feel less helpless about going gently into the bad night. It just seems impossible to me but I am hoping. Tacoma finally shoots back; she puts on the "Caps Lock" so that there will be no mistake about what she is saying: "I am dying and you can't change that. Fuck you and your stupid words. Fuck everyone. I have to stop talking to you and go live. Maybe I still have time to make her remember. I have to try." I log off the Internet and feel that that is not enough. I shut down my computer, close it down so that the screen is blank enough to make the voices go away.

At five thirty we turn on the televisions in the sector, all four of them tuned to different news stations, each anchored in the corners of the room like we are in a sports bar or airport lounge. The vice president and Mrs. Wallace are shown in full color, smiling and shaking hands with the commuters as they board the Staten Island Ferry. Mark looks surprisingly calm, and as I watch him, I begin to look forward to dinner with him on Saturday.

After I left Will last night, I was drunk and upset; I was lonely sitting on the couch Harry and I had bought years before on a bright spring day when we were filled with possibility. Neither of us had ever bought a couch before; Harry had inherited one at his old apartment, but it was black and small and looked more like it belonged in an office than in the light-filled Ansonia. We looked at the 26th Street flea market, but somehow they all looked too worn and sunken, and as Harry pointed out, there are some things you don't want to have a history.

We decided to go to ABC Carpet on 19th Street and Broadway. When I first moved to New York and heard about ABC Carpet, I thought it sounded like a carpet warehouse in New Jersey. But it couldn't be more opposite. I told Harry it was like being seven years old and going to FAO Schwarz, floor after floor of the most beautiful furniture, linens, rugs, objects. It even smelled lovely. Through all of my sublets and housesits, I would go to ABC Carpet and imagine what I would buy when I had a place and money of my own. I would spend hours roaming through the vast floors, pondering the perfect duvet cover and exactly right chair. I found it thrilling that you could get everything from an armoire that had belonged to a czar to a little silk sachet filled with lavender.

Harry tried not to let me see him looking at prices; he pretended to feel the fabric of the sofas, and then he would lean a bit, take a fast peek at the discreet sales tags. He moved from sofa to sofa. And then we saw it at the same time: an enormous deep green one that somehow looked both quite modern and old-fashioned. We dared not to peek. And then a helpful man in a suit came up behind us and said that it was on sale. He explained that many people had wanted to buy it but they weren't able to fit it through the narrow doors of their New York apartments or into the tiny elevators or up too many flights of stairs. Harry and I looked at each other and smiled. We thought of the cavernous elevator at the Ansonia and of our wide, tall front door and knew the grand sofa belonged to us.

We walked out into the sun and down to Union Square, where the farmers market was set up: stall after stall filled with flowers, brilliant buckets of tulips, roses, fat peonies dripping with rain; booths that sold wine, honey, bread, fruit, and vegetables. We bought a loaf of sourdough bread that the old man said had been flown in overnight from San Francisco; we broke pieces off to eat as we walked. And we continued downtown and went west to the Village and our favorite restaurant, a tiny French one that sat on the corner of Waverly and Grove but looked just like Paris. We drank carafes of wine to celebrate. We put the big order and delivery form in the middle of the square wooden table, and Harry toasted, "To our future."

Al comes out of his office to watch the ferry launch with everyone else in the sector, and I am relieved to see that a lot of press have shown up and even look vaguely enthusiastic. We catch a glimpse of Jill beside Mark as she pushes one reporter away, and it briefly looks as if a Secret Service agent is apologizing to him. Al, his arms folded over his enormous stomach, shakes his head, takes off his half glasses.

All the news stations use the segment as it was designed—as a soft news piece at the end of their broadcasts—and each seems to treat it as a wee bit of Americana, most of them use a closing shot of Mark waving to the Statue of Liberty.

I sit at my desk by the heated, tense glow of the metal lamp until late in the evening to avoid going back to Swann Street and the sofa, which would not fit up the stairs, and we had to crane into the apartment, removing the front windows. The phone rings after eight, announces "Unknown Number." When I answer I am hopeful—although I'm not sure for whom or what—and my stomach dives when I hear it is Yuri Cherpinov.

"I have been away on my honeymoon!" he yells, and I cannot tell if he is driving or riding somewhere off in the distance, and I don't even try to figure out what time it might be with Yuri.

"You got married?" I ask blankly, and think it's only been a couple of days since I last spoke to him. I look at the bulletin board in front of me; Harry's photo is still there and he smiles at me, with an amazing squint of his eyes.

"Oh, no, Katerina!" He laughs and I can hear the heavy sound of machinery in the background. "Just lots of love, you know?" I think he means honeymoon as in lots of sex on a brief vacation, but I am not going to split verbal hairs in this conversation, which I want to be over as soon as possible.

"That's nice," I say, and don't want to imagine who or where.

"When do you get married, Katerina?"

"Yuri, I'm really not sure."

"You do not know your own wedding? What is wrong with that man of yours? You make sure he bring you here for your honeymoon. Your husband like Saint Petersburg; he like his vodka very much."

I know Harry has never been to Russia, and I have never seen him drink vodka. "I think you have him confused with someone else," I say because I am so tired of Yuri Cherpinov and his fiction.

"Oh, no, we good friends. He tell me lots of American history lessons."

This freezes me for a moment but I shake it off because I believe Yuri simply takes what I tell him and drunkenly spits it back as fact, and I know that two weeks ago I told him that Harry used to teach American history, to which he had snorted, "What history does America have?"

"Irina is so beautiful!" he offers proudly tonight. "But I call because we are coming to visit you!" I lean back in my chair and think this bad can only go to worse.

"Katerina?" He thinks he's lost me to enthusiasm as the machine noise grinds on behind him.

"That's great," I manage. "When?"

"This weekend? Can you believe it?" He sounds like a little boy so pleased with himself, and he thinks that I am genuinely happy to hear his news. I cannot think of what to say, and it, of course, hardly matters, because anything I could say would not stop this train from coming.

"I come to cover the meeting with your bad president."

And I have forgotten about Camp David; there has been no news about it in my clip package.

"I bring Irina, too; she will be my photographer. Maybe you have dinner with me on Saturday night?"

"I'm sorry, I have plans already."

"We need to have dinner, Katerina—"

I knock the receiver on the desk, once, twice for luck and sound effects, and then I press down on the hook to make Yuri go away. He won't notice for a few minutes that I'm no longer on the line, and I won't answer the phone when he rings back to find me, when he calls from the auto repair place where he's standing, dialing my number, and waiting for his Mercedes to be fixed, souped up, spring cleaned of the Russian winter.

I have an e-mail from Mark's secretary and a second from Harry's father. I read Marge Peterson's one and it confirms that a car will pick me up on Swann Street at seven on Saturday night, one day away. I sit for a while before I can open Mr. Bellum's message sent from his ranch-style house in South Carolina. Harry got him a laptop for Christmas and carefully explained how to use e-mail, but Mr. Bellum already seemed to have studied his manual and took to e-mailing as the great lost art of letter writing. Of course I feel guilt when I see his name on the e-mail. I miss this gentle man who sold his construction company to become a host of a children's show on a local station in Charleston. He loves his puppets, much to Harry's embarrassment. I open his e-mail, which says,

Dear Daughter, I do not like to bother you at work but I have not heard from my son (who is rather scarce during the best) in I believe two months or sixty-two days plus time differences depending on his travel and whose calendar count. Are you well? Is he making a good living and being kind? How are your folks? (I think of your mother because my daffodils are now blooming.) I will not burden you with any more old-man questions. I know how you like Miss Sheeby the Cow, but alas I've had to put her out to pasture (puppets age, too, after all), but I've

added a new girl named Fare Hare who is a clever
pink rabbit. Yours with admiration and as always I
wish I were thirty years younger and had captured
you before Harry had that privilege! Love, Walter

I close the screen and cry. I feel sick and finish off the rest
of the bottle of Pepto-Bismol. I need to find my coat and
get out of the Old Executive Office Building fast before
I can't stop myself and the guards know I am crying on
exit. I need to make it back to Swann Street where there
is nobody watching me.

10

It is just after seven when I reach Observatory Circle, and the night is unusually warm for April. The air seems filled with roses about to bloom and the promise of days that will seem light until the stars come out. Mark greets me at the kitchen door still wearing his suit on a Saturday evening, which does not surprise me because I know his schedule: Friday, before dawn, he flew to New Hampshire to warm up for the primaries; by noon he was addressing the road crew of a new highway outside of Albany and then had lunch with the governor, went to a big mayoral meeting in Manhattan, rode the ferry, had dinner in Vermont, and spent all of Saturday at a fund-raiser in a wealthy suburb of Detroit. He shakes my hand in the kitchen, formal and stiff, and I guess this is because he has only just returned and is surrounded by a noisy gaggle of his staff and helpers, most of whom I know so I feel immediately self-conscious. I wish I hadn't come; my face feels warm; my hands don't know what to do. Mark obviously can sense I feel as awkward as I look so he says, "Catherine, glad you could come. I think you know everyone except for Lucy."

And the beautiful six-year-old in flowered pajamas sits at the kitchen table coloring and finishing a bowl of ice cream. She has dark curly hair like her mother, her father's large blue eyes, and she waves at me, another in the constant stream through her kitchen.

"I'll leave you two girls to chat," Mark says as he exits, followed by his gang on cell phones, "while I finish up a few things."

So I am alone in the kitchen with his daughter and her nanny, Evelyn, a patient, short woman in her fifties who I know has taken care of Lucy since she was a baby. I sit down as the kitchen grows darker, almost night, and the last of the tree shadows sweep across the room as Lucy smiles at me. She looks shyly into her empty bowl painted with melting chocolate ice cream.

"What's your name?" she asks finally, saving me from figuring out how to start the conversation.

"Catherine."

"I have two Catherines in my class, one is nice and one is mean. Do you work for my daddy?"

"Yes, I do."

"Everybody works for him." She draws out "everybody" and exaggerates it proudly with a roll of her eyes. Then, having interviewed me and finding me pretty harmless, she turns to her nanny and says politely, "Thank you, Evelyn." When Evelyn leaves the room I realize that Lucy has heard her father say this to people, and now she too says it to people when she is finished with them and wants to be on her own, away from minders.

She taps the back of the spoon lightly against her lips and tells me, "Daddy said I can play until eight o'clock." She looks at her tiny wrist, where there isn't a watch but she has seen her father do this, too, often, his constant motion of checking time.

The little girl and I sit at the large table with construction paper spread out in front of us. She wants to make crowns. "I won't be the princess," she says after she looks like she's given the matter some thought. "I can be the queen." She looks pleased with her self-appointment; she laughs; at six years old she already knows that the queen is a big step up from princess.

"Well, the queen needs a very special crown," I say, and draw an outline on a green piece, her favorite color she tells me, as I sketch jagged pyramids of crown. Lucy is armed with her school scissors, small ones with plastic red handles and blunt shears; she carefully inserts her fingers, adjusts them to get a handy grip, and she looks like she is fiddling with chopsticks, firming up the mechanics for useful operation. She works on a purple piece of paper; she saws away at it, and odd bits fall away from the whole. "These are the jewels for the good crown," she rationalizes, makes the best of the abstract cutouts.

"Mommy likes purple," she says, stacking the shreds of paper.

"She did?"

"She does." Lucy smiles sweetly. She hasn't intended to correct my tense, but her gentle echo does, in fact, correct it for me.

"What else does she like?"

"Chocolate ice cream!" She screams "ice cream," and I wonder if that means she wants more and if she is allowed to have another bowl. She nods. "She *likes* it but she *loves* me and Daddy and Bettina."

The other night Mark told me all about Bettina, who is Lucy's imaginary and identical twin. She also happens to share the name of Susan's nurse who took care of her, who was at her bedside when she died. And the little Bettina is responsible for Lucy's temper tantrums, infrequent as they are, and also for her regular bad dreams, hot and scary. She calls these "night sweats," and this she has appropriated from adult conversations, cancer talk, and it seems a good enough way to describe her nightmares.

Lucy tells me that Bettina "doesn't remember Mommy anymore."

I scissor away and fold the green paper until the two ends meet each other in a cylinder. Lucy carefully puts two staples to our construction; she secures one staple at the base and one in the middle, and then she smiles broadly at me. She dabs her glue stick around the crown to set her paper jewels, inlay each ruby in a special place.

Suddenly, she stops and looks at me as if she has just remembered something important. "Bettina thinks Mommy's an angel."

"Well, she's right."

"No." Lucy shakes her head firmly; she frowns more like the twin than herself. "She's a fire bug."

I almost want to laugh at the way she says this with such authority, but I keep my lips tightly together as I look at her small, serious face.

"A fire bug," she repeats, and glances out the wide window. "Because I can see her with the other dead people. She flies outside at night like a little star."

I reach my hand over and pet hers. It is baby soft and she grins at me with one tooth missing. Then she stands up on the chair and offers the crown to me; she puts it on my head with certain glee. "Maybe you can see her sometime, too," she promises me in a whisper.

Mark and I sit in the garden after dinner on a cold stone bench, spring gusts swaying through the night trees. I ask if he minds if I smoke, and I see firm disapproval flash across his face but he is polite and says, "Sure, go ahead. But I'll have to break you of that."

"The tobacco lobby won't be happy," I say, because I am still nervous, have been all evening. I can't shrug the shaky feeling of being on a date with him or of being on a date in general. By now I know all of Harry's expressions and like each one. I miss him, sitting on a cold stone bench with another man who doesn't like me smoking. I miss Harry and don't know if the uneasy feeling in my stomach will ever go away.

"I'm sorry tonight has been so chaotic." Mark breathes out as if it were his first chance in days to exhale. He puts his arm around the back of the bench, just behind me. "I was really looking forward to seeing you."

I look at him and smile. He sounds so sincere, slightly embarrassed, and maybe, I think, I could get used to being with someone who looks forward to seeing me.

"I guess this is a little strange for both of us." He laughs a nervous kind of half laugh.

"Very strange." I try to laugh. "I do work for you, you know."

"To me that isn't the hard part." And now he sounds very serious in the shadows. "After all, at least you understand the complexity of my world. A person in my position cannot afford to be with someone who doesn't." When he says this I understand the logic behind it of course, but it suddenly sounds so unromantic, as if he has to pick dates who already have a security clearance from the FBI.

"Even if you weren't in the White House," he adds quickly, because perhaps I have frowned or blown smoke out too hard, "I'd want to take you out."

We both stare out into the dark garden, giant searchlights pointing toward the sky, heavy, electronic fences ringing the perimeter, and it seems as if Susan and Harry were swirling around in the spring gusts, whispering to us. I close my eyes as if to erase both of them. Mark leans a fraction of an inch closer to me and I can tell that he smells like lavender soap.

"Do you like Washington?" I ask because somehow his response will mean a lot.

"The city or the job?"

And I laugh. "Both." I look at his face to listen for his answer.

"I love both of them," he says before I kiss him.

On Christmas Eve when I was seven, it began to snow just as the pony parade started. I tipped my head back in the dark, wearing my angel costume, sitting on Tilly's patient back, and I felt the flakes land on my face in tingles. I waited in line with the other children. We would ride first down the short main street decorated with hundreds of lights shining from bare trees and everyday buildings. We would follow our leader, Aunt Sally Ann, who each year led the pageant proudly.

She always began talking about her costume near my birthday, in the summer; she planned her Blessed Mary outfit many months in advance. And that year she wore a dress of velvet pale blue, gold rimmed, and a wire crown that was bejeweled with broken glass and my marbles, which I thought had disappeared and were lost forever.

I watched her from my place in line, and the snowflakes flecked on her dress like tiny polka dots. She sat on Trigger, and even for a small woman, she was too big for the pony, but she draped her legs over him like a sidesaddle seat, her back straight, head held high, and she carried a doll wrapped in white, the Baby Jesus. She had wanted to carry my own little brother but my mother wouldn't let her, and I was shut in Uncle Teddy's room while they argued. Aunt Sally Ann screamed, slammed a heavy wooden door, and cursed her niece, my mother.

She began the slow procession down the lighted street. Trigger walking with his head down showed the way to our ponies, breathing great snorts of breath. All the people in the town stood on the sidewalks, holding candles that flickered in the still and cold; they smiled and watched us angels pass, march toward church and Christmas. I saw the town's mayor, Bob "Tibby" Tibidoux, and he was smiling at his little grandchildren, two on a brown pony just behind Aunt Sally Ann. And she beamed back at Tall Tibby, returning his unintended smile. She smiled big, wide in the imaginary footlights on Christmas Eve. I knew she was supposed to marry him, long years before, but that she had gone to New York instead. When she returned, without her suitcases and with a stare that no one recognized, he had already married someone else. There was a picture of his bride in the *Calhoun Courier,* the woman, still lovely, who stood beside him on the sidewalk, on Christmas Eve. And as we rode on through the town, I saw Aunt Sally Ann look back from on top of her tired pony; I saw her glance back at him, over her shoulder, at the old man who hadn't waited for her dreams.

⌒ *Harry has always known that Washington is really two cities: one that is public and one that is secret. President Wallace and President Regov meet at Camp David on Saturday. There are snapshots of them smiling, but there are unpublished transcripts of them fighting. On Sunday morning Harry knows exactly where the two Washingtons will intersect for him.*

11

By Friday—I refer to this time now as Week Two—I stop expecting to hear from Harry. I know he will resurface at some undisclosed point, in our apartment to collect more things or on our gated compound to attend to his all-important business. *We will talk, of course, but you cannot change my mind on this.* I've stopped believing I can; the part of me that believes I even know Harry is being wiped away (over these past months and after his departure) as if I were being given a new set of fingerprints. Sometimes I think I've made him up, imagined New York, his loping walk and smile of love aimed just at me.

I usually think this in daylight. For the past few late nights I have been going through our drawers trying to throw things out, and that's when I find evidence of him and of us. I sit on the floor with a full ashtray and a bottle of wine in front of overstuffed drawers, pulled out of the desk, the bureaus. Sometimes almost till dawn, I sift through letters and photographs, old invitations to parties that Harry and I had looked forward to together. The drawers are crammed with such things, remnants found, moments lost; they are like forgotten wells filled with water now fast draining. We moved our New York apartment almost intact. In our hurry to get to Washington, we hadn't done any sorting or left much behind; we just transferred our drawers with their junk layers, dim scraps, useless keys, unopened bills, undeveloped rolls of film. I find menus from our favorite delivery places.

I sit on the Swann Street floor, so far from those dinners, and try to throw things away. I try to stick the past in a large Hefty garbage bag; instead, I put the menus neatly in a cardboard box. I'm not sure why but I stack them—Ajanta, Empire Canton, Barbecue West, Nacho Mamas—in a box for him so he might find them, the relics of the years when we sat on the couch and decided what to eat together, like hungry children who had the great candy store of New York at their fingertips.

In the daylight hours of Week Two, I get notes from Mark. They all come through in-house mail, sometimes twice a day; they all get delivered in the brown envelopes that warn intruders of years ahead in federal prison. They are letters of courtship, old fashioned and touching. Some are one sentence long, "The azaleas are starting to bloom in the East Garden—I believe they were planted by Mamie Eisenhower." And some take up a couple of pages; the one that arrived on Monday discussed our Saturday night: "The truth is I don't know how to date. Perhaps it is presumptuous of me to think that you are ready to get close to someone else, and perhaps only in time can we find this out. I look forward to whatever time we can spend together."

I begin to think about him more and more. By Friday I sharply miss his notes because he is in Texas and away from the safe passage of in-house mail, and I find myself counting hours until I see him on Saturday night. This surprises me. This frightens me as I go back to sifting through piles of my past, as I go back to digging through bygones, alone before dawn.

On Friday night I call Laura, who is back in San Francisco. I decide to tell my best friend about Mark. Laura has always wanted Washington to be glamorous for me. And if there was the initial, unjaded "I'm here" feeling about working in the White House, I knew what I was getting into when Harry and I left New York. Being with Harry, though, and his first-before-fading boyish delight was all the excitement I needed when we settled on Swann Street.

I knew all about Washington's decidedly unglamorous ways. I was very familiar with its tourist population that actually runs the city, which is staffed entirely by out-of-towners, a mish-mash configuration of average, of the best from Cleveland, Little Rock, West Lafayette, Cut and Shoot, Slingerlands, Tarzana, and Troy. It is one long parade of fine civil servants and lawyers who once were class presidents back home, who "know how to get things done!" and who never make waves. Even the more exotic launching pads—London, Tehran, Rome, colonies (former and quirky)—lose their shimmer in the resolutely beige atmosphere of the nation's capital. It is a professional liability to have any color here, so people, anyone possessing some even faint shade to begin with, drain it quickly when landing in this place, on touching down in the government, the world's largest bureaucratic machine.

I have explained all this to Laura, but I think certain movies have infected her and have given her a suspicious subconscious that ignores what I tell her. She has believed films of pomp and circumstance, filibusters, sincere presidents, fallen heroes, dangerous spies, CIA rogues, delicious secrets, sharp-thinking specialists, and reporters who always find the truth while dodging bullets. No one, it seems, wants to tell the story from the bowels of the Old Executive Office Building, or from the thousands of dull corridors in the Pentagon, or from any of the countless bland, busy buildings that make up the city and its enterprise. The constant assimilations of the town, the rigorous sameness, and meek, day-to-day bloodletting would surely stun the audience into boredom, ennui, and such a film would leave them restless for the excitement of their own lives.

But Laura persists. When I call her at one in the morning, she does not sound surprised that I have had a couple of dates with the vice president and excitedly asks, "Have you been to any fun parties with *him*?" She will keep referring to Mark as "him" in her Washington indulgence of paranoia. "People are probably listening to us," she whispers, and then laughs at the thought of men with big black headphones on, hunkered down in a van, late at night, with too much coffee. I don't have the heart to tell her that it doesn't matter who was listening because we weren't saying anything, and at any rate, my telephone conversations were not being monitored. So far, no one, internal or external, cared about my relationship with Mark. I already have a security clearance and could be in rooms with him unquestioned and, besides, as he keeps pointing out, we are "both unmarried adults."

"No," I answer her. "Mark and I haven't gone to any parties at all."

"That's good," she says with a kind of sympathetic disappointment. "The two of you should spend as much time alone together as possible."

I read her a few choice excerpts from his letters, and she sounds girlish and approving despite her unease at being listened to by the phantom men in the big headphones. "He's so romantic," she enthuses. "He sounds a lot like Javier," she declares as a compliment, speaking of her longtime boyfriend who is a popular hatmaker (I have five of his creations, beautiful ornaments that I only wore in New York because they are one of the many things so inappropriate to Washington) and is now helping Laura produce her films.

"It makes me feel happy that he's making you sound more like yourself again," she says softly.

A few weeks before my eighth birthday, my father took the atlas down from the bookshelf in our living room, and he opened it up to show us where we were going. I stood with my baby brother—soft and helpless—on my hip, and the atlas was clear as my father pointed to where so much of the picture was blue. He showed us Delaware, not much land but lots of that water; he told us that most of the little state was made of beaches, sand, and swimming, for us especially. He said that we would also see the ocean. He would see it, too. "Just a different one." And he flipped through many pages to find his, his huge piece of water and thin, long sliver of land that crooked like a small broken shell and had funny names attached, Dong Hoi, Binh Dinh, Nha Trang, Phan Rang. And I said them over and over for my brother like a lucky little song.

My mother and father had been loading the car since before my window grew light, and I looked out at them from half sleep. They filled the trunk with suitcases, beach chairs, a folding crib, and I watched my father try to close the lid. He pressed himself against its crowded odds; his face fixed; his smile frozen into a narrow sketch. My mother laughed. She stepped back from him and giggled in the street, in the dawn when the dark sidewalks dewed gently and the air hung fresh before humidity. I looked through my lace curtains and saw him give up his struggle; he went from the car to her and reached out his arms. The shady trees moved above them, and I remember that they looked like they were dancing.

My father belted me in the large car; he adjusted the big nylon strap to fit across my skinny bare legs. "There," he announced, "just like in an airplane." I had never been in an airplane, but I felt safe for the journey with my brother strapped in his own baby chair next to our one beagle in the wide backseat. The wife dog, Jackie, had died early and was wrapped, one bright package of dust, and carefully placed in my mother's nightgown drawer so that she would be safe with her parents, Ike and Mamie. I waited for my mother, our pilot, in the hot car that smelled like her: lemons, peppermint, and roses.

And on that morning, as I waited to go to all those miles of beaches, my father's green car pulled up in front of the house, in back of us in the driveway. My mother walked with him, holding his hand, and he waved back to me in my cockpit. Then his car pulled away, drove down the tree-lined street until it vanished into the early heat. My mother ran after it, she chased it to the corner, and I could hear her running in the middle of the street. I heard her sandals as they clattered along the empty, sunken pavement on that morning we were left alone.

⌒

On Saturday afternoon I sit with Will, in his apartment not far from mine, and we watch TV, nearly anything, because he is too weak to go outside after so much chemotherapy. Will is huddled on the couch, wrapped in a cotton blanket that his mother made for him. He doesn't speak about his parents much—his father almost not at all—but he fingers the crocheted afghan draped around his thin shoulders and he probably thinks of his mother in her drugstore-bought glasses on a beaded chain, hanging across her chest like a laminated ID card. He must picture her, on her own couch far off in Petaluma, California, defiantly knitting away in front of the television while his father sits, stone-faced, drinking beer, and watching ESPN. I know that he was a policeman and that his mother works in a local clothing store called the Sophisti-Cat Boutique with a big, pink cat painted on its shop awning.

Will told me that the town—and his family for that matter—is stalled in the 1950s, atrophied long decades ago. The town has a diner, ranch houses, and rows of tattered shops, a restaurant shaped like a chicken, a grocery store with a revolving plastic cow on its roof, and a bright orange motel that sticks out of nowhere. Petaluma is only an hour-and-a-half drive from San Francisco but it might as well be thousands of miles away down a highway surrounded by hot, brown baked hills; a moonscape filled with nothing except for hydraulic windmills, whirling. He hasn't spoken with his father in years. The White House did not impress the retired patrolman as much as Will's other choices in life, which, perhaps he believes, have finally caught up with his son, have made him sick and wasted, have caused his health to fade like all those parched, wheat-colored hills of his youth.

I can imagine his mother finally finishing the blanket. I can picture her sneaking out of the modest, fake-sided house as her husband takes a nap, after much beer, and her driving to the tiny adobe post office. She must have carefully written the name of her only, ailing child on the mailing label and then gently wrapped the blanket around the brownies—Ziploced and aluminum, double-foiled—some bible verses, cherry-flavored Chap Stick, and a fifty-dollar bill. "Please take care of yourself"—her note read in faint, motherly script on a piece of stationery with sunflower borders—"Your father sends his prayers." And, I guess, that's all he would send, through his wife and silence.

I eat her brownies and drink wine that I have brought with me, two bottles, even though Will only drinks red Pedialyte, a baby juice pumped full of electrolytes for rehydration. His apartment is spotless, immaculate as always, and the only photograph in it is of the president. It is framed in elegant dark wood and is placed at the center of the living room, on a high spool table with a vase of fresh flowers next to it. "At least," Will commented wanly from the couch, as usual searching for the silver in the storm cloud rising, "I don't have to buy flowers anymore."

I know better than to tease him about the picture and his home shrine to the president. The president presides over the tidy apartment like a patriarch. He stands in front of an American flag, arms folded, and he stares directly at the camera with a wry, nice-to-know-ya grin, a public smile. The photograph has a message written across it, in clear sure hand; it says, "To Will Bennett: A man whose dreams are those of a nation." I know better than to point out the irony and to try to turn Will's apparent pride into something closer to my own cynicism.

I would like to tell Will about Mark, but I don't quite know how at this early stage. However, of all the communications staff Will is the one who knows him best, has been with him since the campaign, has traveled with him to every state and beyond. Mark trusts him, turns to him, and values Will's sharp sense, good reasoning, and fair play. And, of course, Will knows me.

He gives me an opening after an hour of television and gossipy chatter: "Well, my dear, you certainly seem in a good mood for somebody whose boyfriend just left her." He looks at me sideways and folds his arms.

"Has it occurred to you that I might be talking to Harry again?"

"No."

"Why not?"

"I just don't think that would exactly make you so giggly and excited right now, more like"—he puts his hands to his face and imitates my voice—"'Oh, Will, what should I *do*? Oh, Will, do you think he still *loves* me?'"

"Stop." I hit him on the arm, gently.

"So who is he? I want a name."

I tell him, yes, I have met someone, unexpectedly and delightedly, but that it is early days still. I can't quite bring myself to say his name so I talk on in abstracts, and as I talk I am beginning to become more excited myself. And Will loves a good romance, and I can tell as I babble that he is hoping this will be one.

"Any kissing?"

"A little."

"Good looking?"

"Yes."

"Harry-type handsome or normal-Joe handsome?"

"Oh, Will, I don't know. He's quite attractive I think."

"Single?"

"Will!"

"Well, beggars can't always be choosers."

"Actually, he's a widower; his wife died a couple of years ago."

"Does he have any kids, oh stepmommy dearest?"

"He has a little girl who seems very sweet."

Something comes over Will's face. In the bright spring light he suddenly looks even paler, and I can see two deep lines around his mouth. "How old is his daughter?"

"She's six."

"You still haven't told me his name, Catherine."

He never calls me Catherine and I stammer, "His name isn't important." It shouldn't be but then I stubbornly haven't wanted to think about how important his name is to other people.

"It's Mark Simon, right?"

And he knows he's correct by my silence. "Cat," he says softly and, uncharacteristically, seems to be searching for words. "He's a great guy to work for and to know but not to date."

"Why?"

He fingers the crocheted blanket, sips his Pedialyte from the wineglass that I have poured it into, and he pets my hand, which I snatch away.

"For one thing, he *is* the vice president."

"So?" I know I am starting to sound petulant and like I might stamp my foot.

He looks at me directly, his eyes blink wide and fast, as if I have told him that I'd just been in a horrible car accident. This is not the reception I expected from my good friend. "Cat," he warns like a foghorn, "put it this way: He's a politician and a very lonely man."

My mother drove fast, she always did, and we sailed along the highway toward Annapolis, on to Delaware and our beaches. She played the radio loud, too, with the windows rolled down; she turned up the volume, highest when a song came on that she liked more than all the others. I sat in the passenger seat with all the windows wide, with the speed making the air rush in deafening roars as we neared the Chesapeake Bay Bridge. "It's the longest bridge in the world," my father had told me when we crossed it together one summer before, when I sat in the back like a little girl next to my brother so small; he was just nearly born. This time my mother sang loudly with me strapped beside her like a girlfriend on her fast morning journey to the ocean. She had her thin arm out the window, and she rapped her wedding ring on the steel roof; tap, tap on the top of the car, she kept time with the music as her long hair raced out the window, trailing us like a dark, shining banner. She wore sunglasses and pink lipstick and I knew she was beautiful. She did not look like other mothers with their wide bodies and tight hair, and I was happy that she belonged to me.

"Now you sing, too," she yelled through a laugh, a thundering wind, and the clicking of our wheels as we boarded the bridge that crossed the bay. I could smell the water, the deep salt smell of brightness and breezes, and I could see it beneath us, all around us, us safe above the huge distance between two pieces of land. I couldn't remember my multiplication tables, but I knew all of her radio songs by heart. "Sunshine, we're fine," I sang with her, "so come home please in the sweet summertime." She tapped on the metal, steered with one hand, and bellowed her song to the world, "If your heart shines true and bright, you'll make it back by diamond light."

⌒

I leave Will's apartment at three, after a long silence between the two of us. Of course I understand his worries for me about Mark. I would never have chosen to get involved with a politician. In fact, sitting in Will's living room, I realized for the first time how ironic it was that after all my doubts about Harry's profession I should choose someone with an even more complicated one. Will tried to resume a polite conversation, but neither had much left to contribute, I, too stubborn to address his worries; he, too wary to elaborate.

I am having dinner with Mark at seven; we are going to see a movie but not in a theater like on a usual date, holding hands in the line in front of the cinema, picking seats together inside ("Do you like sitting up close?" "Oh, maybe that's a little too close." "Okay, here're two in the middle."), and sharing popcorn, unbuttered, because that is always safest and neatest. Instead, we will watch a film in the small screening room at Observatory Circle, and it seems to be unsaid that our dates will take place on his compound. If we went out together in public, someone with a camera or a pen might notice; our date could end up in the thick Monday stack of clippings, Edgar shyly wheeling it in my direction, and it is much too soon for that kind of attention.

As I cross Dupont Circle, the fountain finally turned on for spring, its spray dusting new daffodils, for a split second I think maybe I would like to be in the newspaper with the vice president. I want Harry to see. This angry thought comes quickly like a headache, and it stays with me as I walk the few blocks to Swann Street. I pour myself a glass of wine in the apartment, but instead of drinking it, I decide I need to lie down for an hour or so, set my alarm, curl up with the warm cat in the crook of my arm.

In half sleep my mind keeps playing rewind, and I remember when I took the train down to Washington to look for an apartment for Harry and me. I think he was trying to finish grading his NYU students' midterm exams but for some reason—I can't quite remember why—I was taking the train alone to decide in ten minutes to live here on Swann Street. I can remember every other detail of leaving New York that day. On the way to Penn Station the winter rain dumped against the taxi, on all sides, and it was like being stuck in a car wash or trying to row across town in a hurricane. The Sikh driver, in his turban, seemed unconcerned; perhaps he was used to monsoons or maybe he was calmed by the high-pitched wailing music he was playing or he was distracted by his CB radio that kept erupting into Hindi voices.

The rain battered the taxi as if someone were throwing pebbles by the handful, and I rolled down the window even though it was just above freezing outside. I remember suddenly feeling trapped by the downpour and by something that was yelling inside of me. I felt the cold rain shoot against my face, a sharp spray flew in with the sound of traffic, the traffic that could only inch and blare, midday, midtown. It had been just four days since the new first lady called and offered Harry a job in the White House, three days since her people phoned also and said that I would be assured a job, too, perhaps in the communications office of the Pentagon or for the vice president (I had pleaded for the latter, not wanting to spend my days talking about short-range missiles and land-based targets), and already I was heading to Washington to look for an apartment. My whole life was in New York and I loved the Ansonia and its tall grandeur. But I knew I couldn't let Harry move without me because, if I were to be honest, Harry was actually my life, and I loved him more than the rest of it.

But in the taxi, my heart and stomach had crammed together in an amazing force of nature that kept me from breathing right, and I heard someone over the CB call to the driver in plaintive Hindi. It was a woman's voice and he ignored her. The driver yelled back to me; he snickered as the girl went on, "Oh, she will not leave me alone. What is a man to do?" The taxi lurched forward and the begging woman was silenced by the flip of a switch.

I'd get on the Metroliner and go to Washington. I remember thinking for some reason of a professor I had at Brown named Dr. Potter. He was old and esteemed, strict and very much in love with Shakespeare. He had a rule that anyone who was late for his class three times, anyone who would waste people's time that way, would be dismissed, kicked out of his seminar on Shakespeare. So the second time I ran into the class nearly fifteen minutes late, crashed through the back door of the ancient lecture hall, he stopped talking about Caesar midsentence. The room was loudly still. I could only hear the squeaking of wooden chairs, the radiator creaking, and the patter of nervous coughing that ricocheted off the high ceiling. "Miss Porter," he boomed, his voice registering in some kind of Shakespearean octave; he took off his glasses and lay them purposefully on the lectern. "It is the wise man who sees the cannonball coming."

And, as I sat shrunken with dread in the cab's backseat, I remembered his words but didn't know to think much more about them. Now, lying here half asleep on Swann Street, I can't believe that I did not hear this cannon or its fire ringing out — softly at first — over the months and wide fields between Harry and me. It seems incredible to me that signals have been so crossed, that natural switching systems just broke down. When I got in the cab heading to Penn Station that day, I was already steering in some dangerous direction, heading off in the opposite direction from where I should have been going.

12

Just after five the phone rings, stops before the answering machine picks up, and rings again. I get out of bed and begin searching for clothes to wear, and I choose a thin camel sweater, slim black trousers, and a black T-shirt and put them all carefully on a hanger. I smoke a cigarette in the living room to wake myself up and notice that the branches brushing against the front windows are beginning to grow fresh buds, and I open one of the windows, hit my palm against the frame to pry the ancient window open to spring.

In January Harry began to pay the rent on this apartment directly from his bank account, and I am relieved as I remember this; each month it is paid in full. Perhaps he was already planning his escape, but at least I won't have to pay the rent, which I really cannot afford, myself. Some people are paid very well in Washington but not in the bowels of the Old Executive Office Building.

The phone rings again and stops this time after only two stuttered rings. I don't even think of pressing "*69" to call back the person who keeps hanging up because everyone in this city has that option blocked on their phones. No one wants to be traced back to their aborted calls and hang ups. I need to shower before I can talk right now, and I have a feeling it might be my mother who keeps calling. I haven't spoken to her in over a week, and I know she sits on her higher point of the city fretting about me. Of course, a little part of me wonders when the phone rings if it could be Harry. I stand in the shower and let the water wash that little part of me away.

When I finally do answer the phone, after five thirty and with a towel wrapped turbanlike around my wet hair, it is a voice I haven't heard before.

"Miss Porter?"

"Yes?" I say, pulling the towel up above my ear, hoping the voice will become more recognizable.

"This is Agent Albert Udell and I'm calling from the Federal Bureau of Investigation."

I have no idea why he doesn't just say FBI, but it hardly matters because I instantly feel my stomach flip over in panic.

"We need to see you as soon as possible."

"Why?"

"Miss Porter, we would rather tell you in person."

"Tell me what?"

"Miss Porter, it concerns your fiancé."

For some reason I stick more on the word *fiancé* than on why the FBI has called me, half naked from the shower, and what they have to say to me about Harry.

"We will be over to see you within the hour."

"Do you have my address?" I ask stupidly, knowing that the FBI has a lot more of mine than that.

I sit on the couch, shaking and waiting for the buzzer downstairs to screech up here and make my heart skip two beats, three. I have dressed quickly, scooted the junk drawers underneath the dining table, drunk a half glass of wine and then brushed my teeth twice. I tried to call Mark's private number but I just reached the answering service, an operator who sits in the basement of Observatory Circle, and I did not hang up because all calls are screened and logged. So, instead, I told the impassive voice that I needed to cancel the car that was scheduled to pick me up at six forty-five. I was hoping to talk to Mark, hoping he would calm me, tell me not to worry.

The robot voice asks, "Is there anything else?"

"No," I tell her and hang up quickly.

Albert Udell is out of breath when he reaches my door, after he has climbed the three flights of narrow stairs. The man with him does not introduce himself; he is younger and thinner than Agent Udell but wears a nearly identical navy blue suit, standard issue it seems even on a bright Saturday afternoon. Agent Udell insists that I sit on the big couch and asks me if I have had the television on. I don't tell him that Will and I spent the morning and half the afternoon watching Hollywood gossip shows, re-runs of *Friends,* a documentary on the *Titanic,* because I know that's not what he's asking.

He quietly explains to me that there has been an accident, a train crash. Two Amtrak Metroliners, one bound for Washington from New York, the other heading to Boston from Union Station, collided just before the southern side of the Delaware Bridge, just after three P.M. eastern standard time. He uses lots of directional details as if that is how my brain works, with the accuracy of a good, strong compass.

Harry had a reservation on the train from New York, Agent Udell tells me. He watches me closely to see if anything flashes across my face, to try to read my reaction like he must do with serial killers and other people he questions.

"How do you know he actually got on the train?" I ask because it makes sense with all of Harry's recent, erratic behavior. And in my confusion I can't imagine that Harry would ever board a train that would crash. It doesn't make sense to me, that he would be on a train— reading his newspaper or napping with his head against the window—that would collide with another. Nothing makes sense to me except that Harry is the type of person who usually sees things coming.

"Miss Porter." He looks at me with sudden sympathy. "He was supposed to have an important conference call with the White House at three twenty and no one has heard from him."

"Maybe he's hurt or in shock, maybe he just hasn't called?" I wish they would leave so I could turn on the television and drink more wine. Suddenly thinking of Harry hurt or in shock makes my throat tighten, one notch just before tears. "Tell me exactly what happened," I say, trying to recover in front of these strangers.

"Miss Porter," the other man who is still standing and seems to tower over Agent Udell and me on the couch says, "the Washington-bound train derailed; the first three passenger cars went into the Delaware River; the others sustained significant damage."

"Of course," Agent Udell says quickly, "it is still too early to give any specific details, but we felt it was the Bureau's duty to inform you of the accident because both you and Mr. Bellum service the United States government."

I know I'm the one in shock because I want to laugh when he says that, as if Harry and I were prostitutes and the federal government were some fat man who needed our various services, but more than anything, I just want them to leave me alone, so I say, "Yes, thank you," and stand up.

As soon as they leave, I call Harry's cell phone number. It rolls over and says what it always does: It tells me, when in doubt, to call the beeper number. I beep him. I think he might call me back because he has to; he must remember that more than anything I love him, even if he is hurt, even if he is so damaged in the train wreck that he doesn't know his name, maybe he might still remember mine.

~

We all slept in the same big bed of the tiny rented house in Delaware, which was near enough to the beach that the front lawn had more sand in it than grass. My mother, little brother, and the beagle, Jack, would lie on the big bed at night, and my mother read us letters from my father. He wrote long ones but she never read every word. Sometimes she was silent with her eyes on the thin blue stationery that looked like tissue paper from a gift box, and I knew those words were just for her. When there were no new letters and she had read the old ones many times, she would show me fashion magazines. We'd lie on our stomachs and flip through the glossy pages that caught the lamplight in shining patches; I liked the pictures of women running through the city, I liked the ones where they sat on top of elephants, horses, camels, wearing ball gowns and looking off in the distance toward a party. My mother wore a silk robe that my father bought her on one of his trips. It was red with tiny dots of flowers and butterflies, and I would pet her arm as we lay in the bed, my brother asleep against a wall of pillows so that he would not roll onto the tile floor, and I loved the touch of the silk, the smooth coolness of her lovely red robe.

My mother was most excited in the mornings before the mailman came. She cooked us breakfast in the kitchen that had just one pot and cabinets that peeled yellow paint into the sink. She whistled in that kitchen, sang along to her songs on the radio, and watched for Tim the mailman who had a soft Virginia accent like she did. By the time he made it through the sandy patch of lawn and up to the little house that was painted murky green ("Dull like the army," my mother would say, grimacing), she would already be at the screen door waiting for him. I would sit at the kitchen table that wobbled when the matchbook slipped from beneath a metal leg; I would eat my eggs and fruit and listen to the murmur of their friendly voices as they talked of the mountains or small towns or what the waves here looked like that day. Often she would come running back to me holding the blue envelopes with funny stamps that she showed me first. She'd kiss my brother in his tall chair and begin the rattle of sand pails and shovels for our day at the beach. She came back slowly when she was empty handed; she shuffled her flip-flops across the cracking floor like she was suddenly tired, exhausted first thing on a bright summer morning.

I stand on the shore of the Delaware River near Wilmington with a hundred others who stand in the night

looking up at the short bridge, across the water clouded
by smoke, seared by searchlights, in the night deafened by
helicopters, sirens, voices shouting over speakers, loud
equipment that tries to untangle two trains that have
gone terribly wrong on the narrow bridge. It is hard to
believe how wrong until I stand beneath its southern
base. The train bound for Boston has crushed one steel
side of the bridge and threatens to fall into the river. On
the other end of the bridge Harry's train is gone almost
altogether except for one or two carriages I can see
dangling from land like a serpent's tail. They are charred,
pitch black, and I know they must have exploded and
been on fire before I reached this little piece of land.

When the FBI men left, I watched the television
news in the dark. I wanted to call everyone I knew to say,
"I am a coward," to tell them that I was going to sit on
this couch and drink enough wine to send me to tomorrow, when I would wake up and find out that Harry had
decided to stay a day longer in New York to see the daffodils bloom in Central Park or that he missed his train
because he found a new bar he liked close to Penn Station or maybe his cell phone had lost power because, like
always, he had forgotten to recharge it. Without me
around there was no one to plug it in late at night. I
wanted to wake up in the morning and know that even if
he had left me he is still walking the streets hoping to find
me again.

Sam called at six. He shouted into the answering machine, "Soho, you have to pick up." And I drove three

hours with him in his black Camaro, me drinking wine out of a small Evian bottle and clutching my White House pass and a picture of Harry smiling beneath a tall building. (Which one? I keep trying to remember; it is fall, I think, because two red leaves almost touch his face. Maybe near Riverside Park? Why don't I remember that exact second?) Sam raced me north on the I-95, three hours to where the trains had crashed. He told me over the phone, "You can't just sit there and watch this shit on TV."

"I want to," I said.

"Do you love him?" And before I could answer, he told me he would pick me up in fifteen minutes.

We go to a little piece of land in Delaware that belongs to nice people. We stand in their backyards with barbecues, swing sets, and boat slips on the river that are now all ringed with yellow police tape. We are not allowed on the other side of the river where the New York train has blazed through blocks of similar houses belonging to other nice people. The highway was blocked off, and even with Sam's Secret Service badge and my smudged, laminated White House pass, we were directed to the backyards here with a view across to what is left of Harry's train. Sam has his arm around me because I have forgotten to wear a coat.

"How many cars are there on a train?" I ask him when I see the smoky end of the serpent's tail clinging to land.

"Don't know, Catherine." He squeezes my shoulder, and I can feel his giant gold wedding ring and wonder why he is not calling me Soho, what bad news he knows in his secret world that I cannot even imagine.

The crowd is so dense that the woman next to me shifts her cell phone from her right hand to her left so that her arms and elbows don't keep intruding. I can hear her as she dials the tiny cell phone gripped in her hand; she punches keys and yells "shit" and then she cries. I know she is crying because her back bobs against me like a boat against a mooring.

A plump woman, who must own the tidy backyard we're standing in, comes out of her back door carrying a pile of folded blankets. She's wearing one curler in her hair as if she was getting ready to go out when she heard the crush of two trains colliding, as if after hearing the hideous boom of crashing steel and explosions—the kind of sound no one ever hears—and then a tidal wave of a Metroliner falling into her river, she had forgotten about that one curler.

"Here, honey," she says to me, unfolding a small, faded blanket with teddy bears on it, "you look cold."

She helps Sam put it across my shoulders, and I can see a line of policemen who were standing close to the bridge begin herding the crowd away from it, pushing us away from the woman with her stack of blankets and helpless smile. A cop moves through the crowd commanding us, while looking back at the lopsided train straining against the broken bridge, "You've got to get back in case the other one goes down."

We move through other backyards that never thought to have fences between them, and for some reason, I wonder how to get the woman's teddy bear blanket, smelling like fresh soap, back to her.

There are large boats on the river, some with powerful fire hoses trained on the patches of water burning in pools of fire. "It's the fuel," Sam tells me, and other boats have men on them who are diving off backward in scuba gear, men who will try to find people trapped underwater, beneath the flames, to rescue them. I hold my breath, waiting for the first few who went down to resurface.

"I know they're going to find people," I tell Sam, who is lighting one cigarette from the last.

"Soho," he says, taking my elbow, "we'd better go now." He is looking around; his eyes are darting but they go back to the bobbing boat that the divers left. The searchlights illuminate it, and the men on board seem to know what's happening more than we do on shore. They signal each other and gather, run to both sides of the boat. I quickly pray they are calm, just waiting to help their friends with the cold, wet people, help bring the shivering victims back onto the boat. Sam is looking ahead as he always does for danger, for a bullet to come from a crowd; he is watching for a bad truth to unfold and for what I might see.

I have lost track of time since Albert Udell came to the apartment that I found for Harry and me. I realize suddenly that it's been many hours. I realize the truth: No one can survive for seven hours underwater; the divers are going beneath patches of fire to bring up bodies to fill the yellow bags on deck that Sam must see but I cannot.

"Well"—I yank my elbow away from Sam's sure grip, and I feel like running, heading back to the woman who gave me the blanket with her bright back-window lights shining and her child who remembers sleeping safe beneath the teddy bears—"there could be air pockets down there," I tell him. "You know, like when boats capsize, lots of people—"

"Soho," he starts, and the loud flock of helicopters shifts direction with the wind and there is, for a brief moment, what seems almost like silence.

Then I can hear something that I will not forget. At first I thought it was crickets, little chirps calling out across the bridge, the water, this horrible night. I know that the other people crowded around me are listening, too, the people with panic in their eyes who had been making dinner, waiting for someone to come back to them in warm, hopeful households. They are looking up, straining to hear what it is, this chorus coming from all sides of the bridge, above, across the river, like Morse code, like the faint taps of people buried in a mine. And then, all of a sudden, I recognize the sound: hundreds of cell phones ringing, people trying to reach those on the train who will never be able to answer.

⌐

The green car came to the beach on the day after my eighth birthday; it pulled into the parking lot as I buried my legs in the sand. I stayed away from my mother and baby brother, who were napping together near the shore-line, because I was much too big to sleep with my family during the day out in public. I had nearly outgrown my bathing suit. I wished I would and quickly, too; I was tired of its huge ugly sunflowers that decorated my chest where breasts should be; I wanted a two-piece suit so my stomach would show, brown and flat. I wiggled my sunken toes and frowned. They needed paint on them like my mother's; now that I was eight years old, I wanted new toenails, polished pink and perfect.

In the distance, I saw two men in uniform get out of the car. Someone else's father was coming home; there would finally be men on this beach filled with women. And I felt a stab of sharp envy thinking that some girl would have her father back; right in front of me she would show him off and swim with him while the rest of us were left to ignore our mothers nagging us. But the women didn't look happy to see these men; no one ran to greet them as they came onto the sand still wearing their heavy black shoes. The women stood up and called to their children; frantically, it sounded to me; they screamed for their children to come, to get out of the water.

I sat with my legs buried and watched the men slip-slide along the sand; they looked so awkward walking in their big leather shoes; they reminded me of the astronauts I had seen on TV; they strained against the sand like the men who walked up on the moon. The heat blurred the figures in waves as they passed clusters of women and children who huddled next to umbrellas and beach blankets; the two men stopped and asked fat Mrs. Simms something. I saw them pause, just briefly, and fat Mrs. Simms pointed down the beach, her chubby white arm with its underneath wobbling, pointed in our direction. The men continued on their way, space-walking toward me.

I had no way of knowing that it would be a week before I wore my first black dress. It was a little one with capped sleeves, and I wore it with white lacy socks, patent leather Mary Janes, and my father's birthday gift, my new silver seashell necklace hanging down across my chest. And Granny helped me get dressed quietly, she brushed my tangled beach hair in my bedroom at home while the tree branches stayed still outside with no breezes blowing. On that sweltering day I would sit in Arlington Cemetery, on that humid day, hotter than all others in my memory, short but vivid.

I sat on a folding chair in the front line, the one for my family, and I hugged the flag that was folded into a triangle like a pillow. It was musty smelling around the pointed edges, like mittens dried out after being soaked through on a day of sledding. My brother sat on my mother's lap. She was rigid sitting there on her metal chair, stiff as if she had been frozen, and she was powder pale behind her dark glasses. She wasn't wearing any perfume so the air smelled strange and unfamiliar; when I closed my eyes I could not find her—no lemons, peppermint, or roses. My baby brother squirmed and cried; he was afraid of the guns that fired, again and again, into the thick air filled with the numbing drone of cicadas. The two of them together jolted as each shot rang out and ricocheted through the rolling hills that bore white crosses in great lines, all in aerial-straight formation, the dead like troops above the ground.

It would be years before I learned that my father could have abandoned his plane breaking fast that morning. He could have jumped, opened his parachute to the foreign wind; he could have been safe. But he was flying over a city when he got into trouble; a city filled with busy strangers, children in school uniforms and American soldiers in theirs; all of whom he and his copilot, Pete, were getting close enough to see. He must have signaled Pete; somehow and in little time, they must have communicated something to each other with a hand, a thought, one motion, because they turned together, in an instant they turned away. Above streets that were so close, they decided to go on and not abandon the plane on top of people who had just finished breakfast, washed the dishes, and kissed their loves good-bye. They banked. Sharply they left the crowded streets and disappeared off someone's radar screen; suddenly they vanished into morning. My father the pilot and his lonely one-man crew, his best friend for many more years than I had been alive, steered toward the Pacific. The plane went instinctively, I guess, to the ocean, with the bright water guiding them; shining ahead deep and beckoning, it led them to still waters and far from home.

But to us, the men kept coming. The women in their bathing suits followed; flat-footed women padded along the shore behind the men who came to tell us bad news. My mother was still sleeping. So was my brother in his diaper and sun hat, in the crook of her arm beneath the giant, striped umbrella that shielded them. I stood as the people got nearer and sand clung to my legs when I rose up; I remember that it tingled like brown rock sugar melting hot on my skinny legs.

And I stood still on the sand, my feet cemented firmly, waiting for them to pass us by, for them to march on and leave my mother and her baby in peace and sleep with dreams of England or my father and his eyes that smiled at their corners. But she must have seen them, suddenly. They stopped some feet away from her and she stood finally; she covered her body from them; she wrapped her long arms around the bikini skin that glowed bronze and perfect in the sunshine. The two took off their hats. Each removed his stiff-brimmed hat and held it by his side. I remember that their heads, quite bare and bald, glistened in the heat bright-hot and my mother backed away from them.

The women froze in their long parade; like me, they could not move; they could not step closer to the truth or the men with eyes cast down, their medals flashing on the day now finished. My brother, woken from his napping rest, screamed like a siren sounding, warning fire, shark, bad weather coming on that clear beach afternoon. And then my mother ran. She turned from the men and women with sadness ringing them like moons; she ran toward the waves and plunged into them.

With her long hair flying back, back behind her, she went farther until the water crashed against her, sudden and cold; it washed over the cries of her baby and her own sounds that sobbed across the currents, all the way to the other side, to the horizon, but not to him as he lay on the floor of another ocean. I saw her head go beneath the water. Her face and body disappeared into the green ocean, and I knew that she had forgotten about us on dry land. I found myself running, too; I went right past the men and my brother, away from the women who waited; I went fast toward the water. And on the day after my eighth birthday, I chased her; I ran after my mother to save her from the sea.

13

By Sunday afternoon I can-
not watch the news anymore; in fact, there is very little I
can do except go to Mark's house. For twenty-four hours
the divers go down into the dark river and bring back up
what they can find. I don't know what they will find for
me in the tangled steel, in the lonely thick sludge at the
bottom of the river, and I have gone from frightened to
numb every time the telephone rings.

My mother comes to see me in the morning, feeds
the cat, tidies the apartment, tries to get me to eat, but
after a few hours I want her to go. Her face is gray pale,
and her mouth keeps twitching as she tries to etch out a
smile and words of comfort. When she turns on the vacuum cleaner, its loud shrillness shocking both me and the
cat, I tell her, "Mama, please don't."

I can't stand looking at her like this, so jittery, so help-less, and I snap off the machine; I try to reassure her; I lie, "I've got to get some work done to distract me, okay? I'll phone you later."

I wander around the apartment looking for things that will remind me of him but each remnant—a razor I have not thrown away, the half-eaten bag of his beloved Oreos, those sad, hole-filled socks—makes me believe that he is out there somewhere in his suit. I look through the worn envelope of photographs he left in his drawer.

I have looked at them a hundred times (without him knowing), his private collection of boyhood snapshots, him with proudly shorn hair at Marine boot camp, uni-versity moments, his previous life. Standing by the front windows, the tree now bursting with new leaves, I finger through them, and suddenly I know there is one missing. I try to remember when I last looked at them, and I know that it was just a couple of weeks ago, that when he left the apartment at four in the morning, I sat up in bed in my nightgown and stared at him blowing out the birthday candles when he was seven. And I know which one is missing, the one of him when he went to Stanford; he is standing on the deck of the Tiburon Ferry, his thick hair is tousled by wind, his eyes are bright like his big, young smile as he looks toward San Francisco and shore.

Mark greets me at the back door; he is by himself in the kitchen and the house for once seems empty and quiet. "It's just us tonight," he says gently, "and Lucy is already in bed." I will sit with him at the kitchen table; we will sit for hours drinking wine; one of the busiest men in the world will not answer the phone; he will sit still and hold my hand, listen to my worries; he will not say anything when I just want to be silent.

I sleep in one of the many guest rooms; I lie in a large white bed, in his borrowed pajamas.

"You shouldn't be alone right now," he said as the clock ticked by midnight. And as we went upstairs, a grand curved staircase from another time, he added, "You should sleep as late as you like."

But I don't sleep; I suddenly miss Harry more than I have missed anything or anyone before. I suddenly feel a terrible pain in my stomach that shoots upward and settles in my chest. The pain tells me that Harry is really gone.

Sometime very late and in the darkness of a strange house, I hear Lucy call out from her room down the hallway. Lucy begins to cry louder, almost a full-scale wail; she calls out "Daddy" from behind her door. I go out into the hall and see that Mark's own door is open; I wait, holding my breath, listening to the little girl cry, thinking a Secret Service man might appear suddenly from downstairs. But the house is quiet except for Lucy. I finally peek into Mark's room and see his back rising and falling steadily; I think about waking him, but I realize he is in some deep part of sleep, a place away from dreams.

I open Lucy's door tentatively. I know she wants her father and that she will be startled by me standing there in his blue pajamas, a rumpled stranger in her doorway. Her eyes are open, and she looks very small in the large pink room lit by a nightlight in the shape of a moon; she has taken off her covers and lies stiffly, arms at her sides, on her flowered sheets. She doesn't look upset to see me; she says, choking back sobs that catch her involuntarily, "Bettina keeps kicking me." I remember her imaginary twin and sit down next to her.

"Well, she shouldn't do that," I say. "There's plenty of room for both of you."

"She's mad at me."

"Why's that?"

"Because." Her chest heaves lightly in the aftermath of crying.

"Because?"

"She thinks I like you."

I smile small in the darkness, the room smells like flannel and a child's sweet powdered scent, just washed.

"So." She touches my arm, her little fingers play with my pajama sleeve. "Maybe you could sleep next to me so she won't kick me." I walk around to the other side of the bed and lie down in the flowered little girl's bed.

"I'll tell you what," I say, settling down next to her, putting my head on a frilly pillow and curling my legs so that my ankles don't drop off the bed. "I'll sleep between you and Bettina so that she doesn't bother you anymore."

Lucy breathes a long, tired sigh. "She can kick you,

instead." And she backs up against me, to fit with me, safe and warm enough.

The telephone rings when I am in Lucy's room. Through half sleep, the kind you have in a strange house, in a little bed, I can hear it, sitting on the table next to Mark's pillow, ring down the hallway. He must have an odd sensation waking to the ring. A call near dawn, with the rest of the city black and silent cold, can never be good news. I leave Lucy's room to her tiny snores that sound like a kitten and carefully shut the door. I wander to his voice and his bedside lamp glowing; I hear his calm murmur as I approach before he hangs up.

"Catherine?"

"Lucy was scared." I am sleepy and cannot think. "I went to Lucy." I am not entirely sure I am even awake.

"Catherine," he says sitting up, and I realize his pajamas are identical to the pair he lent me. "The call was about Will."

"Will?"

"It was his friend Peter calling for you. The operator put him through to this line because you're a guest in the private quarters."

He says it so matter-of-factly as if my whereabouts were common knowledge even though I hadn't told anyone I would be staying at his house. Then I realize there are legions of people who don't care where I am but care very much who's with the vice president.

"You'd better get dressed and I'll have a car take you over to Georgetown Hospital." He is standing now, ready to help with another crisis. Will lost consciousness; earlier he had nearly faded away; they've revived him for now, parts of his body were recovered enough so that his heart beats again. Mark explains this to me as if I am Lucy, wide-eyed and frightened.

"Can you come with me?" I blurt out before I realize how much I am asking.

"I can't."

"Evelyn is just downstairs." I go on like a panicked child, "Please come."

"No, I'm sorry, Catherine; I just can't go to a hospital."

And I realize of course he cannot go in the early hours of the morning to watch someone who might be dying—today, tomorrow, next month. The truth is he could not even go for Susan. When he told me this, I at first felt perplexed, but then I understood he probably did not want to believe that she would actually die. When Bettina called at three A.M. and said her time was close to over, he told the nurse that he should remain with Lucy, that he needed his sleep to be strong for the day coming and for all the days afterward. But he didn't sleep, he just could not say good-bye. He didn't go to the hospital until after he had had coffee, Lucy had woken peacefully, and, by that time, Susan had left without him.

———

The hospital is crowded. This seems surreal to me, as if it really is daytime, and it is impossible to tell whether it is or is not from inside, without windows and in the bustle. The central waiting room is full; doctors dart around, clipboards in hand and nurses in tow, and the announcement voice calls out, crisis and predicaments through all the shiny hallways. I get directions from the front desk, from a man with glasses, green scrubs, and an air of business. He gives me directions to oncology, where Will has been transferred from emergency care; he explains to me patiently how to take the third elevator to the fourth floor and that I should follow the signs to the Ford Wing. I walk and feel like I am still in Mark's borrowed pajamas; I am wearing real clothes but they feel too loose, leftover, and jumbled. They smell like smoke and I pledged to stop when I entered the hospital, and I pledge it twice again when I head toward the oncology floor.

I board the last elevator; it rises, jolts to a stop, pauses before the doors snap open, and I feel a surge of nausea. At least it wouldn't be unusual for someone to throw up in the hospital, I think, with the antiseptic smell and bright windowless light. But as I walk out of the elevator, look right and left for the Ford Wing, I forget about my own sickness when I see Peter sitting in the beige waiting area. Usually he has a good poker face, a prosecutor's one that's firm and unreadable. But sitting on a long, empty row of benches, he looks stricken. His legs bounce up and down, his hands ride along; they rap, thump, and bounce against his knees nervously; it is as if he is playing horsey with a child, but, of course, there is no happy child laughing on his knee. His eyes are swollen and wide at the same time. He looks like he has witnessed something that, prior to this night, he has only heard about in testimony. He looks like he has seen something terrible, something that is usually just about the words of what other people witness.

He stands when he sees me and I hug him hard. "Cat, I'm sorry that I called you with everything else you're going through." His voice is unfamiliar and small, shrunken really. "But I thought you might want to come. Just in case . . ." He is at a loss for even the most lawyerly of words. "Sam is with him now."

"Sam?" I pull away and look into Peter's ragged face.

"Yeah, Sam O'Connor was nice enough to sit with him while I waited for you."

"But why?"

"So I could watch for you."

"No, I mean why Sam?"

"He's been great. His mother is over in another part of oncology, and he recognized Will right away when we came in."

I didn't even know that Sam's mother had cancer, and I feel some guilt for not knowing this, but also I feel a stab of jealousy because he was here for Will when I was not. "But they're not even friends," I say, giving in to the second feeling. My pettiness somehow anchors me in the fluorescent, spinning room.

"Maybe seeing the Secret Service makes Will feel better. You know, safe."

I know that this is probably true for Will, he must feel protected by the president's guard. I sit next to Peter on the hard benches. "Plus," he says, "Sam was the one who told me where I could find you."

The monitors whirl and hum when I enter the barely lit room. Sam is sitting with his back to me and is hunched over Will, singing to him softly. Will's eyes are closed and covered with white tape in case the lids should flutter; he has an enormous plastic device in his mouth that looks like a faucet, and it is taped, too; it seems to disappear far down his throat, snaked into some other place. I stop at the doorway and feel like an intruder watching Sam comfort him and seeing all the machines that click away in front of me, so many vast machines that I feel as if I've wandered into the engine room of an ocean liner. Beeps sound every few seconds, and between beeps, before Sam turns to see me, I hear his low baritone singing. I hear the old Irish words come out steadily; bending over Will he sings, "My house is made of flowers and you climbed into its dome. The fireflies stayed outside until they called you home."

I wake up with my cheek stuck to the thin plastic cushion of the waiting bench and my shoes hanging over the end. I think I fell asleep using Peter's leg as a pillow, but I don't remember when I wake up not knowing anything, most of all where I am or what time it is or even the day of the week. It is Monday and it is just after noon. My eyes are glued shut by the parched contacts that I have been wearing since the morning before; my cheek is hot and sore, imprinted from the plastic. When I do pry my eyes open, sticky and blurred, and prop myself semi-up with a shaky arm, I see Sam. He sits farther down on the oncology bench and calmly reads a magazine; his left hand faces me and it is naked; there are no twisting snake heads shining.

"Hey, Soho." He smiles over at me. "How you holding up? You don't look so well." I nod and he continues. "Hey, my brother's about to come over with a big pitcher of his killer banana daiquiris to keep us going; you could probably really use one."

And all at once, hearing "banana daiquiri," I don't feel well at all. When I sit up fully, Sam is already sliding over to me as I throw up on the carpeting. Just like that, no warning. In one rapid movement, the Secret Service man both comforts me by rubbing my back and manages to perfectly cover my crime on the floor with his opened *Sports Illustrated.* Connected to this seamless action is another; he waves his arm at a strolling doctor, a short Asian man who comes as beckoned with Sam's firm, "Hey, buddy, can you give us a hand?"

I sit on the steel table in a paper robe as the doctor feels the glands in my throat. He asks me a long series of questions; he has taken blood to answer even more questions.

It seems that I can't keep ignoring this and certainly not that. I tell him a fictional date about the arrival of my last period (I honestly just can't remember dates anymore) and he asks medical details, amounts, flow questions, sexual history, and so on. He seems focused on my lack of facts, blurry memory. I ask him, "Is there something wrong with me?"

Dr. Bin-Lo, who I realize looks much younger than I, grins. "No, most likely you are pregnant." He smiles at me as if this should be very happy news.

Will has the tape off his eyes but it looks like it has abraded his pale lids. For some reason, as I hold his hand, I keep dwelling on his eye burns; I keep looking at the angry red marks that the tape has left behind. And I do realize that this is the least of his problems when he opens them and looks back at me so weakly.

"Hiya, Cat," he finally says, through such dry lips that I think they are part of his teeth. "I know I'm one to talk but you look like shit."

The apartment smells like trapped, stale smoke, and all the windows are closed tight. The sun-through-glass has cooked the living room all day by the time I get to it at four on Monday afternoon. The red light on the answering machine beats fast; all the accumulating messages make the little heart race like mine does after I've climbed three flights of stairs with the weight of the last few days and what I have just learned from Dr. Duk Bin-Lo.

I open my refrigerator and it is empty except for half a bottle of wine and some milk that I only ever use for coffee. I rinse a wineglass under the tap; I use my fingers to try to clean the glass, scratching it to try to erase an old imprint of lip. I know I will have to listen to the messages; I know I will have to call Harry's father. I haven't yet because I wanted the men to tell me something concrete, but now I don't even know what that might be. I open the refrigerator again to get the wine. I stand with the door open to the strange, lighted coolness with its funny smell of invisible food. I take out the milk carton and look at the expiration date, which seems to be today; it has "Sell by 30 Apr" printed in smudged purple ink. I pour the milk into the glass; I want the wine; I want a long tart swallow and then a few full glasses, but I pour the milk instead because I know this is what you are supposed to do for a baby.

14

When I wake up on Tuesday, I sit on the deep green sofa and stare at the wall of perfectly hung photographs. I get up and look into each of the faces that Harry and I chose to frame long ago, Contessa Vanessa, Charles at his last picnic with his mother smiling, the blond twins, good and evil. And I realize I will have to make a decision. I will have to make many. The FBI has called to tell me that they need to see me; they have found "evidence of Harry" at the bottom of the river. Can I come to the Old Executive Office Building to identify their discovery?

Evidence of Harry.

I search the faces on the wall to find him again. But they suddenly look like what they are: strangers to me.

People we made up stories about on hot, windy days as we walked through a city I would no longer recognize. And I don't know what Harry did in Washington; why he left me; why he never called me from New York to say good-bye, but somehow it hardly matters now. As I stand in the living room on Swann Street, I have no firm evidence of love.

I cannot have this baby. I don't even remember when Harry and I conceived this life, or exactly the moment when we lost the one we had together.

"We are all very, very sorry," Al says on Tuesday afternoon, wearing the benevolent half glasses and his chubby hand resting on my shoulder; we rise in the empty elevator from the lobby in the Old Executive Office Building. The doors snap open at each floor, but Al shoos his hand at the people trying to board. "Take the next one, will ya," he growls at workers as we slowly creak our way up to the ninth floor. I have never been to the ninth floor, to the situation room, where I have been summoned today.

"We're so fond of you here," Al says as the light on the elevator's button board flicks from five to six, and I can feel my stomach jump like it does when an airplane takes off and I brace myself against being hurtled into the sky, high, higher, fear making me grip the armrests and pray. "The vice president would be here today, but he couldn't cancel his trip to Denver." Al looks at me sideways. "As you may know."

And I do know. Mark called me last night and told me, asked if I wanted to come over to the house. But I couldn't. I needed time to think and pace and think.

"Take as much time off as you need," Al continues as the lights go from eight to nine. "I will have to bring someone else in. Hey, maybe I can borrow Sherrie Meager from the West Wing, but, hell, that's not your concern."

Agent Udell is standing by himself in the large room that looks as bland as any corporate conference one with its giant wooden table, beige decor, recessed lighting, and mild hush of climate-controlled air-conditioning. For some reason, the first thing I notice is that all of the seats have water glasses and china cups placed in front of them and that in the center of the vast table there are pitchers of orange juice and coffee, as if we get to use the room for a few minutes before an important lunch meeting.

The second thing I notice is the large plastic bag that sits on a side table, which instead should have trays of croissants and fruit on it. As we walk toward it, at first I have trouble making out what is inside. Then, I know. As Agent Udell clears his throat, I realize that it is Harry's briefcase. He never owned one in New York; he carried everything—books, students' papers, his lunch, mini packages of Oreos, a Walkman with a homemade tape of his favorite songs, "my soundtrack for the city," he called it—in a worn nylon backpack that he had had since Stanford. I gave him this briefcase for our last Christmas in

New York because he could not carry the backpack into the White House and his new life.

Laura and I spent five rainy hours combing the city for exactly the right one. We giggled in a plush store on Madison Avenue when a cranky woman with hair like a helmet told us our dripping umbrellas were "soiling the parquet" and tried to keep straight faces as a man on Fifth Avenue told us that leather goods were his life and he lovingly petted the "Rolls-Royce of briefcases," which I could never imagine Harry carrying or me ever having enough money to buy. After a couple of hours, we wound our way downtown and away from the expensive heights of Madison and Fifth Avenues; we stopped to have wine at the favorite tiny French place on Waverly and Grove.

"I can't believe we're shopping for briefcases," Laura said, tugging at her hair, which had become curlier with the rain, and taking out her little silver mirror to quickly apply red lipstick. "So serious," she concluded, smiling not very seriously at all.

And I couldn't imagine it, shopping for a briefcase for my boyfriend to carry into the White House. I needed Laura there to laugh at me, drink wine with me, bolster me against feeling like I might someday be carrying one myself.

"You're not going to start wearing *suits,* are you?" She put her hand to her mouth as if she were going to sneeze, and then tipped her head back and began to laugh, a chuckle that grew into an uncontrollable, soundless laughter. "You know, with skirts that go down to the *knees?*"

The rain splashed against the large windows, but we didn't care how hard it rained because we were inside the warm place that smelled like bread and coffee and had postponed our search for the perfect briefcase. We both kept laughing until the young French waiter, who was trying to become a model, came over with two more glasses of wine and said, "These are on me."

We did find the perfect briefcase; late in the afternoon we found a row of leather shops on West 4th Street, all run by the same Pakistani family, and I bought a simple, slim black briefcase that Harry loved on Christmas morning. Now I see it sitting in a plastic bag flanked by two men who don't know what to say.

Agent Udell tries first; he tells me that the divers recovered it from the bottom of the Delaware River. I won't go too near to it. I don't want to be close to it. But even from where I stand, cower, by the conference table, I can see that it is mottled and stained, dirty from sludge beneath the dark water.

"Catherine." Al takes my arm. "They need you to identify it and its contents as belonging to Harry."

"It's his," I say, still anchored to the table.

"Perhaps you should sit, Miss Porter, and we can get this over with quickly."

Al pulls out a chair for me like a waiter would, and Agent Udell places another plastic bag in front of me on the varnished wooden table. He clears the water glass and coffee cup away and shows me Harry's address book, soggy and unglued beneath the plastic covering, and I can see his sure handwriting on a loose page, blurred but still familiar.

"Yes, that's his."

"And this?"

The bag contains one black glove that I had given him for his birthday right after we first met.

"Where's the other one?"

I know the two men must look at each other helplessly; Agent Udell clears his throat and shows me another bag; this one is filled with Harry's keys that are on a Marine Corps key ring, a collection of pens and some change, three quarters, a dime, and a stray button. My throat begins to tighten at the sight of the little, clear lost button. Had it fallen off one of his shirt cuffs as he was going or coming from work one day? Why had he never asked me to sew it back on for him? My face is so hot, and I realize I never sewed anything back on for Harry; in fact, he once stitched up a hem of my trousers for me after he noticed that I had tried to patch it with Scotch tape.

I do not ask them where his Saint Christopher medal is; I think of the little silver medal shaped like a four-leaf clover that belonged to Granddaddy and know for sure that Harry would have had it on him; he would have rubbed it as the train picked up speed.

"This is the last one, Miss Porter."

He puts the smallest bag in front of me, and I can see that the box is Tiffany blue; even wet and wrinkled I can see it is a little box from Tiffany's.

"I don't know," I say, the tears now dripping on the slick, bright table, but I am beyond caring whether these men see me crying or not.

"Do you recognize it?"

"No."

He takes it away and opens the bag, opens the lid of the box and inside is a velvet jeweler's box. He hands it to me. Inside is a platinum wedding band; slim and perfect, it shines in the sterile light of the conference room.

"Do you recognize it?" he repeats.

"Yes," I lie, because I don't understand why Harry had this ring in his briefcase; why he was carrying around a wedding ring after breaking up with me. I don't understand these past two years or why I am sitting here now in the situation room of the Old Executive Office Building.

"You recognize it as belonging to Harry Bellum?"

"Yes."

"Miss Porter." Agent Udell suddenly sounds measured, like he is starting a cross-examination. "In his wallet we found the sales receipt for this ring; it was purchased in New York five days before he, uh, five days before the accident. And you've seen the ring before?"

"Where is his wallet?"

"We didn't need to show that to you because it had his driver's license in it."

"Where was his wallet?"

"In his briefcase."

"He never put his wallet in his briefcase," I say stubbornly to get him off the subject of the ring. "New York training: If someone stole the briefcase, they'd have everything. He kept his wallet in his back pocket."

Al chimes in from behind me and I can tell he is irritated that my manners have slipped with the Federal Bureau of Investigation, the Department of Justice. "Catherine, if they say they found it in the briefcase, then they did. Why are you making this harder on yourself?"

"I'm the one who's making this hard?" I feel like an eight-year-old and sound as testy as I suddenly feel.

Agent Udell ignores my outburst and continues his line of questioning, "Have you seen this ring before, Miss Porter?"

"Yes," I tell him, and this part is not exactly a lie. When we walked by Tiffany's on a Saturday so hot the pavement was steaming, I stopped. "Anything you like?" Harry had asked sweetly, pretending not to be frightened of me admiring wedding rings. I pointed to one that looked just like this ring, this one that has come up from the dark, cold river.

I want to run now. I want to leave this building that looks like a wedding cake, retreat down the back stairway, nine flights to the street, run down the wide cement stairwells that smell like the old, damp clutter of this place. They are secured stairwells, and I will have to hit a button each time I reach a floor, as if I were passing through cars on a train; I will have to press one to get to the next antechamber of this submarine. I will go fast; I will run, hit, run down steps. I want to get out of this building with speed, and I won't face the maze of hallways, the elevators, the workers who think it is bad to cry in the middle of the afternoon, who think that there is no place in Washington for emotions. This building is so strange to me now without even a trail of bread crumbs to find my way out. And in this foreign land, in the situation room I have found what I have needed. I have found evidence of my Harry.

"Miss Porter, the ring?"

"I do recognize it," I answer, not lying. "We chose it together."

PART III

*I Look
for Home*

15

Last night I dreamed of a little girl. She was riding a Ferris wheel with me, the two of us snuggled close in a seat that swayed above the city well after dark. She was old enough to talk but still so tiny, dark curls tucked against me, my arm around her as the wheel turned, up, down, night breezes catching us; I tried to keep her warm as we watched the city beneath.

"Mommy, look up," she said. "Look at the sky."

And there were stars; there were bright planets and clouds that raced across them all. I looked at her, and she stared upward, glanced backward with wonder as the wheel swung back down.

And then I woke up too quickly and I lost her.

———

Today I stand in my mother's backyard. We have been shopping and have always done this together in good times and bad ones. Perhaps we feel that nothing too horrible can happen to us between the shoe and perfume departments in Saks, Neiman Marcus, and Bloomingdale's. Maybe we find it better sometimes to browse rather than talk. My mother always tries on new perfume; she keeps something that she calls her perfume museum; she wears one scent for exactly a year—birthday to birthday—and then closes up the bottle, labels it by date and moves on to another. That way, whenever the mood strikes her she can uncork L'Air du Temps and remember the first year she was married to my father or unscrew the heavy black lid of Arpège and revisit 1971. There aren't any bottles that represent 1974, when my father died, through 1975, and I know this is because my mother stopped wearing perfume altogether.

It is hard for me to remember that time, scentless and silent. I do remember that sometimes I would cook dinner for my brother. I would make him Campbell's soup and neatly fold a paper napkin beneath his spoon. I would give him ice cream for dessert and clean his chocolate-smudged face. I would cut roses from the garden for my mother. I took each stem like my father had done and trimmed them with the nail clippers. *Your mother doesn't like the thorns.*

A week before my ninth birthday, my mother decided she was going to San Francisco. She was only thirty, three years younger than I am now, trapped in her sadness, trapped with two children in a city she never liked. She explained to me that she was going to stay with the wife of my father's copilot. "She is lonely and has no kids," my mother said to me as she packed in her bedroom before we went to stay with my grandparents for the rest of that long, hot summer.

By fall my stepfather was calling our house. My mother returned from San Francisco with brightly wrapped presents for us; I remember the first time she hugged me I could smell something that reminded me of cookies, vanilla perhaps; she smelled sweet and brand-new. Each night after we went to bed, she would sit in the kitchen waiting for the phone to ring. I would lie in bed upstairs, waiting with her for it to ring. And when it did, I could fall asleep to the sound of my mother's soft murmur, faint laughter.

I wait to tell her that I am pregnant until we are standing in the backyard, as her two beagles, Eleanor and Franklin, run away from their bath.

"I can't think of any good advice to give you," she says, not looking at me as she sprays the hose on one of the dogs who stands on the back lawn shivering.

"I wish you could," I say because I do, in fact, want her to give me some advice, any advice, good or bad.

"Honey, you have made your decision." She pours shampoo into her palm and lathers up the dog.

"Mother?"

She carefully washes each beagle's long velvet ears.

"Mama?" I sound like the nine-year-old I feel like being.

She rinses the dog and turns to me; she holds out the towel and says simply, "Could you dry him, please?" and then she retreats; she turns and heads for the French doors. The beagle looks up at me; dripping water from each ear, he considers his options; and he scurries after her, head down; he chases after his fleeing master.

Catherine opens the book that Harry gave her, A Collection of Twentieth Century Speeches, *when she began to write ones for the vice president. She has looked at it often. She has read the words of Franklin Roosevelt, John F. Kennedy, Winston Churchill, Martin Luther King to inspire her. When she looks at it this time, in the darkness of Swann Street, she sees that there are passages that have recently been underlined. Harry has chosen certain words. Robert Kennedy talks in 1966 from Cape Town about a "tiny ripple of hope," and above Harry's dark underline it reads, "There is a Chinese curse which says, 'May he live in interesting times.' Like it or not, we live in interesting times. They are times of danger and uncertainty . . . and everyone here will ultimately be judged—will ultimately judge himself—on the effort he has contributed to building a new world society and the extent to which his ideals and goals have shaped that effort."*

People will tell me that I won't be able to have any closure until they find Harry's body. I will not believe them because I don't want anyone to find his body and I don't want to have anything like closure. I can only listen to people who will tell me what I want to hear: that this has been a mistake, a big bad blunder by the FBI. But my own mother does not say this or Harry's father or Will or even Laura, who believes like I do in miracles and martinis. Instead, they listen to me cry; each says that I should come and stay with them because they don't want me to be alone in this apartment with its stale smoke and Harry's favorite videos playing to replace the news on TV.

I can't leave right now. I can't think of taking down the photographs, putting the deep green sofa and our bed in storage, of throwing out all the menus with their dumpling grease stains and fossilized cabbage from ancient days of moo shu pork. I've stopped drinking wine but I did smoke one cigarette after I ran from the Old Executive Office Building the day before yesterday, escaped from Al and Agent Udell, went down the back stairway two steps at a time leaving them behind with my wedding ring trapped in the teeny plastic bag marked EVIDENCE in red; after I ran down 17th Street in my short skirt and high heels, black stockings so out of place on a bright spring day. Me so out of place running and crying and running all the way back to Swann Street, where I could smoke because I can't think of a baby just yet.

Mark came that evening to my—Harry's and my—apartment. Sometime in the late afternoon the phone rang and a voice on my machine announced itself as Secret Service. I ignored it. Then there was a knock on my door, which I couldn't ignore because the knocker, who had bypassed the heavy front door downstairs and its buzzer for entry, kept knocking. When I did open it, there was a man whom I recognized as a friend of Sam's, a vice presidential guard in a suit and tie who did not call me Soho but said, "Excuse me, Catherine, I have to inspect the premises because the vice president is scheduled to arrive in ninety minutes."

Scheduled to arrive.

"I don't want any visitors, please," I told Tony, and he, the man who could be Mark's bullet double, looked at me with a mix of pity and stubborn duty. I told him this because I was not sure what to say to Mark right then.

"Ma'am," he said, "I have to inspect the premises before the vice president can come in."

He disappeared into the bedroom and looked concerned that there is an old building backing up to the two windows near the bed; he pulled down the shades. He examined the front window and seemed relieved that the big calm tree has all its leaves and crowds the view from across the street.

"Thank you, Catherine," he said as he exited, walkie-talkie in hand like an efficient forest ranger, which he yelled into, "All clear at Sector Swan Five."

Mark did arrive exactly ninety minutes later. He was preceeded by a Secret Service agent and trailed by another, both of whom immediately disappeared into the second bedroom that is lined with our bookcases, that holds hundreds and hundreds of Harry's treasured books.

"Catherine, I've been so worried; I needed to see you as soon as I got back," he said, looking as honest and lovely as I remembered from just a few days ago, and somehow this made me feel terrible, like he would soon enough learn that there wasn't a place for emotions in Washington.

"I'm happy to see you." I told him the truth and would have to tell him other ones.

He sat on the sofa and looked around the room. "What a beautiful apartment," he said, kindly ignoring its new disarray.

"Mark?"

"Yes, darling?" he said so sweetly, and put his arm around me as I sat beside him.

"I haven't been avoiding you but . . ." I couldn't figure out precisely how to say what I had to say.

"I know grief is a very powerful thing, but I hope I can help you through it."

"Yes, thank you, but it's that . . ."

"Tell me," he said with such trusting eyes.

Today I open all the windows in the apartment to the deep May air that smells like lawns and new flowers. I am so tired of my stale environs, wallowing, the piles of tissues and laundry that cram my once immaculate apartment like a crowd of ghosts, cover the rooms in a huge cloud of regret and dismay.

Sam came over yesterday, unannounced and unasked, pressing the shrill buzzer until I let him in. Then he commanded me to put all of the laundry in one big garbage bag and the dry cleaning in another. "Sheets, too," he directed like a boot-camp sergeant. He must have ordered the Chinese laundry man, too, had him call in more troops to do my wash, because Sam arrived back just three hours later carrying a giant, neatly folded pile and ten dry-cleaning bags. I had to admit that clean clothes made me feel human again, that tearing into the blue wrapping paper and smelling the fresh detergent was very reassuring.

Opening all the windows feels like a step, too. Josie eagerly jumps onto the big tree branch and looks at me as if I have just released her from a box; she climbs high into the thick green leaves. I make myself breakfast, which I never do. I ordered groceries online and the refrigerator is full. I know I will have to start eating better now; I make eggs and eat strawberries that taste like early summer.

On Friday morning I resign from the White House. I call Al to tell him that he can expect a formal letter on Monday; I will compose it over the weekend and send it by messenger to the Old Executive Office Building.

"The vice president will be disappointed," he says.

No, I think, he will be relieved. When I told him I was pregnant, blurted the news out in this sunny living room, he got up from the deep green sofa. It felt like I was staring at his back for an hour. When he turned around, I could see that his eyes flickered between surprise and something else, something close to sorrow.

"Should I say congratulations?"

"Yes, I think so," I told him, thinking of the wedding ring and my dream of a little girl tucked snugly against me.

"Catherine . . ." he started, and looked at the floor and then at his watch.

And I knew my choice had left us with no choices. Seeing his face, that looked as if it were cast in shadows, made me question my decision for just one moment. If this was happening to any other two people, it would be hard for the man to accept that his girlfriend was pregnant with somebody else's child; soap opera plots thrive on such things. But, of course, Mark is not any man. As he looked at his watch, I knew he was quickly calculating the political implications of this situation—he had to. I knew that no matter how the facts were spun, how much public sympathy could be eked out of both of our circumstances, many voters would never accept our relationship as right. And Mark is, after all, public property. America expects the vice president to be different from its own families, something better than the plot of a soap opera. Too many voters would think he was not man enough if he accepted someone else's illegitimate child. We wouldn't need poll numbers to tell us this.

"If there is anything I can do for you," this good man told me as the Secret Service came into the room to take him away, "anything you need, please call me." He held my hand for a second and kissed me on the cheek before he left, before he returned to his own shining city.

16

In June I borrow my moth-
er's car and drive through the hot back roads of Virginia
to my grandmother's house halfway up the mountain. I
need fresh air and drive with all the windows open. I listen to music, find myself tapping my engagement ring
on the steering wheel and singing loudly to old songs
that are caught in the corners of my brain like cobwebs:
"Sunshine, we're fine, so come home please in the sweet
summertime."

I have pieced together some of Harry's puzzle. I
never liked jigsaw puzzles; I got frustrated by all those
endless random pieces of blue sky that had to be filled
in before you could find a concrete one, a tiny sliver of
boat, a head of a cow in the pasture. Sometime in May I

phoned Kendall Stein at his Metro Desk extension at the *Washington Post*. I still don't know precisely why I did it. Perhaps I thought a journalist could find out more about Harry than I already knew, could help me fill in some of the concrete pieces rather than giving me more ones of dark sky.

I do know that Harry could speak Russian; he could speak it fluently and write in it with conviction. This I found out for myself. Late at night I simply put Harry Bellum into a search engine on the Internet, scrolled through mentions of his appointment to the White House, three pieces in the *Washington Post* about the train crash (these I did not reread); I found lectures he had given on American history that were published on the NYU website; I passed by other Harry Bellums who had web pages—one raised dogs, another was a plumber in Indiana—and then I found what I could have known all along if I had ever done an Internet search on the man I loved. Somewhere buried in the Stanford Center for Russian Studies were papers written by Harry. Some were coauthored with the head of the center, Vladimir Abramov; all of them noted that they had been translated from Russian.

Each I read. I sat in my nightgown, Josie lying next to me, fast asleep across the dining room table, and read Harry's words, written so long ago in another language when Russians were still called Soviets. The papers discussed the threat of nuclear theft if the Soviet Union were to collapse; they quoted KGB defectors; they warned that the same people who were powerful in the black market could become more powerful still. I stuck on the words of one major general who had been in the KGB for two decades who said, "These bastards think in dollars and deal in blood. The Soviet Union made them hard and the United States made them greedy and now all you Americans will look back at the Cold War with nostalgia!"

I met Kendall at a place around the corner from the apartment, a café at the back of Kramer Books, where I used to go in high school because the distracted, gay waiters didn't care that we were too young to drink and would serve us margaritas and admire our shoes. I chose the place thinking that the same waiters were probably still there and wouldn't care about our conversation nor would the other people who were there in the middle of the day, students nursing coffee and reading Foucault, unemployed people searching the want ads for a future.

I regretted calling Kendall as soon as I saw his overly eager face. He ordered a Scotch, and I asked one of the vaguely familiar waiters, who stood tapping his foot impatiently, for a glass of water. Harry and I had been there only once. The night we moved into the apartment we went there because it was open late, and he teased, "I want to see where little Catherine used to come and drink in her school uniform." We sat for hours, dirty from unpacking, cold because the landlord hadn't turned on the heat yet, and Harry told me he was worried that I would miss New York. "I will," I said, looking into my third glass of wine. He held my hand and thanked me for moving with him. "I love you," he said. "We can still have fun, I promise."

"I've got some information for you," Kendall whispered as if he were going to hand me a secret file beneath the table.

"I don't need to know much," I said, trying not to excite him with too many questions about Harry, suddenly feeling like a bad Nancy Drew, suddenly feeling like I probably knew enough already. "I just wanted to see if you ever dealt with Harry when you were a White House correspondent."

"No," he said taking a gulp of Scotch. "Never did, which is odd in itself."

"Odd?"

"Yeah, I dealt with all the president's men." He snickered.

I drank my water quickly and wished for wine.

"What I did find out is that Harry was never discharged from the Marines." He smiled and he suddenly looked like he had at Brown, confident and sure.

"So?"

"You don't understand," he said to me as if I were still wearing my school uniform. "There's no honorable discharge date, nothing. It means he was still in active service."

My stomach fluttered and I wondered if it was the first vague kicks of the baby. I put my hand to my stomach beneath the table.

"You know"—he went on, not waiting for my response, craning his head to attract the waiter who was sitting with two men who were arguing—"it is not unusual for the president to be surrounded by people in military intelligence."

"Yes, Kendall," I said with as little sarcasm as I could manage. "They wear uniforms and they're called the joint chiefs of staff."

"And Harry wore a suit."

"He wore a lot of them." I laughed but then a wave of cooking smells came out of the kitchen, and I felt like I might be sick, so I sat back in my chair a little and took a deep breath.

"Do you want to know what I think?"

And at that moment I was sure I didn't.

"Harry being on that train had something to do with why it crashed."

I don't remember what I did when Kendall said that. I remember that one of the arguing men jumped up, and his chair clattered to the floor; he stormed out of the café with our waiter running after him.

"Kendall, come on," I did manage at some point. "It was an accident."

"Really?" He looked at me smugly. "Stranger things have happened," he said before I told him good-bye and left him alone with his conspiracy theories, swallowed by them like a big shark. *Sunshine, we're fine, so come home please in the sweet summertime. If your heart shines true and bright, you'll make it back by diamond light.*

I turn up my grandmother's familiar long drive. I always wanted to bring Harry here, to where I know each tall tree and pasture, but somehow we never made it. Maybe that's why I have chosen to come here right now, to one of the few places where I have no memories of Harry. I have stopped being able to think clearly on Swann Street, surrounded by the photographs, by Harry's hundreds of books that I go through looking for clues, that I flip through at night to see if he has underlined any passages for me like he had done in the *A Collection of Twentieth Century Speeches.* He had saved books from his whole life, and I find *The Adventures of the Hardy Boys* and *101 Experiments to Do on Insects.* I discover a biography of Thomas Jefferson written in large type for a second grader and cry until morning.

When I called Granny to ask if I could visit for a couple of weeks, she sounded thrilled; *delighted* is a word she uses frequently and with feeling. She is full of coiled energy at eighty-five; arthritis stops her here and there but not much and not often. In June I know she is already planning for Christmas. She told me on the phone that she is making a whole new set of ornaments, all birds this year: seagulls, cardinals, robins, and sparrows. "No crows," she said firmly. "They're bad omens." She has been putting feathers and sequins on them, and her sister Beatrice helps her with the seamstress duties, basic work on the flock, but Granny is in charge of all concepts in design.

When my grandfather died ten years ago, Granny stayed in bed. "Right through Christmas," she would recount with an embarrassed shake of her head. "And I'm still making up for time," she'd say, and get back to work. Everyone calls her sister Miss Bee, and she had gone to live with Granny and Aunt Sally Ann when her own husband, a short, kind man named Leon, died of a heart attack. "We were planning our trip to Europe, and he just collapsed," Miss Bee said sadly about his sudden demise.

Sally Ann didn't go so quickly. "I'll decide when it's time for me to die," she told Miss Bee, and muttered other things to herself. She got into bed after breakfast one day and didn't get out again. "I'm tired of walking around wearing diapers," she told her sisters, and climbed into her frilly bed wearing her flannel nightgown, with her rubber boots still on, I imagine. Granny and Miss Bee waited on her, which couldn't have been easy because she only liked scrambled eggs one way, and she'd only eat Jell-O still soft, hard ham, and bread toasted for ten seconds, warm and white.

"Hopefully she's finally at peace," Granny said two years ago when her sister died, many months after she chose to go lie down. She died in her sleep, deciding, I guess, that whatever she was dreaming about was better than waking again. Perhaps she was on stage; perhaps she is bowing in the footlights, accepting roses from the man named Tennessee or a diamond ring from the mayor of Calhoun.

Catherine looks for Agent Udell's business card. She walks home quickly after leaving Kendall Stein and searches the deep silver dish that sits on the hallway table. She finds keys, cards from friends about Harry, dry-cleaning claim tickets, and she keeps digging. Suddenly she wants to know exactly what the card says. And there it is at the bottom of the dish. It is official enough and what she remembers, "Agent Albert Udell, Investigation Unit, Federal Bureau of Investigation," and it has many Washington phone numbers on it and the Justice Department seal. Then she finds the second business card, handed to her by the stranger who never introduced himself and about whom she had almost forgotten. It reads simply, "Simon F. Bradford." There is no identification on it whatsoever, just a telephone number. She feels a more virulent panic in the hallway. The number has a Virginia area code; she dials the number quickly and a voice answers, "Langley 252." She hangs up the phone and it instantly rings and keeps ringing. She backs away from the phone that she and Harry bought in New York and does not answer it.

17

In July I move into my
mother's house, my birthday is threatening, and John
Kennedy Jr.'s plane has gone missing. On the day this
news is announced and flight plans, trajectories, are
shown on TV, Will is well enough to come over and sit
with me on the back brick patio. He is only well enough
to sit but not inside because he is cold all of the time and
the air-conditioning hurts his skin. Peter tells me this quietly as he brings him into the house, kisses him, gives me
his bag like a baby's full of supplies.

When I returned from my grandmother's house, I decided to move out of Swann Street.

"Where will you go?" Granny asked as we walked
through the woods one early morning when it smelled
like dark moss and bright summer.

"To Mama's for a while," I told her, not really know-ing the exact answer. "And then I'll decide."

"Good," she said, taking my hand as we walked close to the creek that I used to catch crawfish in with my brother. "Sugar, just don't get stalled there for too long," she told me without a trace of reprimand in her voice. I knew she was thinking of Aunt Sally Ann, whose life had stalled in Granny's house and then stopped entirely. Per-haps she was thinking of her own son, Teddy, who left the warm kitchen as a young man just to drift far up north, just to grow older without coming home again so she could see his progress. There hadn't been any, my mother told me. He pumped gas on some frozen road above Lake Superior; he ranted in his letters to my mother about his broken snowplow, his bad luck, the government that had long since told him he could come back, could be part of the country he ran away from, but by then he had already stalled in another one.

"You can't find your clues in the clover," Granny told me cryptically. "At least you can't stand in the same patch and hope to."

I packed up all of Harry's books and mine. I put them in strong brown boxes that will go into storage. First I took the photograph of the twins off the wall and care-fully wrapped it in plastic bubble paper. I absent-mindedly popped a few of the bubbles as I taped up the last of the photos. I left out only one and that is the pho-tograph of the black couple getting married that Harry gave me for our engagement; that one I wrapped in a soft velvet shawl and put in my suitcase.

My brother Paul came from New York to help me pack. When I called to arrange the details, I got his wife on the phone whom I had not spoken to since Harry went beneath the river. (I will never be able to say, "Since Harry's death.") She sent me her condolences on perfect white stationery, and when I get Marie-Ange on the telephone, she launches into her house decoration troubles: The decorators had mixed the paint for the guest room disastrously, and instead of Vero Gold the walls had turned out yellow. "Yellow." She sniffed as if the very thought were impossible.

She went on in her firmly French-accented English to tell me that she was having a fabric crisis householdwide and how all of this incompetence was very stressful. She had fired whole work crews and reported in detail about their petty crimes and blunders. For a six-room apartment she had walls torn down, fireplaces added, windows moved. She went to Paris to get soap and towels for the bathroom, even though they were in a shop around the corner on Madison Avenue. She traveled all through Italy to find the kitchen tiles and ceramic trim for the important nooks and crannies. She went to Russia for cheap odds and ends. "You never know when one of those basic peasant colors will just strike you," she explained, as if the mere fact of this might transport me.

"Could you put my brother on the phone," I finally

said, admiring her efforts but not wanting to hear about them as I packed up my own lovely objects.

"I'll get Paulie," she sniffed. The nickname is not as bad as the way she says it, which sounds something like "pulley." "Oh, Pulley works so hard so we can have a lifestyle," she would tell me, or, "Pulley is the big money-maker at his bank." And big was "beeg," and my poor brother seemed to always be at the bank while she labored at the lifestyle.

I had been happy to see my brother. I hadn't seen him since Christmas, and that was for only two hours with Marie-Ange holding court. But standing in the door of Swann Street wearing his suit and tie, he suddenly looked much older than twenty-six. "I can't believe you don't have an elevator," he had said, out of breath.

As I packed dishes, glasses, and a teapot, he sat on the sofa and went through my finances. It was hard for me to think of my baby brother in a tie talking to me about mutual funds and high-interest bonds. The White House had given me a final check that was the equivalent of nearly two years' salary; I was paid through the end of my contract. I was shocked until I realized Mark must have had something to do with it. And then I sat on the floor and wished I had something else to remember him by. The check came in the box full of my office belongings; I imagined gentle Edgar carefully packing up everything of mine that was not White House property: my change of clothes, half-full bottle of Chanel, the shoes I wore to the inauguration, picture of Harry on the Ferris wheel behind the Louvre, books, packets of Pepto-Bismol, fashion magazines. All of the letters Mark had sent me that I kept in my locked bottom drawer were not in the box. They were, after all, White House property.

After Paul finished giving me investment strategies, took off his tie, had two beers, he asked me, "Are you sure it's a good idea to move in with Mom?"

"It's only temporary."

"Cat, you know what I mean."

And I did. Paul often described our mother as loopy. "Come on," he would always say, "I was named after a Beatle, for Christ's sake."

Sitting next to him on the sofa that I would have to leave behind on Swann Street because I couldn't bear having the crane remove it again from a place where the doors were too narrow, I realized that Paul could not remember our father. There is no way he could. He couldn't remember our parents in the backyard together laughing in the snow, building a polar bear igloo that they laid my brother in, wrapped him in a blanket so that he could take a nap outside with us. Paul can't remember our father's long arms or the way he looked when he hugged us. And for some reason I have never told Paul that Daddy used to sing to him every night because he was a fussy baby and would not sleep. Our father sang him the same thing each time: "Too high little monkey up in that tree; when you look down, you can't see me.

I'll come and find you way up high. Daddy will get you, bring you down from the sky. Mommy will kiss you, hold you close when you cry. Now sleep little monkey safe in our tree. When you open your eyes, you'll see morning and me."

Will and I sit on the patio outside on this blistering early evening in mid-July; we recline on wooden deck chairs, Will wrapped by my mother in a big blanket even though it is still ninety degrees in the shade. And I tell Will that I think John Kennedy will be found. I imagine that he will swim ashore, that in long, strong strokes he will come out of the sea.

"It's possible," Will says, looking into the bamboo that has grown more treacherous since spring and now looms in deep rows. "His father did rescue all of those people from that PT boat and he had a broken back and everything." This makes sense to both of us in the backyard, as if what the elder JFK did could somehow save the younger one now.

Of course Will knows that I am thinking of Harry, that I am always thinking of Harry, that I am obsessed with every detail of his departure from our life and then from his own. We haven't had a memorial service; neither his father nor I can think how to organize such a thing, and we can't have a funeral because they still cannot find "bodily evidence" in the river. My caseworker, a kind woman from Amtrak, tells me that sixteen people are still lost, missing in the swift river currents, and offers to put me in touch with these other families. I thank her but don't agree with her that speaking with them will bring me comfort, warm or cold. I cannot tell her that I will not open this door to grief.

Will finds it comforting that Harry bought me the wedding ring. "He obviously didn't mean what he said in his note," he tells me eagerly from beneath the wool blanket.

"I don't know what he meant," I say because I get tired of this jigsaw puzzle, this one with so much sky and no firm land. I have told Will about Kendall's theory: that the trains crashed because Harry was on one. "Yeah," he responded, "and the aliens took Elvis to be with President Kennedy."

"What I have never understood," I say in the backyard, "is why they found his wallet in his briefcase; he would never put it there."

Will doesn't answer, perhaps because I have already voiced this question to him a hundred times, or maybe because he doesn't want to tell me that Harry was probably still alive right after the trains crashed; trapped and injured perhaps, frightened surely but he must have had the sense and a few moments to put his belongings together before the train plunged into the river. I did know that this was probably the answer, the worst truth of all.

My mother would never tell me the details of my father's death. And for that, too, I had had so many questions. In college I was finally brave enough to ask Granny about it, about how they were able to recover the bodies in the vast expanse of the Pacific Ocean, bring them back to Arlington Cemetery for an honor burial. She had been drying her hands after doing the dishes on Christmas Day; my mother was far enough away—out in the barn with my grandfather—that I could even ask this question.

"Sweetie," my lovely grandmother explained patiently, as if she had been preparing her answer for years, "it took a long time for that plane to go down. Your father was able to put on his life vest." And I know this must always haunt my mother. What was my father thinking, that perhaps he could survive the plunge into the freezing ocean or that he wanted his body to be found? I knew by her years of tears and night wanderings that grief was also mixed with anger. He saved people on the ground but he left us behind.

Will finally asks me his own question because he knows what I have found out about Harry, his fluent Russian, broken secrets. Will asks a question that no one has had their own kind bravery to ask me yet: "So do you feel like you might not have ever really known Harry?"

"No," I say after a pause, from behind my dark glasses that break the glare in the predusk heat, "I did, at least I did before we moved here." I say it thinking of the smile he would give me when he was trying to wake up, on mornings in New York after we had had too much to drink the night before, when he would open his eyes just slightly, groan, and put his arms around me, warm, curling his body behind me as I turned over. "I had a terrible dream," he would tell me. "I dreamed you weren't here," he would say before we both fell back to sleep.

"Still, Cat, it must not give you a very good feeling about men and their ambitions." Will looks like a very old man covered in his plaid blanket and I feel like the two of us are outside on some huge ocean liner, passengers with time to sit in our deck chairs and watch for land on the horizon.

"Well, I don't have such a bad feeling about men, Will," I tell him, and I do believe this, even though I sometimes feel cast out, adrift and homeless, and even though I sometimes don't feel much of anything at all during these hot, lonely days. "I just find them pretty disappointing. Except for you, of course." I look over at him and smile, but he has closed his eyes as if he is enjoying the lull of water and the rocking of our boat.

"But, Cat, I'm going to disappoint you, too, I'm afraid." He says this matter-of-factly, the light slowly dimming as the sun begins to set. "You know, I'm going to have to go and die on you."

I can smell barbecues cooking somewhere else. It is quiet back here, the yard buffered by the evergreens and bamboo, and for a long time Will and I stare into it. Occasionally the flock of crows, high up and hidden, scream threats at each other across the sky that unfolds behind them like thin, washed silk. And I sit on through the evening with my friend and realize that both of us are waiting for due dates of a different kind. We will both spend our summer waiting. After a while, I stretch my arm to his deck chair and find his hand beneath the blanket. I hold it and we stare on, focused on nothing for a moment but what is in front of us, a sea of bamboo. As the day fades fast we wait for the fireflies to come out and light up the dark flowers; we wait for them to come out of the black bushes and fly.

18

In August Sam cuts down bamboo in my mother's backyard. He comes about once a week to see me; we talk; sometimes we walk up to have lunch on Wisconsin Avenue a few blocks from here. Sam tries to make me laugh and often succeeds; he always offers to "have a go at the bamboo," and today my mother has agreed because the bamboo now stands ten feet tall and grows taller each day in heat and relentless sunshine. Sam went to the garden supply store and brought back some long, expert-looking hedge clippers, and he attacks the forest like he knows exactly what he's doing.

I watch Sam through the French doors; I watch him work as I sit on the couch reading *Vogue* in the well air-conditioned house. I finally had to buy some maternity clothes. I put it off as long as possible and simply bought two pairs of jeans a size larger, two cotton skirts with elastic waistbands, but overnight it seems as if my entire body is reshaping itself. Last week I began leaving the top button of the big jeans open and covering it up with any shirt that was roomy enough to accommodate my swelling form, but no one has to tell me how unflattering this look is becoming.

"I don't really need many clothes," I told my mother rather crossly when she suggested last night that we go shopping. "It's not exactly like I have any social engagements," I added for extra petulance, and was surprised that my mother proceeded cheerily along and said we should go to Tyson's Corner for "more selection." I knew she meant that the vast mall in suburban Virginia — filled with idle teenagers, hundreds of shops, and giant department stores anchoring the compound at each corner — might have maternity clothes I would actually wear, something without bows, polka dots, or slogans like LITTLE ME! with an arrow pointing down the belly.

So this morning we set out, me in my elastic-waistbanded skirt and a T-shirt that looked embarrassingly tight across my chest, my mother slim and perfect in a linen camisole and matching trousers. It was already ninety degrees at nine thirty in the morning; the humidity was already thick and suffocating so early in the day. And even with the air-conditioning blasting in my mother's new Volvo, I could feel the scorching sun through the roof.

"This will be fun," my mother, trying helpfully in my silence, said as she flipped through radio channels to find the station that plays her seventies music. "There," she announced happily when she heard "Band on the Run," and turned up the volume, "and we haven't missed the beginning!"

Driving to Tyson's Corner, listening to my mother singing with Wings, made me feel incredibly tired and depressed. As we drove through upper northwest D.C. down toward the river, I felt as if I were in some true time warp, except instead of being eighteen on my way to the mall to buy new clothes for my first semester at college, excited and armed with a long list of new fall fashions I had studied in the magazines, I was pregnant, thirty-three years old, with my mother driving me to buy maternity clothes. I felt ill with the sun glaring and my mother singing. We crossed Chain Bridge and I looked down at the fierce river far beneath the bridge and remembered that when I was six I drove over it with my father right after Hurricane Agnes and the roaring water was so high it nearly touched the bridge. I remembered how frightening it was, the water so close, but my father did not look scared; he looked excited and said, "You won't see a river look like that too many times in your life!"

My mother drove fast along the road at the end of the bridge, the narrow road lined with forests that takes us to the highways and the suburbs. As we passed Robert Kennedy's home, set back on many acres of grass and trees, my mother turned down the music and said, "You know, we can look for the things you'll need for the baby."

"No," I said as "Silly Love Songs" came on to complete the Wings "Three for Three Thursday." I looked out the window and realized I would have to accept what is happening to me and that the baby is going to come whether I am ready or not. But not today.

"No thanks, Mama." I tried to sound like a pleasant daughter as Paul McCartney warbled away. "I can get all that stuff from catalogs."

When I answer the front door in September, I don't know who I am expecting to find. Nobody rings the front doorbell, comes calling across our porch, except for the trick-or-treaters on Halloween and people who don't know us; those that do climb up the back stairs and ring the old bell outside the kitchen or rap on the screened door. Through the open windows of the house, I can tell that this is the first real day of summer lifting. I can tell that it is cool outside as I pad through the house in my sock feet, black maternity jeans, and a cardigan that belonged to Harry.

I want things to start lifting for me. But so far the only thing I have to account for the summer by the end of September is that I have grown bigger, much bigger, with the baby eight weeks away. But as she grows—I always think of her like that, a little girl—I feel like I stay in the same place; all of my energy goes to her directly, to these in-body movements; I am anchored to her and to my own depression. My summer trips from this house consisted of going to lunch with Sam; visits with Will at his apartment or hospital because he was, by then, too sick to come to me; the grocery store three blocks away; the drugstore across from it; and my own doctor just two short bus rides away.

I have read many of the novels on the shelves throughout the house. Many of them are mine from high school and college. I reread *Anna Karenina;* I avoided Dickens; I put down *Lolita* when I realized it was underlined in my fourteen-year-old hand; I closed it when I saw hearts drawn on the front pages with my initials inside each heart along with someone else's whom I could no longer recall. I have gone through baby catalogs, baby Internet sites, and bought lots of little white clothes and some pink ones, too.

"What if she's a he?" both Sam and Will have asked, but I am sure she is who I think she is. I ordered cotton blankets, bottles with ducks on them, soft toys that promise "intelligent play." I haven't committed to furniture, strollers, highchairs, infant swings, but have circled the ones I like and Post-ited the pages of the catalogs. Everything that was delivered to the house I stacked neatly in the basement and left the invoices taped to the boxes so that I will know what is inside of them.

Most July, August evenings, I walked the beagles with my mother, but those were particularly nervous treks through Cleveland Park. Each time we walked around the block, I was afraid I would run into someone, a dog-owning White House correspondent or news producer whom I dealt with in a former life, who might touch my arm, avoid looking at my stomach, and say, "I'm sorry for your loss."

Sometimes on those walks my mother would be silent. We'd watch the dogs relieve themselves, mention the weather that, for all summer, had been hot and cloudless, stifling even after dark. And her silence spoke volumes about her concern for me, my future.

The summer receded with no progress but that of the baby. It felt to me like airplane time, on trips so long that you begin to settle in and live on the plane — eat, sleep, wake, watch movies, sleep — as if it that were your temporary life, your new world before landing. But even now so late in September, I haven't thought ahead to my touchdown, arrival, my destination. This fact alone makes my mother silent. Milt retreats to his upstairs study on nights when my mother drinks vodka with ice. She has always said that she sips it to go sleep, and my brother and I grew up revering it as some kind of a medicine. But now she drinks more of it, starting sometimes long before dinner, and by nine o'clock she's on the couch with it, watching movies on the VCR. Sometimes they are old romances; sometimes they are about Vietnam, and these she watches in a trance; she doesn't even flinch at the brutal parts. I retreat down my stairway near the front door, and as I go, I hear the bombs screaming out through the house with the rocket launchers answering at full volume.

Often during the long summer evenings, I'd stand in the kitchen and talk to Milt while he made dinner, still wearing his tie. He is a kind man, shorter than my mother but filled with a firm energy that makes him seem taller. When we had these conversations, it was often hard to separate my stepfather from the psychiatrist that he is.

"Be easy on yourself, Catherine," he told me sometime late in August. He advised me as he expertly chopped two carrots at once while looking me in the eye. "You have already done a lot and you have a great deal more to do."

"Do you think I might be depressed?" For some reason I wanted his medical opinion but realized I probably shouldn't be asking my stepfather to give me one in the kitchen.

He cleared his throat as he darted to the sink to drain the pasta, as he thought of how to straddle the divide between what he might say to me professionally and personally.

"Did your mother ever tell you how we met?"

"Not exactly," I said, because she never told me any details about her relationship with Milt.

He covered the pasta and leaned against the counter, folded his arms. "Well, you know that she was staying in San Francisco with her friend Lil?"

I nodded; at least this much I did know.

"She had been there for about two weeks and had been riding the same cable car each night. Up and down Nob Hill she would go so she could see the city and talk to the driver who was a Vietnam vet." His body relaxed and he smiled at the memory. "That year the American Association of Psychiatrists was holding its annual conference in San Francisco, and that night a few of my colleagues and I were on the cable car to go back to our hotel from dinner. And there she was."

I imagined my mother alone on a cable car filled with psychiatrists a year after my father died; the year she spent in bed; a year punctuated by trips to other beds in hospitals I was too young to know about.

"She was so beautiful," Milt went on, smiling.

And I thought of her holding on to the pole of the cable car as it climbed Nob Hill, the bell ringing, her long hair flying back. I suddenly felt so sad for her as I stood in the kitchen, thinking how lonely she must have been, riding the same cable car every night filled with different strangers.

"Why didn't we come to live with you when you got married?" I asked him, because I have always wondered why such a competent man would change his life so dramatically and move into a house with a widow, two young children, and one tall ghost.

He looked at me quizzically before he went back to making dinner. "Because," he said simply, "this is your home."

When I moved into my mother's house, which by September seemed like years ago, I took over the basement, where my father used to keep his model airplanes and baseball-card collection. I moved into two little rooms with a bathroom, and some days, most nights, I sat down there in a rocking chair and watched television, read my books and magazines, or talked on the telephone. In this temporary room I made imaginary friends: Oprah and her guests who bravely remember their spirit and encouraged me to think of mine and, for a while, I became attached to Lance Armstrong when he soared through Paris, cancer free, and finished off the Tour de France.

Will and I talked on the telephone three, four times a day; we joined each other often in our separate isolations. In July we both held our phones together when the news programs broadcast John Kennedy's memorial service. The cameras just spent their airtime trained on the outside of a church, but we watched the whole thing and commented about it over the phone. We spoke about who was arriving, why they were invited, and what they were wearing.

An Irishman sang "Danny Boy" and Will was silent, his receiver held against his face, which I could not see, as he watched another man's send-off, as he listened to the deep baritone sing out to the mourners who had looked at history and wished for a happier ending.

"You know," Will said after the song was finished, "John was born at Georgetown Hospital." He mentioned this to say something, anything, at last, but even its fact reminded us of his own fate and his many months of suffering at the same hospital that had brought a president's son into the world.

My strange, random fixations were like pregnant food cravings. I followed one person, one story, until I wore them out and moved on to the next. I began to think about Robert Downey Jr. when he was sentenced to three years in jail because he did not stop using drugs when he was told to; the judge decided he would have to be locked up, that they had given him every chance to rehabilitate himself. He'd failed and the judge said that the actor had misled and conned all of the doctors and lawyers into thinking he was better, that he was well enough to stay on the outside. I wasn't sure in this story whose fault it was; I wondered how they could expect a good actor to do anything but give a convincing performance. I wanted to write him a letter to lend my support, to encourage him to stop destroying himself, but then I decided I might not be the expert he needed. I still thought about wine all of the time and cigarettes even more, every minute, if that could be possible. Every bit of energy and intelligence I might have was going into not doing these things and, by the way, not for myself. For myself, I would smoke and drink wine still, then throughout the long summer, especially on those nights in the basement.

What would I have had to say in such a letter? I could have told him that I am an unwed pregnant woman who lives with her mother and devotes all of her waking time to not poisoning her baby. But that sounded, even to me, pitiful and morose. It certainly did not sound remotely dignified, and so I eventually abandoned the effort to cheer up Robert Downey Jr. in prison.

I moved on to Richard Nixon. For a good solid week I fixated on him and his troubles; during the twenty-fifth anniversary of his resignation, I read everything about him with an eager and morbid fascination. I thought about that paranoid man hunkered down in the Lincoln Bedroom, a fire burning in the summer heat, air-conditioning blasting to cool it all down; him sitting there slumped in his chair, drinking Scotch and listening to the last act of *Swan Lake* on the stereo. I saw the pathos of the story: a mean, ambitious man in a meaner, more ambitious town. I thought of Nixon as he chased after the imaginary threats and tried to trick and sabotage the actual monsters, and all the while going mad in his pursuit of shadows, going insane from fighting off the bogeymen.

I resorted to watching *Friends* each night at eleven. In New York I never watched it and laughed at people who actually thought it resembled New York life. But in the basement I began to cling to the show as if it really did take place in a big Manhattan apartment and a fun local coffeehouse with so many close friends laughing. I came to rely on it for company. Sitting by the air-conditioning vent through the humid summer, with Josie, who hid from the beagles downstairs with me, I looked forward to the characters and their harmless antics, mild adventures, and their comfort of each other. The summer evaporated and can only be counted by pounds, fetal movements, and the episodic rotations of TV.

Early in September and very late at night, I'd sneak up the back steps of my mother's house trying not to make noise on the wooden stairs. I would go out of the kitchen door and into the backyard, still humid, dark, and so quiet; I hoped that I would think better out of my downstairs prison, where I always put the past couple of years into rewind, where I tried to fix everything in hindsight. On those late nights I stood in the middle of the backyard and stared up at the sky, stars, and planets that shimmered like diamonds, with late-night planes bringing people home through the sky, wing lights twinkling. I thought about the astronauts' wives. I wondered if those women ever got mad at their loneliness. As they stood on the ground, pregnant and hot, I wondered if they ever looked up and cursed the men who left them for bigger things, for their own egos and glory and space.

By the end of September I stop rewinding, stop wondering who Harry was and what happened to him on that day. I have to stop because my energy is just too low. By now the baby kicks most of the time; her demands grow larger each day; she seems to want a bigger life and is taking it from inside of me, almost like an alien. She turns me into her to survive, to get out, to make it into this world.

I begin to read a how-to baby book but it makes me feel so lonely. Certainly you're supposed to run all of this new knowledge by another person, the one who is supposed to be excited about this other life, too. Certainly you're supposed to lie in bed, while the man goes to the kitchen to make you a salami and cheese with mayonnaise sandwich, and read about the birth stages, the right way to breast feed, and what necessary supplies to buy together. He is supposed to lie next to you in bed after delivering the sandwich and want this information, him lying beside you looking through another book as he tries to think of names.

When the doorbell rings at the end of September, I am trying to eat in the kitchen. I have to force myself to do this a few times a day because I read that, if the baby does not get enough calcium, she will take what she needs out of my bones. I try to give her enough. I eat cheese on bread, lots of both, and read the calcium content on the back of ice-cream cartons. When I put a big scoop of Rocky Road into my mouth, the doorbell rings.

I go through the front hallway and to the door, guessing that it is probably someone trying to clean our gutters or chop our trees or sell us cut wood for later fires, sell us kindling on this first cool day. The cardigan is just about buttoned over a faded T-shirt that I bought in a market stall in Paris, but I don't think much about how I look anymore and I don't check in the mirror in the entry. The beagles follow me; Frank howls and brays but Ellie is silent as always, bringing up the rear. My mother named them Franklin and Eleanor and I can't help sometimes thinking of them as the real ones, back now wearing their beagle masks, eager and forlorn.

Behind the glass storm door is a short man in a long, black duster coat, unseasonable even for the new cool temperature, and he is holding a big stuffed pony. The strange waxed coat and spotted toy both look expensive and puzzling standing on my front porch in the brisk sunlight. The man is bald, beaming, and wears a diamond earring. He bounces his pony up and down behind the glass door.

"Yes?" is all I can manage as I peer around the heavy wooden door, ready to push it shut, should the stranger go for the handle of the thin, glass storm one that stands between us.

"Katerina! Is it you?" the instantly recognizable voice implores, and he thrusts the pony closer. "I bring you this for your baby. I look everywhere for you." He says this as a kind of reprimand, as if I have been hiding just from him. His voice is loud and it is shocking now to see it coming out of a human form, let alone this one in front of me who looks like he has spent so much time looking through men's magazines that he has started to believe them.

"Yuri," I say, swallowing my ice cream. I open the storm door to a gust of new autumn and his cologne, which is heavy and floral. I quickly look in the mirror and discover that I look somehow worse than I imagined, that I look like images that I have seen of those old Soviet-era women.

"I think you probably like horses," he says as he hands over his gift proudly, and I recognize it as a very expensive German toy and it wears a tiny name tag that says "Pokie."

I awkwardly take the stuffed animal from him and invite him in, not knowing what else to do. As he steps into the house I notice that he is wearing designer, very blue jeans, and little boots that look like they belong to the Beatles, short and square.

"Thanks. Thank you, Yuri." I lead him into the living room, and he looks around nodding, perhaps disappointed at the spareness of American decoration.

"I call you and call you. But no one in your office will tell me what happened to you. They pretend they don't know who I am." He raps on his chest before he sinks into the sofa. He continues with force. "So, I call up important people." He winks at me and smiles wide. "Finally I get the answer I'm looking for." He punches a stubby fist into the air, rubs his hand across his surely balding, now-completely-shaved head. "You know, Katerina, Yuri Cherpinov never give up." He laughs happily at this thought, at this notion of himself, and I sit tentatively on a wooden chair that I think I might be able to struggle out of again.

"So, I now find you." He winks and sits up very straight. "And you are like they say: with child." He points at my stomach and I try to wrap the cardigan further around my belly. "You look beautiful." He claps his hands and seems sincere enough that I blush and push strands of hair behind my ears, as if this will help and renew me.

"What are you doing here? In Washington, I mean?"

His eyes dart quickly to the floor and he sticks his tongue inside his cheek. He looks like he is thinking fast, from Russian to English and back again. "I tell you the truth," he says after some time, and he puts his hands together as if he is praying. "I come to speak to you about Harry Bellum."

I suddenly feel like I should not be talking to Yuri Cherpinov in my mother's living room. I don't know if I should have let him in, if I should be scared of him, paranoid.

"Katerina." He blows out air in some kind of sad resignation. "He get involved with very bad men." He twists his head from side to side as if he has a stiff neck; he keeps craning it until I hear a crack. "Very bad." He finishes with a threatening look, his eyes bulging in a kind of wordless anger.

I don't understand what he is trying to tell me, and I don't think I want to hear any more about Harry's secret life. I look at my watch and it is almost time for Oprah. "Listen, Yuri, maybe we can have dinner before you go, but unfortunately I have to get dressed to meet someone."

"Katerina, are you listening to me?" His eyes are now wide with horror and impatience.

"Yes, but I think I'm in quite enough trouble already—"

He looks alarmed. "What?" He lowers his voice. "They have your house, how you say, bugged?"

"No, no, I'm kidding, joking. I meant the baby—" I suddenly feel completely tired and wish he would just leave me alone with the pretty pony and what is left of my illusions.

"These men still look for Harry." Yuri paces in front of the French doors; he peers out into the trees as if the crows can help him make up a truth.

"Harry is dead," I say, and realize it is the first time I have said it.

"Maybe." Yuri looks at me. "Maybe not. You see, Russians do not make threats; they make promises."

I feel chilled, ice cold at the end of this long summer. "Harry died on the train," I tell him again, because I have only finally come to believe it myself.

Before Yuri can argue, there is a loud knock on the back door. Sam pushes open the screen door and calls inside, "Hey, Catherine?" He walks into the living room carrying a big bag of Chinese food. "I thought you might like some lunch."

"Will you join us, Mr. Cherpinov?" the Secret Service man says to the Russian before I have even had the chance to introduce them.

"No," Yuri says abruptly, his eyes focusing on Sam in a cold, firm way. "I was just leaving."

"Good," Sam says rudely, and I realize he has never come to my mother's house unannounced; he always calls on his weekly visits and I just saw him yesterday. "I'll show you to the door."

19

We stand in the rain to bury
Will. He stayed with us until the middle of October, but
then he just could not; his body was so worn, his face
whittled away beneath the depths of shadow; he was too
tired to live anymore, I think. We urged him to go. Peter
stood by him; the picture of the president had been
brought to the hospital, and it also smiled right next to
Will. On his other side, as close as I could get with my
stomach big enough that it kept me away from the steel
railing, I could only stretch my arms out to him, across
him. I had asked Will about what Yuri told me in my
mother's living room. I had asked everyone who would
listen and each person looked at me sadly, helplessly. Will
said simply, "Yuri is a drunk and wants good copy for his

magazine. Honey, I wish for you that Harry weren't dead but people do die."

One late night we told Will to stop fighting his troubles; we said that it was all right to stop; we knew he was brave but he could stop fighting if he wanted to and we would be all right.

"Go to sleep, you," Peter said gently, touching his forehead, which by then looked bruised like the rest of his blue shrouded face. I left the room so that Will could believe that he and his love were falling asleep together one more time.

The day of his funeral is the color of gunmetal, darkly damp, filled with the fog of autumn breath, and our feet get wet as we huddle under wide black umbrellas. We stand graveside, in a row: Peter next to his parents, me and my mother, and Sam by himself. We are the only ones Will invited to see him off—"my family," he called us, with Sam as a late addition to the tribe; Will probably thought that any family deserved some Secret Service protection. Will always said that Washington was a city of thousands of acquaintances but only a handful of friends, just enough to hold in your palm. And here we are in the rain, his small handful who will not be the same again without him. *My house is made of flowers.*

The vice president sent a thick bouquet of roses to Will's apartment; he had remembered that Will liked pale peach ones the color of the faded summer sun. I stayed

with Peter in the immaculate apartment for the week between his death and funeral. We stayed up late, as late as
I could, and talked about him, packed things in perfect
cardboard boxes that Will had asked us to buy; he wanted
ones that were not crushed or marked from some other
move. I was in the living room when the vice president's
roses arrived, and I read the tiny note, which said, "There
is no greater loss than that of a friend."

"You should keep it," Peter said quietly. And I did. I
tucked it carefully in my purse instead of in the box we
were packing for Will's parents. In it we put a laudatory
letter from Al and the president's framed photograph.
They couldn't come east, Will's mother had told Peter on
the telephone, her voice grew fainter and indescribable,
Peter said, his own voice catching on the memory. As I
packed the box I tried to think of what his father would
say when he saw the president grinning at him, declaring
that this retired policeman's gay son embodied "the
dreams of a nation." I wondered and I put the blanket
Mrs. Bennett had knitted on top to keep the contents
safe for their long journey to Petaluma. *And you climbed
into its dome.*

The ceremony is short—as Will requested—and
Peter's mother cries as she watches her son's love taken
away, put beneath the drenched ground in his favorite
suit, a blue cashmere one from healthy times. Peter's parents are hardy, good people who look like two solid
bookends, and his father holds his son with big arms

when the priest finishes his prayer. Sam sings like Will asked him to. And when he begins, the rain pounds harder on my umbrella; my mother's slim arm is around my back, she smells so warm and familiar, like lemons, peppermint, and roses. Sam doesn't want an umbrella; he stands in the graveyard and just gets wet as he sings, the gray rain soaking him in the cold. As he sings, two black Suburbans and a limousine move slowly down R Street and stop in front of the cemetery. The tinted back window of the limousine opens just a few inches, and although I can't see him, I know it is Mark inside. He has come to pay his respects, just for a few moments, before the cars move on; he has come to say good-bye.

We walk out of the big gates to the street, into Washington, and we leave Will behind to rest; we leave our friend alone in his new world, among others who have lived and died in this city. *The fireflies stayed outside until they called you home.*

I want to see my father again; I want to visit my daddy and ask him to help me. I want him to tell me what to do, this time, every time. I walk into the Arlington Cemetery Visitors Center and have to find his white cross on an enormous map, pinpoint his exact place in the vast geography of the dead. I can't find him. I am too directionally challenged to read a map, which may be why I did best in Manhattan, safe in its certain grid, steered north, south, east, west by the city's own compass.

A tall female guard with lovely hands, dressed in a tidy National Park Service uniform, asks me carefully, "May I help you?" She must see my distressed look every day; she touches my shoulder, her long fingers used to comforting those who cannot find their own crosses.

"My dad is buried here." I hear my own echo in the strangely lit hall with its American flags and diorama displays of President Kennedy's funeral procession.

"I can take you to him," she says, looking at a list of what seems like a million names, and then expertly finds my father in her own book of maps that looks like a tourist guide of any city.

She leads me outside to the grand promenade, and I follow her into the clear, chill of October onto the road where President Kennedy's coffin traveled on that cold day, silent except for the horses' hooves, silent except for the riderless horse who whinnied in the frost.

We climb, this kind stranger and I, up the long steps toward the grounds of General Robert E. Lee's home. The glossy tourist pamphlets tell us that as revenge for the Civil War, the Union buried its dead on Robert E. Lee's lawn so he couldn't go back there; he couldn't possibly live in a graveyard; he could never go home. I stop for a moment to catch my breath and I turn around. I look at the city behind me. Across the river the white monuments glitter as if caught in diamond light. They are familiar cutouts against the deep blue sky: the Washington Monument, the Lincoln, the Jefferson with its rounded dome and Grecian pillars. Will would love this view. He would love the postcard perfection of it, the patriotic and distant beauty of the world's most powerful city.

"Why don't you rest for a few minutes." The guard looks at me, pregnant and panting. "Unfortunately your dad's grave is still six sectors away."

We stand in front of a steep green lawn. In the center, by a path, is one simple white cross. On it are only the dates of Robert F. Kennedy's life; beneath it, a small plaque. It is so different from the lonely grandeur of his brother's grave, where the path leads to the right, to its eternal flame and marble shrine. I read the plaque and it says just:

In our sleep, pain which cannot forget
falls drop by drop upon our heart until,
in our own despair, comes wisdom.

"I am so angry at him," I tell Sam, who is behind the steering wheel as we leave Washington, cross Memorial Bridge, point toward Arlington Cemetery for a moment, and then turn right, onto the highway, and drive into Virginia.

"At who?"

"Harry," I say, looking out the window at the cold landscape, two days after Will's funeral, where the trees etch across the monuments like dark spiderwebs, their leaves gone so early, and blow stiffly in the winds that come from a sullen, mud-colored Potomac.

"I don't know what the hell I can even believe about him anymore," I shout belligerently at the president's special guard, at my friend who is kindly driving me to the airport, to Dulles, an hour and many suburbs away from Washington.

"Soho," he begins.

"Don't call me that." I have turned into a child or a crazy person but I can't quite stop myself.

"Catherine," he continues, speaking softly as if he has learned that this is how to control an assassin's rage, how to keep the violence from exploding like a land mine. "I know it's really, really shitty, but I think you're going to have put some of this behind you."

"Where do I put it?" I shout as we ride along the line of the river, my belly feeling like it is growing with each mile, like it will grow right into the dashboard. Sam stares ahead and does not answer. He cracks the window and an icy wind ricochets with a roar.

"Because of Harry's ego we came to this city in the first place." The force of this nasty thought rams behind my eyes and I feel like my brain itself will burrow right through the sockets. "And look where it's gotten us."

I don't know where all of my determined, destructive thoughts have come from or why they have taken so long to simmer into a boil that now is fast and scalding. I stay awake at night with this anger, and when I do fall asleep, I have vivid nightmares that bad things are chasing the baby; she is so little but she can run and the bad things chase after her.

I look out the car window, steamed over with my own breath and fury. I wipe a peephole clean; I stare at the frost-dusted forests, naked but thick with so many bare trees that have been growing since long before the Civil War.

When the thoughts and nightmares started, I decided to leave Washington. I could not sit for the final weeks of my pregnancy within remembering distance of the White House, Swann Street, Observatory Circle. My mother, masking her own eagerness, suggested that I go stay with Laura in San Francisco. Laura had been asking me for months. There are very few places, my mother's house sometimes included, where I would feel welcome enough to do such a private thing: to have an infant and take care of her, to bring another person into this world. But Laura insisted. She assured me that her apartment is "huge," that she can borrow a crib from friends on the other side of Russian Hill.

My doctor had a friend from medical school whom he described as the "top OB/GYN in the Bay Area," and he called Dr. Evans as I sat in the office. My doctor must have noticed that my agitation grew steadily over the months, that it was growing bigger than my baby. He wrote a letter to the airline allowing me to fly in late pregnancy. He patted my back and said, "You'll be fine," as I left his office for the last time.

Harry's father and I e-mailed throughout the summer. When I told him about my San Francisco plans, he sounded thrilled, his e-mail filled with exclamation points. He called one night, which he rarely did ("Not much good on the phone, daughter," he would say in a long letter or e-mail). He cleared his throat and sounded serious, and farther away than South Carolina.

"I've saved a lot of money," he started. "Not many people to spend it on now," he continued without a note of self-pity. "It would give me the greatest pleasure if I could support my grandchild." He sounded so dignified and as if he had put months of thought into how to approach me with this idea and how to carry it out. He would not accept my refusals. He planned to put a sum into my bank account each month that would more than cover an apartment, health insurance when my White House policy ran out, living expenses.

I did not know what to say and I was crying, so anything I said right then would have made so little sense over telephone wires to South Carolina.

"Walter, I do plan to get a job," I sputtered.

"Not too fast, daughter. And when you do, you can put it away for the little one's college." He sounded proud and excited; he sounded almost happy.

He said he would come visit me just before Thanksgiving; he would stay with his sister in Marin County. I hung up the phone in the basement and for the first time had a glimmer of something that looked like a future.

"Perhaps," Sam says calmly, lighting a cigarette and steering on with it between his fingers, "Harry felt he had a duty to his country."

"Oh, sure," I say mockingly, "'Duty, honor, country, blah, blah, blah.'"

"You're quoting!"

And I realize I am, I'm quoting one of the passages Harry had underlined in the speech book he gave me. I realize I am quoting General MacArthur's famous speech given at a West Point graduation:

Duty, Honor, Country—those three hallowed words reverently dictate what you want to be, what you can be, what you will be. They are your rallying point to build courage when courage seems to fail, to regain faith when there seems to be little cause for faith, to create hope when hope becomes forlorn.

I feel weak and suddenly I am tired of my own anger, exhausted by my own situation. The pressure throbs harder behind my eyes. There doesn't seem to be any place to put my thoughts and I feel like screaming; I feel like rolling down the icy window and shouting, loud and long. I try at least to breathe differently and look straight ahead.

"What really happened to Harry?" I ask as Sam tries to stay away from the giant trucks that rocket along the interstate. I ask him because I know he will tell me the truth.

Sam makes a sound like a quick sigh, and I cannot look at him because I think his eyes might be more pitying. He speeds up to pass a slow blue van with THE MOORE EVANGELICAL MISSION painted on it. I look at the faces inside as we ride side-by-side with the van; for a second we are glued to them in the wrong lane and two women stare back at me from their slow, smudged window. They smile in a plastic way, as frozen as the day, and I am relieved when Sam accelerates and leaves them behind, looks in his rearview mirror, shakes his head, and laughs. "Jesus junkies."

"Catherine," he says, touching my shoulder softly. He doesn't answer my question directly but answers it precisely: "I'm so sorry he's gone."

I try to concentrate on the lonely, cold landscape that flashes by. I try to focus on the tattered stores and diners decorated halfheartedly for Halloween, on the broken churches, rusted fencing, and peeling billboards, and miles of nothing at all. I let many things go by—commuter subdivisions, airport exits, and then wide farm fields— before I can speak again, before I can put words to my own horrible emptiness. Eventually I say what has been nagging and gnawing at me all summer, fall, and nearly winter: "I miss him so much."

"I know."

I think of my father gone for so long; I think of Will asleep beneath the ground, and of Harry under the river sludge or circling high up somewhere behind the moon.

"Sam, what am I going to do with a baby?"

"Take good care of her." He smiles at me, sideways, as we travel along the highway. "You'll be a great mother. Will always said so."

I shut my eyes as the plane takes off. I rest my forehead against the window and feel the shudder of leaving earth, the jolting lift of getting to the sky. I think of how Harry would have spoken to the pilot by now, would have introduced himself to all his aisle mates; I smile a little bit when I think of this but do not wake the woman next to me to tell her my name. I will travel alone over six hours of landscape, high above the vastness of a continent. High above it all, I will sleep as strangers murmur around me with their dreams and arguments, as we, my baby and me, go west to where the new part of country might not remind us of the old.

20

San Francisco stuns me as
New York once had, when I would be walking on an average errand and a building would strike me, a glimpse up
an avenue would keep me for days. I leave Laura's apartment high on Russian Hill and scale downward. Tipping
back at a slant, I descend into the city with its shadows
and fog, its district for finance, its squares surrounded by
grand hotels and shops, narrow streets filled with Chinese bowls and Buddhas for sale, windows dressed with
hanging ducks and partial pigs, crusty from the barbecue.
I buy old photographs from a shop I find on Gold Street,
I buy faded ones of earthquake days, ancient ones of forgotten weddings. I find a postcard of the Golden Gate
Bridge lit up at night and think it looks like thousands of

fireflies glowing, which I might send to Mark's daughter, Lucy, for I can still remember the private zip code at Observatory Circle.

I troop back up a different hill—Nob or Telegraph—into the pure blue air, the wind and open view of the bay and mountains, of the Golden Gate that leaves me breathless from my pregnant climb and the impact of the perfect vision.

After two weeks, Laura and I see a FOR RENT sign around the corner from her apartment. The building is small and lovely, the front door is open, and Laura says what I am thinking: "Why don't we just have a look?"

An efficient real estate agent in a bow tie shows a nice-looking couple out the door. "I'm sorry," he says to them curtly, "but Mr. Sykes just won't accept freelancers."

Before he comes back to us, I have seen enough of the apartment: beautiful high ceilings in the large main room; French doors that open onto a perfect garden with a tall palm tree; a deep bathtub on old-fashioned legs; a huge bedroom; and a smaller one that looks out onto the sunny garden.

Laura pinches me. "That would be perfect for the baby," she says in a loud stage whisper, knowing that I've already found my home.

"Can I help you, ladies?" the agent asks us, clipboard ready, lips pursed, all business, if you please.

"I'm interested in the apartment."

I can tell he is trying not to look at my stomach. "Will it be for you and your husband?"

"No, just me." I see him making a note on the clipboard.

"Occupation?"

"I'm not currently working," I say and add quickly, "I'm about to have a baby."

"I'm sorry, miss." He looks at his watch. "Mr. Sykes is terribly particular about his tenants. You can understand that he requires them to be employed."

Laura can see that I am looking out to the garden. I think of Josie climbing high up into the palm tree.

"Catherine used to work in the White House," she says quickly. "She was important. She was a special adviser to the vice president," Laura tells the now-interested man.

"Show him, Catherine." And I know she is asking me to get my White House pass out of my wallet, the one I nearly packed away until my brother said, "Don't be stupid, you never know when it might be useful." And as I hand it to the prissy real estate agent, I know my brother has learned a lot in the ruthless canyons of Wall Street.

"Well, Miss Porter," the man tells me, says in a new, soothing tone after carefully reviewing my all-access laminated White House pass, "I think we can arrange something. Would you like a one- or two-year lease?"

"Two," I say, thinking of the baby taking her first steps in the perfect garden.

That night Laura and I sit in her living room. We laugh and collapse on her huge sofas. She drinks wine and says,

"I guess Mr. Sykes voted for President Wallace." We talk about our good luck of living around the corner from each other; we look out the windows at the lights of the Marina District that flicker below us, twinkle beneath fog like tiny phosphorous fish in the dark ocean depths, that shine so much like diamonds.

The phone rings and we let the answering machine pick up. I hear Walter Bellum's voice, a warm, familiar bellow that says, "I've arrived safely and will call you in the morning. It certainly is beautiful out here, daughter."

The next day Harry's father and I arrange to meet on the ferry landing near his sister's house in Marin. I decide it is time for me to ride on the Tiburon Ferry. I will take the bus across the Golden Gate Bridge and into the green hills and sail on that ferry, the one of Harry's clearest memories. Every journey is new for me now. I start to think of names for my baby as I walk through the fine sunshine to wait for the Marin County Express.

The bus shelter is almost empty this morning, on a day that has a kind of sharp brightness, a sort of light I have never seen before, a light that floods down the long boulevard in front of me.

There is just one woman at the stop, and as I get closer, I can tell by her wide smiling face that she has Down syndrome. She is small, stout, and wears a denim skirt that is too long and almost touches the pale pavement; she waves a bus pass at me as I join her in the glass shelter.

"I like your sunglasses," she says.

"Thank you."

"My name is Gloria and I like the sun, too," she goes on, and turns her head back toward it, cranes her neck from underneath the shelter's roof, and aims her face to the warmth of the sunshine.

"Hi, Gloria."

"I know there's a baby in there." She points at my short black raincoat. She smiles shyly and then is eager to show me her laminated bus pass, which is attached to a neon purple cord. She lets me examine it and then she puts it proudly over her head and carefully adjusts the pass across her chest so that it hangs to her satisfaction. "I know how to get home by myself."

"That's great," I say, searching in my pocket for exact bus fare, fingering the coins as if I'm reading braille.

"My mommy showed me. I look for the rainbow and then I get off at the very next stop."

"The rainbow?"

"I'll show you when it's time," she tells me with authority, and then she laughs. She looks expertly up the wide avenue at the bus coming in the distance. "Where's the baby's daddy?"

"He's far away."

"So's mine!" She shakes her head firmly, side to side with some hair swinging for emphasis. "Far away," she repeats, as if it is, indeed, a real destination.

————

I do not know what I'm about to find out as I ride next to Gloria, as we innocently cross the Golden Gate Bridge. I cannot know that Walter will be with another man at the ferry landing or that Harry's father drove from South Carolina in the middle of the night to meet this tall man from the Central Intelligence Agency. I will never know about the airplane journey Walter had to make. Gloria puts out her hand and it is soft, small, and sure.

I will ride the ferry with Walter and the stranger. The tall man's shoes are big and black and official, the kind of shoes that bring bad news on a bright, hot day. A helicopter will fly over the ferry and the sound will be so deafening, blades struggling against bay winds and gravity, and I will have to ask the stranger to repeat why he is so sorry. Walter will try to light a cigarette into the wind, even though he gave up smoking twenty years ago; his hand will protect a flame that just flickers.

I'll stand on the deck of the ferry as it swings around the crook in the bay and goes toward the city, leaving the green hills of Tiburon behind. The air will blow cold and clear across us, the father of the man I loved, a stranger from Washington, and me, air filled with salt and ambiguity. The man from the CIA in his raincoat, a light brown one that twists and tangles in his legs, shouts against the wind and tells me Harry was not on the train. When the trains crashed, they used the incident for Harry to disappear. I cannot know more details. I hear "national security" as the helicopter chops heavy air above us. I back away from the man and go to the railing of the ferry. I turn my back on him in those black shoes and look down at the roaring water that seems as ferocious as the river from my childhood, when my father steered me safely home.

I will know that Harry is dead. I will know they tried to get him away from the people who had taken nuclear things from some Russian city whose name I will never be able to pronounce. I do not want to know where they found his body; I remember it warm. I will close my eyes when the ferry chugs toward the golden city. I won't cry on the deck; I will later when I put on the wedding ring that the tall stranger gives back to me; I will when I see Walter's face. He looks like he has had to say good-bye to his boy, his only child. I will cry when Walter tells me how his son tried to protect me and our country, how he tried to guard a world trembling with meanness, criminals, and terrorists.

Before I know everything, Gloria starts to look anxious when we turn off the bridge and the bus twists along hill-hugging curves in the highway. I cannot know that I will see Harry again in two days. I will see him in our baby who is born perfect on a late November night when the foghorns cry out low and deep; her eyes will be so much his: large, bright blue, and wondering.

⁓ *"Colonel Bellum," the man says as he gets out of the green car that creaked up a steep gravel path. When he steps out in full uniform, he feels the full force of the November heat in Australia. Harry watches him climb toward the porch that he has waited on all day for some news. He was trying to remember that song Catherine used to sing when she was happy, the one that starts with,* Sunshine, we're fine, so come home please in the sweet summertime . . . *Harry holds the Saint Christopher medal in his hand; he puts it to his cheek, so close for luck.*

Gloria grins broadly. She points excitedly at the oncoming tunnel that burrows beneath a splendid green mountain; she says, "There, there!" and across the top of the tunnel entrance is a rainbow painted like an enormous smile on the cement traffic-tunnel, "I'm home."

⌒ *"Sir," the uniformed Marine tells Harry one day before Thanksgiving, "you know she will be safe as long as she believes you're dead. The maintenance man in her new building will be one of our people. He will look out for her." Harry nods and does not know why he can't remember the rest of the song. He hums the tune and doesn't know why he can't remember the words; he tries to remember what else he has forgotten.*

Before Harry turns to go back to the house, the intense heat making him feel so far from hot ovens, turkeys, yams, and home, the Marine salutes him and says, "The president has authorized you to see a photograph of the baby. Her name is Rose."

Before I know anything, Gloria waves good-bye. Her big grin is caught in the morning sun, and as the bus pulls away, I look back. I want to see that smile one more time. Before I can look forward, I put my head against the window and watch the pavement passing beneath. After we pass the rainbow I look out of the driver's window. I face forward. I want to see what lies ahead, what is right there in front of me down a long bright stretch of road.